Heat Wave

DONNA HILL
NIOBIA BRYANT
ZURI DAY

Dafina
BOOKS

Kensington Publishing Corp.

http:///www.kensingtonbooks.com

DAFINA BOOKS are published by

Kensington Publishing Corp.
119 West 40th Street
New York, NY 10018

All Kensington Titles, Imprints, and Distributed Lines are available at special quantity discounts for bulk purchases for sales
promotions, premiums, fund-raising, and educational or insti-
tutional use. Special book excerpts or customized printings can
also be created to fit specific needs. For details, write or phone
the office of the Kensington special sales manager: Kensington
Publishing Corp., 119 West 40th Street, New York, NY 10018,
attn: Special Sales Department, Phone: 1-800-221-2647.

Dafina and the Dafina logo Reg. U.S. Pat. & TM Off.

ISBN-13: 978-0-7582-6543-2
ISBN-10: 0-7582-6543-3

First mass market printing: July 2011

10 9 8 7 6 5 4 3 2 1

Printed in the United States of America

Contents

Summer Fever

Donna Hill

Chapter 1

The summer sun was setting over the crystal blue water, casting a brilliant orange and golden glow across the horizon. The sand glistened like iridescent diamonds as far as the eye could see, dotted by one- and two-story beachfront homes with Mercedes, Lexuses, Corvettes, and BMWs parked in the driveways.

Nina Forbes cruised along the narrow street, checking the scattered addresses against the slip of paper she'd taped to her dashboard. Her GPS—that she'd named Gerty—said in its almost human voice, *"Your destination is on the right."* She slowed her '97 Honda Accord, turned onto the driveway, put the car in park, and stepped out. "Wow," she said on a breath of awe; 8802 Sheepshead Bay Road was a home straight out of the movies.

The two-story glass and chrome structure glistened and sparkled against the waning light like a hidden treasure in the sand. Yet, curiously enough, with all that glass, she couldn't see inside. She walked around to the trunk, took out her two suitcases, and went to the front door.

Her best friend, Rita Lennox, had given her the key along with a list of instructions for her four-week stay. Rita's boyfriend, Drake, had arranged for a surprise vacation to Hawaii, and Rita hadn't wanted to give the plumb assignment of house-sitting to anyone else. The house belonged to one of Rita's wealthy real estate clients, who turned the house over to Rita during the summer while he vacationed elsewhere.

"You'll love it," she'd said. "The house is fabulous. The beaches are gorgeous. Everything you could want is right there, restaurants, shops . . . All you have to do is water the plants, keep an eye on the place, and enjoy a free vacation."

"You sure it's okay with whatshisname—Carlos?"

Rita had waved her hand in dismissal and laughed. "Carlos has so many different properties he only remembers the Hampton beach home when I remind him about it during vacation time."

"Well . . . if you're sure." She'd held out her hand and Rita had dropped the keys into her opened palm.

Nina drew in a breath and stuck the key in the lock, turned the key, and pushed the door open.

"Jackpot!"

Sleek, low leather and rattan furnishing dotting gleaming hardwood floors; chrome and glass tables, standing lamps, and a funky chandelier were all straight out of *Designed to Sell.* The open floor layout led from the entryway to the living room—with a two-sided fireplace that faced the dining room on the other side and the biggest built-in flat-screen television she'd ever seen—then on to the massive stainless steel and granite kitchen.

The layout allowed a clear view straight through the entire first floor onto an indoor pool and yard beyond, complete with a fire pit, industrial grill station, hot tub, and an array of seating.

Nina dropped her bags and did a happy dance. And to think she'd had second thoughts about staying in a strange house for the summer. On her teacher's salary and since helping her mom put her younger sister through college, taking a summer vacation had stopped being an option. This was more than a dream come true, she thought as she climbed the winding wooden staircase to the second level, which boasted three bedrooms, three full bathrooms with Jacuzzi tubs, an exercise room, and a small laundry at the end of the wraparound hallway.

Nina chose the bedroom closest to the stairs. She opened the door and stepped into heaven on earth. The room was bathed in the soft afterglow of sunset. One entire side of the room was glass, and she walked over to close the floor-to-ceiling curtains when she remembered that she could see out, but no one could see in.

The other side had a sliding glass door that opened onto a small balcony that faced the back of another house a few hundred yards away. Lights were on in the house.

Nina pushed open the door and stepped out.

The warm breeze off the ocean and the distinctive scent of the beach and the soft sounds of music wafted up to her.

She stepped closer to the railing and saw the figure of a tall, slender, shirtless man walking across the backyard deck in the house across from her. He opened the top of his grill and was enveloped in aromatic smoke. The mouthwatering aroma joined the other tempting scents and Nina's stomach rumbled in response. She hadn't eaten in hours and she was starving.

She started to step back inside when the man she'd seen waved and called out, "Hello."

"Hi." She waved back and wished she could make out his features in the twilight and wondered if he had a great face to go along with the chiseled physique. He turned a corner and disappeared into his house.

She wondered if that was Ian, the neighbor who Rita said was edible if she didn't have a man of her own. According to Rita, he only stayed at the house occasionally, but he owned a lounge in town.

Nina stepped back inside and shut the door and, just in case, she drew closed the cream-colored silk drapes. She took a quick look around, then headed downstairs in hopes of finding something to eat.

Much to her delight, the fridge was full and the cabinets and pantry were stocked to near bursting. She had her choice of anything from a basic salad and deli sandwich to a full-course meal.

She found a package of grilled Italian chicken and decided on a salad. Next to the fridge was a smaller one that was stocked with chilled wine. She took out a bottle of white, placed it on the tray with a glass and her hearty bowl of salad, and went to her room. Her room. She giggled at the thought. This was going to be a blast.

Ian was up bright and early. Those exquisite moments before and during sunrise were his favorite parts of the day. It was the time when he was most inspired to paint.

He set up his easel and paints and took a sip of coffee. He looked at his half-completed abstract of the lounge he owned in town. He hoped to make some headway before it got too warm. He glanced over at the house across from him. He'd been back to the Hamptons for nearly three weeks in preparation for the summer rush, and it was the first time he'd seen signs of life from the house. And if his eyes weren't deceiving him, a very sexy sign of life.

He'd met Rita, who'd usually come in the summer, and the woman on the balcony last night was not Rita Lennox. As an artist, part of his job was to understand fine lines, balance, and proportion. The mystery lady on the balcony had all that in spades.

While he sipped his coffee and added new dimensions to his painting, he realized that he'd begun etching in the body of a woman captured among the bold red and black squares and circles, golden trumpets, and silver drums.

He stepped back, the image having taken him by

surprise as if the brush had a mind of its own and had brought his dream to the canvas. He glanced toward the balcony. When the hour was appropriate, he'd stop by and welcome his new neighbor to the Hamptons.

Chapter 2

Nina awoke energized and ready to take on a full day of touring the town and walking the beach. She couldn't remember the last time she'd slept so well or so soundly. *Must be that pillow-topped mattress*, she mused as she stepped out onto the back deck.

She drew in a long breath of sea-washed air and stretched. The day was magnificent. She glanced across to her neighbor's backyard. No sign of the handsome stranger. At the thought of him, she got a fluttering feeling in the bottom of her stomach as vague images began to play in her head. She'd dreamt of him last night! Or at least someone she imagined him to be. She frowned in concentration, trying to recall what the dream was about. She seemed to remember seeing and not seeing him, if that made any sense. And she was trying to find him in the many rooms of the house and out on the beach. Each time she got close enough to touch him, he would vanish.

Nina shook her head. Crazy. The front doorbell rang. She certainly wasn't expecting anyone and no

one knew she was here except Rita. She went downstairs to the front door.

"Yes," she called out as she approached. She
pushed aside the curtain that covered the front
window near the door. Her body jerked and heated
all at once. It was the man from her dream . . . the
man from the house across the way. She was sure of
it. She stepped to the door and pulled it open.

No, this vision in front of him was definitely not
Rita Lennox. Her wild spiral hair framed a face of
dark brown sugar, with eyes as wide and luminous as
the future. The body-hugging pink T-shirt outlined
her toned body that he calculated was about . . .

She tilted her head to the side. "Can I help you?"

"Yes . . . I mean, hello. I'm Ian Harrison. I live
across the way." He shifted his weight from one leg
to the other. "I, uh, saw the lights on last night. I
thought Rita was about."

He had the coolest British accent and she had a
hard time concentrating on what the hell he was
saying and not on the curve of those lips or the way
his brows swept across dark, deep eyes. Rita was right.
His skin was the color of smooth Hershey chocolate. Totally edible.

"Is she here?"

Nina blinked several times to clear her head and
vision. She ran her tongue across her bottom lip as
her eyes trailed down his carved torso. OMG.

"Is she here?" he repeated.

"Who?"

"Rita."

"Oh." She tossed her head and sputtered a nervous

laugh. "Sorry, no, she's not. Actually she's in Hawaii."

"Hawaii. Nice."

They stared at each other.

"Didn't mean to intrude," he finally said, breaking the trance they were both in. "I should be shoving off."

"No! I mean, you weren't intruding. I was just getting used to the place." She smiled and folded her arms.

He smiled and her stomach did a little dance.

"If you need anything, I'm just across the way."

"Thanks."

He turned to leave.

"See ya," she called out.

He glanced over his shoulder. "See ya."

"Nice to meet you."

"You too."

She stood there for a moment, watching him walk away until he turned the corner. Slowly she closed the door. A tingling sensation began at the bottom of her feet and inched its way up her legs, her thighs, until it settled and stirred in her center. Ian Harrison. Hmmm.

Ian couldn't keep his mind on what he was doing for the rest of the day. His thoughts kept jumping back to the woman next door. When he'd come face-to-face with her, he'd been totally thrown off his stride. She was a vision and he'd lost all sense of intelligent conversation. He'd been so enthralled by her that he'd forgotten to ask her name.

He shook his head. No point in getting all wrapped up in thinking about her. A woman like her was sure to have a man somewhere about. Besides, he was only there for a few weeks and then it was back to Barbados, where he had a life and a business to run. Anyway, he needed to get his head out of the clouds and go over to the lounge and check on things. Opening night for the season was in two days and he wanted to make sure that everything was in order. He got his car keys and the folder that had the information on the vendors, inventory, and contact numbers and headed out.

Nina heard the rumble of a car engine and hurried to the window just in time to see a black BMW pull out from the driveway next door. She felt like jumping in her car to see where he was heading, but that would seriously be stalking. Then again, she did intend to head into town. She grinned, ran and grabbed her purse, and darted out. There were only so many places to go and one main road leading in and out of town.

She hopped into her Honda and pulled off. Maybe she would "casually" bump into him in town. Moments later she was on the main road. She tried to peer around the two cars ahead of her to see if she spotted his Bimmer. This was crazy, she thought as the cars eased down the narrow roadway and she moved behind them. She didn't see his car. What if he'd turned off to go visit friends? Or was driving out of town totally? She pulled up to a stop sign. Never in her wildest dreams would she have thought she would have stooped to trailing some guy like in a James Bond flick. She laughed at her own silliness. Rita wouldn't believe it. She hardly believed it herself. It was so out of character for her. Must be the air. That was the only logical explanation.

Nina took the turn into town. The quaint streets hosted myriad shops and restaurants, from the sole proprietor to well-known cafes and designer outlets. She pulled into a parking space and got out. Everywhere that she looked oozed class and style, from young mothers pushing state-of-the-art strollers to the casual jogger sporting designer running gear to the couples and groups of friends as they strolled, window-shopped, and sipped white wine under the canopies of the outdoor cafes. Suddenly she felt totally out of place in her Old Navy T-shirt, five-year-old white shorts, and Payless sandals.

She drew in a breath. The hell with it. She was just as good as anyone, she determined as she walked across the street, head high and shoulders back. The outfit didn't make the woman. Besides, the elite Hamptonites could use a little urban flavor. She dug in her worn shoulder bag and pulled out her shades, slid them on, and proceeded to blend in.

More than two hours later Nina returned to her car laden with shopping bags filled with two new books—*Glorious* by Bernice L. McFadden and *The Warmth of Other Suns* by Isabel Wilkerson— a bathing suit, sunscreen, juices, fresh flowers, toiletries, and two T-shirts that she paid entirely too much money for, and she had yet to spot Ian. He could be anywhere, she concluded before getting in the car. Probably went to meet his girlfriend and they were somewhere planning their long, romantic evening together, she thought, slamming the car door harder than necessary.

She turned on the car. It sputtered and shut off. Her heart jumped. She tried again with the same result. "No. Do not do this to me." She drew in a breath. "Okay, sweetie, start for mama. Don't embarrass us today. Okay?" She squeezed her eyes shut, said a quick little prayer, and gently turned the key. The engine sputtered then hummed to life. "Thank you," she said on a breath of relief, put the car in gear, and eased out onto the road back to the house.

She was taking her packages out of the car when she saw Ian's BMW easing down the street. He stopped the car in front of the house and got out.

"Hey." He strolled over. "Need some help?"

"Umm, sure." She handed him a bag.

"I see you found your way around town."

Nina laughed and took the other packages from the backseat, tucking one under her arm and carrying the other. She shut the door with a shove of her hip and started for the house.

Ian hurried around her. "Let me get the door."

"The keys are in the front pocket of my purse," she said, angling her head toward her bag, which hung on her shoulder.

He stepped closer and reached into the small pocket. He was close enough that she could smell the clean soap-and-water scent of him . . . and something else . . . all man.

Ian pulled out the keys and opened the door. He stepped aside to let her pass. She turned to him in the doorway. "Thanks." She set her bags down and reached for the one he had.

Ian handed her the bag. "No problem."

"So . . . how well do you know Rita?" If she could keep him talking, she thought, then maybe she could figure out how to get him to ask her out or in or something.

He shrugged slightly. "Enough to say hello, chat from time to time." He paused a beat. "How well do you know her?"

"She's my best friend since high school."

He grinned. "Guess that's pretty well. How long will you be staying?"

"Most of the summer."

He nodded.

"And you?"

"I own a small lounge in town. I'll be here for the summer business. It opens for the season day after tomorrow. You should stop by."

"A lounge? Really?"

"Yeah. Basic menu. Bar. Entertainment." His gaze moved slowly over her face.

"Sounds great."

The corner of his full mouth curved. "We open at seven."

She nodded.

"Harrison's on Market and Seaview."

"Okay."

"So I'll see you then?"

"I'll try to fit it into my very busy vacation schedule," she teased.

He laughed. "I'll save you a seat if you tell me your name."

"I was wondering when you were going to ask. My name is Nina. Nina Forbes."

He held out his hand and she placed hers in it.

"Pleasure to meet you, Nina. I mean that. And my offer is still good."

She frowned slightly. "Offer?"

"If you need anything."

She raised her chin. A slow smile moved across her mouth. "I'll definitely remember that."

"Good. Good." He backed up as he spoke, then turned and walked away. "I was planning on grilling some steaks tonight. Stop by if you want," he said over his shoulder. He walked to his car and opened the door.

"Maybe I will."

He offered her a hint of a smile and got back in his car.

Nina walked inside. Steak for dinner.

Chapter 3

Nina unpacked her shopping bags and put her things away. *Ian Harrison.* His name and the picture of him kept running through her head. The man was simply gorgeous and she had a hard time believing that there wasn't some lady friend waiting in the wings. But if there was, would he invite her over for steaks and to his club as his guest?

Men have been known to do worse, she concluded as she undressed for a shower. She could testify to that. After the disastrous relationship with Randy McKnight, she'd backed off getting serious with anyone. He'd done a real number on her that left her angry, resentful, and wary.

She turned the shower on full blast and stepped in under the pulsing spray. Randy was what most women would consider a dream come true. He had a solid job as the communications director for Councilman Harris. He was educated, dressed well, drove a Jag, was easy on the eyes, and was great in bed. Unfortunately, he felt compelled to share himself equally with any woman who thought the same thing that she did. A fact she may never have known had she not gotten a phone call from his "fiancée."

Nina turned her face up to the water. It took her a while to shake off the effects of that humiliation. But from that point on, she was determined that whatever relationship she entered would be on *her* terms. She would start and stop when she got good and ready. And Ian Harrison had pressed her ready button.

She smiled to herself as she lathered her body and massaged it with a loofah sponge. A few weeks of a summer fling was just what she needed. Ian Harrison had no idea what he'd gotten himself into.

"Sure, about eight," Ian was saying into the phone. "Grilling some steaks . . . a bottle of wine is good. See you then. And bring some music," he added.

He hung up and continued seasoning the steaks. He took out some potatoes and the fixings for a salad, checked to make sure there was enough beer in the fridge, then went out back to start up the grill.

The light was on across the way. Based on what he imagined the layout of the house to be, he guessed it was a bedroom. He wondered if Nina was in there and, if so, what she was doing.

He shook his head. It was simply crazy the way this woman, whom he'd barely had a real conversation with, had invaded his head, which is exactly why he had invited Keith and his wife for dinner as well. Although she hadn't exactly said yes, she hadn't said no either, and he couldn't take the chance of being alone with Nina all night. Not yet, anyway. Besides, he didn't want her to get the wrong impression. He was quite sure that given the opportunity, he would have to see for himself if her skin was as soft as it looked and if her mouth was as sweet and her breasts were as lush.

"Get a grip, old boy," he said aloud, blinking away the taunting images. He poured lighter fluid on the coals and lit them. He watched the flames rush up, then simmer among the chunks of coal. Satisfied, he closed the lid, took one more look up at the window next door, and returned to his house to change.

Nina watched him until he walked inside, thankful for the one-way glass. He was alone. She smiled and wondered if it was too soon to "stop by." He never actually said what time, but since he'd already gotten the grill started, maybe she could offer her services to help out with dinner.

She hung up her robe and looked for something to put on.

Ian wrapped a towel around his waist and draped one around his neck. He was pulling open his dresser drawer when he heard the front doorbell. He took a pair of boxers out of the drawer, put them on under the towel, and trotted downstairs. Keith was early as usual. Anytime the man heard "free meal," that wasn't his wife's cooking, he was there.

"Hang on," he called out and opened the door. "Oh. . . Hey." He flashed a crooked grin.

Nina swallowed and tried not to stare at his bare chest. She focused on his eyes and that wasn't much better. "I'm sorry. Obviously, I'm early."

"Not a problem. I was getting out of the shower." His gaze stroked her. "Thought you were someone else," he said absently as the subtle fragrance she was wearing messed with his head.

They stood in the threshold, neither of them moving.

"I can come back if . . ."

He snapped back to attention. "No." He gently took her hand. "Come in. Please."

She forced herself to concentrate on moving one foot in front of the other and not on the idea that he may be naked under that towel or her overwhelming desire to run her hands across his broad, hard chocolate back or the jolts of electricity that kept running through her fingers and up her arm, but she didn't want to let his hand go. And she didn't.

He shut the door behind her and led her inside. "Have a seat. I'm going to run up and, uh . . . put on something more presentable."

Don't change on my account, she thought but didn't say. "Take your time. Is there anything I can do?"

"Nope. Got everything under control. Make yourself comfortable. I'll be right back."

Ian turned and went up the stairs and it took all of Nina's self-control not to try to peek under the towel. She put her small purse down on the sectional couch and walked around the open space.

She ran her hand along the sleek stereo system that was so high tech it looked like something from NASA. She didn't dare press a button. The living room opened onto the eat-in kitchen. Nice and neat, she noted. Turning the other way, she crossed the room to the sliding glass doors that opened onto the back deck. She slid the doors open and stepped out.

From where she stood, she could see her bedroom window and was immensely relieved to confirm that you really couldn't see inside. She walked farther out on the deck and saw the smoke curling from the grill. She opened the lid and stirred the coals just a bit. They'd already begun to turn white with the heat. She lifted the cover of the big tray that sat on a table next to the grill. At least eight steaks were marinating in seasonings and a sauce that made her mouth water.

Eight steaks? Quite a lot of food for two people. Obviously *two* was not the magic number. Then it hit her. When he'd opened the door, he'd said he thought she was someone else. At the time she paid it no attention, simply figuring that he must have meant a delivery. Apparently he meant *other guests.* A twinge of disappointment settled in her stomach. She'd been looking forward to some alone time with her next-door neighbor.

She turned at the sound of the glass door opening behind her.

Ian had put on a black T-shirt, a pair of black cargo shorts, and sandals. A quick flash of heat shot from her center straight to her head. Her face was on fire. She blinked and looked away.

"I was going to be ambitious and get the steaks started, but I didn't want to be one of *those* kinds of neighbors." She smiled sweetly.

He stepped fully onto the patio deck and crossed the space to where she stood. His bottomless eyes slowly rolled down her body from head to toe, setting off tiny pings of electricity beneath her skin. He opened the lid of the grill. Heat engulfed them, clouding their images for a moment in smoke and dancing flames. It was like watching each other in a sensual dream.

Ian picked up the long fork, jabbed it into a piece of the succulent meat, and almost reverently laid it down onto the hot grill. Nina watched him, mesmerized, imagining all manner of things that had nothing to do with grilling steaks. He did it again and again, until the rack was lined with thick beef that simmered and sizzled. She never thought watching someone grill steaks could be such a turn-on.

Nina ran her tongue across her bottom lip just as Ian closed the lid, and he wondered what her tongue would feel like running across his chest, down his neck, along his . . .

They both jumped at the sound of the doorbell as if they'd been caught doing something very naughty.

Ian cleared his throat. "Must be Keith and his wife. Be right back." He dropped the fork on the countertop and hurried out.

Nina's legs felt weak. She sat down in the closest available seat. *Whoa.* What was that all about? Her body hummed and her heart was racing as if she'd run around the block a half dozen times. On second thought, it probably was a good idea that Ian was having guests. She needed a drink.

The sound of voices drew closer. Nina hoped she didn't look as shaken as she still felt. No man had ever had that kind of visceral effect on her before. He hadn't touched her, yet she felt as if he'd been over every square inch of her body and branded her with his intentions.

"Nina, this is Keith and Lauren Jackson."

Nina pushed up from her seat. "Nice to meet you." She shook Lauren's hand and then Keith's.

"So you're house-sitting, Ian told us," Lauren said in a faint accent that Nina couldn't quite place— one of the Caribbean islands to be sure.

"Yes. My friend Rita usually does it, but she had to go away. She offered it to me."

"And who could say no," Keith said with a smile.

"Exactly."

"Can I get you all a brew?" Ian asked, looking from one guest to another and stopping with Nina.

A hot flash zapped her. "I'd love something cold."

"Sounds good," Keith said.

"I'll help you," Nina offered. She followed Ian over to the cooler.

"You can grab that tray," he said with a lift of his chin in the direction of a serving tray on the food cart. "Bottom shelf."

Nina bent down to reach for the tray and Ian zeroed in on each curve. His gaze turned into radar and tracked every movement—the angle of her hips, the soft rise of her behind, the muscles in her thighs down to the dynamite dancer's legs.

She stood and Ian's groin tightened. Damn, she was beautiful.

"This it?" She held out a rectangular wooden tray.

His throat was incredibly dry. "Thanks." He took the tray and placed the icy-cold bottles of beer on top.

"Anything else?"

To Ian her words sounded like a soft plea that he wished he could satisfy. "Not now."

Nina purred under the soft caress of his response and the warm invitation of his eyes.

"We're dying of thirst over here," Keith called out.

Ian swallowed over the tight knot in his throat while he undressed Nina with his gaze one more time before returning to his guests.

Nina drew in a slow, steadying breath before joining the others.

Keith was putting some CDs in the player and Ian was opening Lauren's beer. Nina eased into a seat next to Lauren. Ian held out a bottle of beer to her with a raised brow.

"Thanks. Yes."

He popped open the cap and handed it to her.

She took a quick sip to cool the fire in her belly. This was going to be a long night.

"So what do you do when you don't get a wonderful house-sitting gig?" Lauren asked. She turned sideways in her chair to face Nina, resting her weight on her hip. She drew up her knees.

Nina laughed lightly. "I'm a high school English teacher."

"Really? So am I."

"You're kidding. Where do you teach?"

"In Harlem. What about you?"

"I teach in Brooklyn."

Lauren shook her head in amazement. "Small world. Do you live in Brooklyn also?"

"Yep, all my life. What about you?"

"We moved to Harlem about fifteen years ago, when it was actually Harlem." They both gave each other knowing looks. "It's pretty much unrecognizable now."

Nina nodded in total understanding. "Where were you before you came to Harlem?"

"I lived in England. A transplant from Barbados," she added. "That's where we met Ian."

"In England?"

Lauren nodded. "He was working on designing an art gallery."

Nina's finely arched brows rose in surprise.

Lauren glanced briefly over her shoulder at the two men, who were deep in conversation, then turned back to Nina. "He's extremely talented and"—she paused for a beat—"passionate." Her eyes sparkled in the light. Her smile wrapped around the mouth of her beer bottle and she took a long swallow.

Nina felt as if she'd been stuck with something sharp. What was this woman trying to infer? Had something gone on between them? Her heart began to pound.

"When Ian gets in his zone, there's no tearing him away. He becomes totally immersed in whatever it is that he's doing. Pours all of himself into it. He becomes . . . consumed. Like a man totally in love." She took another sip and set the bottle down. "But for Ian, it's always work, work. He says he doesn't have time for anything else." She shrugged her left shoulder. "I can't tell you how many women I've tried to set him up with." She laughed and waved her hand. "He's left many a broken heart in his wake. I can tell you that."

Nina's racing heart began to slow. She stole a glance at Ian and felt as if someone were slowly stirring her insides.

"Sounds like a very complicated man," Nina said wistfully.

Lauren appraised her. "How well do you actually know him?"

Nina's gaze skipped over to Lauren and back to Ian. "We've only just met."

A slow smile moved across Lauren's mouth as she watched Nina study Ian. From the vibe she was getting from Nina and the caressing way Ian had said Nina's name during the introductions, she was pretty sure that having just met was only a technicality.

Chapter 4

The two couples had a fun-filled evening, with Keith and Lauren filling in a lot of blanks about Ian and how they'd met, kept in touch throughout the years, and reconnected again in the States.

The steaks were incredible and Ian humbly took his bows—literally—and swore that he would never give up his secret ingredients no matter how much they begged.

The music was just right, the night was perfect, and the company was intelligent, funny, and worldly. Nina was enthralled by their vignettes about Europe and the Caribbean, their take on world affairs, and their knowledge of art and music.

She'd always considered herself well versed in life, but among them, she felt lacking, yet they never made her feel as if she was an outsider. She definitely needed to get out more, she thought to herself as Keith and Lauren prepared to go.

"Please call me," Lauren said. "We could do something during the days." She squeezed Nina's hand and moved closer. She lowered her voice. "He has his eye on you. Haven't seen that in our Ian in a very long time." She kissed Nina's cheek and stepped back. "Lovely to meet you."

"You too . . . and I will."

Ian walked Keith and Lauren to the front door. Nina made herself busy picking up plates and cups, consolidating leftover food. She was putting a beer bottle into the recycle bin when two strong arms snaked around her waist. A hot kiss was dropped on the back of her neck. A shiver shimmied up her spine.

"I've been wanting to do that all night." He turned her around.

"Have you?" she was barely able to ask when she fell into the bottomless well of his eyes.

His thumb gently rubbed her waist. "Yes."

If he kissed her she would let him. She wanted to know the pressure of his lips against hers, experience the taste of him. She held her breath.

"It's late. You must be tired."

Everything shifted. She felt unsteady, unsure of herself and his intentions. Was he telling her the night was over?

"A little." She forced herself to smile, determined not to exhibit the mortification she felt.

"I'll walk you home."

His thumb still brushed along her waist as he spoke, but now it annoyed her more than teased. She wanted to give him a good shove, but manners prevailed. Was he messing with her head and libido, or was her imagination on overdrive? She took a step back. "Ready when you are."

Ian opened the gate that enclosed his backyard and they walked over to her deck and up the steps to the rear door.

Nina fumbled in her purse for the key, wanting to tell him to beat it and leave her the hell alone. She didn't have time for . . .

"What would you say if I told you I wanted to make love to you?"

Her bag clattered to the hardwood deck, spilling the contents. Her tube of lip gloss rolled one way, her compact went another, and a mint, a pack of tissues, the keys, and a tightly sealed condom in a gold and red package landed near her feet. If she was mortified before, she didn't have a word for what she felt now.

"Let me help you."

"It's okay. I got it." She bent down and quickly scooped up her belongings and shoved them back in her purse. She was sure that if someone had shone a light on her face, they would have seen flames of embarrassment dancing beneath her skin. She stood and wanted to duck inside and call it a night.

Ian took her hand to stop her from putting the key in the door. "You didn't answer my question."

Her gaze jumped to his. She tried to swallow but couldn't. She could feel his body heat bouncing off him.

"Question?"

"Yes. It had to do with two healthy adults who are

very attracted to each other spending the night . . .
and maybe the morning expressing that attraction." His mouth moved into a soft, sensual smile
that was impossible to resist.

He stepped closer, so close that his image blurred.
She knew she should stop him. What would he
think? Too late. She didn't care.

His mouth moved against hers—strong, secure,
full, and sweet all at once. She moved into his embrace as his muscled arms wrapped around her.
Pinpoints of light popped behind her closed lids
when her body came flush with his and she felt the
beat of Ian's arousal against her own. Expert fingers with the power to loosen taut muscles and her
last vestiges of reason moved up and down her
spine. The heat of desire roared through her, melting Nina's body into his.

Slowly and with great reluctance, Ian eased back.
He stroked her cheek.

"Better than I thought," he said on a husky
breath. He brushed his thumb across her bottom
lip. "I was always told the best gifts are worth waiting for."

He wasn't going to leave her like this?

"I'll see you in the morning." He pressed a kiss to
her forehead, turned, and walked across the yard
to his house.

Nina didn't know if she wanted to throw something or scream. Her body was vibrating. He'd in-
tentionally led her on, heated her up, and left her
like a . . . She huffed in fury, jammed her key in the
door, and went inside. So he was a tease. He wanted
to play games, she fumed all the way up the stairs.

She pushed open her bedroom door and threw her purse onto the bed, then stormed over to the balcony that faced his house. Lights were on. She folded her arms. A slow smile moved across her mouth. She lifted her chin.

"Then let the games begin."

Chapter 5

Ian couldn't remember the last time he'd had to take a cold shower. Walking away from a desirable woman who appeared as ready as he was wasn't how he operated. He stood under the water, and if he didn't know better, he'd swear that the water steamed when it hit his body.

He turned his face up to the spray. Nina Forbes wasn't the kind of woman you had a one-night stand with. As much as he'd wanted to strip her naked and feast on that lush body, that's not what she deserved. He'd left a string of brief encounters in his wake . . . but there was something about Nina . . .

He turned off the water. The shower had done him no good. He was still hard as a rock. Heat thumped in his veins. It was going to be a long night.

The morning brought only mild relief. Ian felt a little better, but his desire for Nina hadn't lessened. If anything it had intensified throughout his restless night. He'd dreamed of doing everything short of illegal to her body. The idea that he barely knew her, hadn't spent any real time with her is what had his head all screwed up. Had she been any other woman, he would have taken what she offered, let the weeks play themselves out, and moved on.

Something that he couldn't explain stopped him, and the inexplicability of it had him tight as a drum. He put on a pair of shorts and his sneakers and went out for a jog along the beach. Maybe he could burn off some of his pent-up energy. He didn't even think he could focus on painting, which usually soothed him.

Ian took off along the shoreline at a slow jog, hoping to clear his head and organize his thoughts. He had to figure out what he really wanted to do about Nina other than taste every inch of her. The truth was, he lived on the other side of the water. He had a thriving business that occupied most of his time. During the summer, he came to the Hamptons and ran his club, relaxed, and indulged himself in his art. That was the portrait of his life. Where could Nina fit into that tight frame? Maybe all it could be was a hot summer fling. She seemed up for it. So why was he stressing himself?

Nina was stretched out on a lounge chair on her back deck. She still had a hard time getting over what had happened at the back door the night before. She'd shifted from stunned to angry to embarrassed to disappointed and back to basically pissed off. The worst part was that she felt used. Ian had worked his British charm, gotten her all worked up just to see how far she would let him go, and she'd been foolish enough to put all her cards on the table. What she'd done spelled "easy."

She reached for her glass of orange juice and took a sip. It's not that she was prim and proper or anything, but in truth, she wasn't the kind of woman who slept with a man she barely knew. So why Ian Harrison? Why was she so ready and willing? And what in the world must he think of her now? She groaned in misery. If she hadn't agreed to watch the house, she would pack up and leave. She didn't know how she was going to face him. Her only choice was to make herself as scarce as possible. There was an entire town to explore.

Nina pushed up from her reclining position and spotted Ian jogging toward his house. She made a move to dart inside before he saw her, but she didn't move soon enough.

"Nina!"

His voice was carried along by the morning breeze and lifted the tiny hairs along her arms. She started to pretend that she hadn't heard him, but something stopped her.

He was coming in her direction and it was as if she'd lost all willpower. Seeing him, with the sweat from his run glistening on his chest, the muscles of his thighs bulging and contracting as he ran, was hypnotic and whatever idea she had in her head to make a beeline for the house got all cloudy and fuzzy.

Ian jogged to a stop in front of her, took the

towel from around his neck, and wiped his face. "Hey."

"Hey."

His gaze darted around for a moment then settled on her. "How'd you sleep?"

"Great," she lied. "And you?"

He shrugged. "I've had better nights."

"Hmmm. Well, I was getting ready to . . . do something inside." She started to move away.

"Nina, about last night."

Her stomach jumped. She arched her right brow. "What about it?"

"I shouldn't have come on to you the way I did." He saw her tense. "At least not the first night we'd known each other." He glanced down for a moment, hoping to get his thoughts in order. "Look, I have a thing for you. Simple as that. We're both adults. I live way on the other side of the ocean ten months out of the year. So if anything does jump off between us—"

"I'm game if you are," she said without flinching. She planted her hand on her hip, practically challenging him to be good at his word.

The corner of his mouth curved slightly upward. "Always."

Her eyes moved slowly over him from top to bottom and back. "I'm busy right now, but my afternoon and evening are free. Any plans?" She quietly relished in seeing the macho façade shake just a bit.

"How about a late lunch? I have to go over to the club shortly, check on a few things. Get ready for the opening." He paused. "Actually, depending on how long you're busy, you can come with me. We can grab something in town."

She tugged on her bottom lip with her teeth. "I can be unbusy in about an hour."

"I'll be out front. We'll take my car."

"See you in an hour." She walked away, fighting back a sunshine smile.

So this was going to be an adult summer fling, she thought as she went through her wardrobe to find something that would take her from afternoon to possible evening. It was clear that Ian wasn't into commitment and she was cool with that. She couldn't see how it would work otherwise. It was like he said, they lived on different sides of the water. And she knew she wasn't into long-distance relationships. Getting her groove back with Ian Harrison was what she needed. When the summer was over, they'd go back to what they were doing and hopefully take some good memories along with them.

Nina picked out a soft magenta sundress that hugged her waist, flared out around her hips, and kissed her knees. The thin spaghetti straps accentuated her shoulders, and the deep scooped neckline gave a teasing hint of cleavage. A vanilla-toned open-weaved shawl if it got cool later on, sling-back sandals, and small clutch purse the same color as the shawl were her accessories. She added thin silver hoops and a silver chain with a teardrop in the center to finish off her outfit.

She looked at all of the pieces laid out on the bed. It was cool, classy, and just enough sexy without being obvious. Now all she had to do was wait out her "busy" hour.

Nina took her time getting dressed, worked a little extra on her hair, gave her nails a fresh coat of clear polish, and just as she was putting on her sandals, the front doorbell rang. She took a quick look in the full-length mirror in the bathroom, put an extra slash of lip gloss on her mouth, grabbed her purse, and went to the door.

"Right on time," she greeted.

Ian's eyes lit up when he saw her. "Lovely," he said, the single word both husky and possessive.

Nina offered him a smile, stepped out, and shut the door behind her. She walked by him to give him a quick whiff of her scent and did a slow stroll to his car.

Ian snapped himself from the hypnotic trance of her hips and hurried behind her, getting to the passenger door just as she did. He opened the door for her and Nina slid onto the butter-soft leather seat like a movie star on her way to Oscar night. He drew in a deep breath and shook his head in amazement at his luck.

"I shouldn't be too long at the club," he said, putting the car in gear and easing out onto the two-lane road.

"It's not a problem." She leaned back and let the breeze blow over her, hoping that it would take her temperature down a notch. Being this close to him was creating havoc at all her pleasure points. Her nipples were hard, and jolts of need shot through her as they brushed against her clothing. And he hadn't even touched her. She crossed her legs in hopes of calming the pulse that was beating between her legs.

"How did you get into teaching?"

Nina blinked to attention. "Um, my aunt was a teacher. She was my favorite." She smiled at the memory. "She was the one who got me to love books and reading and getting an education. I followed in her footsteps. I wanted to change lives the way she changed mine. I've always believed that education was the way out."

Ian stole a quick look at her. Her tone, the conviction about her beliefs, and the obvious affection that she held for her aunt added a new dimension to her. It took her beyond the femme fatale to a more rounded, thoughtful woman. That realization shook him in a way that he could not explain.

"Lauren was telling me that you have an architectural business and you paint and you own a lounge. Busy man."

Ian laughed. "You could say that. But I enjoy what I do. Took over the business after my father passed about ten years ago."

"Oh, I'm sorry."

He nodded. "It's been a while."

"What do you design?"

"Mostly resorts, condos, and townhouses."

"Only in Barbados?"

"So far. I've been thinking of branching out." He shrugged. "Expensive." He turned onto the main road in town.

"So what made you decide to come here and open a lounge?"

Ian laughed. "One of my other passions," he

confessed. "I'm a would-be musician, culinary school dropout, and fledgling artist. I figured if I mixed them all up together I'd come up with something. Turned out to be the lounge. Plus it adds some *culture* to the Hamptons, if you know what I mean."

Nina giggled. "So basically, the lounge is in response to those unsatisfied needs."

Ian stole a look at her before pulling into a parking space. "I do what I can to satisfy my needs."

A thrill ran through her. She chose not to comment.

Ian unfastened his seat belt. "This shouldn't take too long." He got out, came around, and helped her out of the car. "It's right up the street."

They walked along the street, stepping around the tourists who lined the narrow walkways until Ian came to a stop in front of a glass-front building sandwiched between a high-end boutique and an organic grocer.

"Harrison's," Nina said, looking up at the silver lettering on the awning. "Very original."

"Must I be brilliant too?" he teased. He turned the knob on the door, then stepped aside to let Nina pass.

Her eyes adjusted to the dimness. It was a typical lounge setup: horseshoe bar, circular tables, low couches and side chairs, a few booths, and a stage for entertainment. But what set it apart was the amazing artwork that hung on the walls. In every available space there were brilliant pieces, from abstracts to landscapes to portraits. Instinctively, Nina knew that they were Ian's.

"I need to check on the inventory," Ian said, breaking into her perusal. "Be right back."

"Sure." She walked around and took a closer look at the pictures, totally impressed with his skill. He had talent and it obviously didn't stop with simple sex appeal. There were dimensions to Ian Harrison. He was a businessman, a skilled artist, a creator of visions. She drew in a deep breath and slowly released it. He was more than she bargained for. She didn't want to think of him beyond a sexy man whom she wanted to make love to. If she thought of him beyond being an object of her desires, she was going to get all messed up in the head and confuse a hot fling with something more. And they'd both agreed that was not possible.

She was examining a seascape that resembled Ian's house set against the ocean when he came up behind her.

"Hope I didn't take too long."

She turned, and when she focused on him, her insides did a little tap dance, her heart beat a little faster, and she felt breathless all at once. "I had no idea that you had such an impressive body of work. This is no hobby," she said, regaining her composure.

"I suppose if I didn't take over my father's business, I would have tried to pursue a career as an artist. But you can't always do what you want in life. At least this way," he said, looking around at his work, "I still get to share what I do."

"I'm a believer in doing what makes you happy. I think you can have it all."

"Do you?" he said, taking a step closer. He dipped

his head and brushed his lips lightly against hers. He let his finger trail along the side of her face.

Her breath caught as her lids fluttered over her eyes and tingles ran through her.

Ian's arm curved around her waist and eased her to him. "I think I like your philosophy."

"Mr. Harrison."

Ian looked over his shoulder.

"There's a call for you in the office."

"Thanks, Sam." He turned back to Nina. "I'll be right back."

He started to move off. Nina clasped his arm, stepped up to him, and kissed him, slow and easy, and then moved away. "Hurry back," she said on a breath.

His gaze raked over her. "Before you know it."

Nina watched him walk between the tables to the back and through a door. She twirled around in a quick circle, her skirt fanning out around her legs. She lowered her head and shook it in disbelief. What in heaven's name had gotten into her, she thought even as she felt the smile pulling her mouth in opposite directions. The man made her think and do things that were totally out of character. But what the hell? You only live once, right? This was a chance of a lifetime, from the free vacation in a fancy dream house to meeting the man who could get a blind woman's panties in a bunch. She hugged herself and looked out the window at the streams of happy strollers passing by. It didn't get better than this.

That's where she was wrong.

Chapter 6

Nina and Ian walked hand in hand along the cobblestone streets, stopping to peek in the different shops and boutiques before coming to where Ian took her for brunch.

Mixed with the thrill of getting to know each other, there was still the element of feeling easy and comfortable together.

They talked about their respective lives on opposite ends of the globe, their favorite books, music and movies, politics, hopes, and dreams. Ian told her how he'd gotten started painting. It was during his junior year in high school. His mother was very ill and part of her recovery was art therapy.

"She liked to paint in the mornings," he began, his memory drifting off to the sunrises that glistened across the Caribbean, washing the white-washed porch in an orange glow. He focused on Nina, who had a half smile on her face. "She wasn't very good," he confessed, "but she enjoyed it. I would sit with her on the weekends while she worked. I guess it started when I would make suggestions to her as she painted—about color combinations or objects. She started letting me use her paints to show her what I meant. Before long I was painting. I still have no idea where the skill came from. I somehow was able to see in between the lines, beyond the eye." He shook his head as if still amazed by it all.

"Some talents come naturally," she said and took a sip of her wine, looking above the rim of her fluted glass into his eyes.

Ian tried hard to keep his thoughts clear, but when she said things like that accompanied by that "come hither" look in her eyes, he lost all concentration. Fortunately the busboy came and cleared the table, giving him a moment to regroup. Nina was reapplying her lipstick, which didn't help.

She dropped her lipstick into her purse and clicked it closed. She drew in a long, deep breath that made her luscious breasts rise and fall and sent his imagination into a million directions. He shifted in his seat.

"Have you ever taken one of the cruises along the water?" Ian asked as they prepared to leave.

"Only in New York, during the summer. There's always a jazz cruise on the Hudson." He was right on her when she stood as he helped her out of her seat. What she wanted to do was turn around into his arms and sample him right then and there. His scent was driving her crazy.

"I was thinking, if you want, we can do one of the cruises this evening, listen to some music, dance a little. It's my last free night for a while. Tomorrow the lounge opens and . . . I'll be all tied up."

The heat of his breath brushed her neck and hot-wired her brain. She wasn't sure what he'd just said—something about tying her up—but she agreed anyway.

"Perfect. I'll make reservations and pick you up around seven. They shove off at eight."

"I'll be ready."

He pressed his palm against her lower back as he guided her outside. "I know," he responded in a thick whisper.

"Mind if we stop at the market before heading back?" Nina asked as they walked to Ian's car.

"Not at all. One of my favorites is about two blocks down, near that light." He pointed, but all Nina could see was the way the muscles in his arm rippled like the ocean, and she imagined herself held captive by them and carried away to some remote locale where it was just the two of them, exploring the hidden treasure of each other's bodies and . . .

"This is it."

She came up short, not realizing that they'd come to a stop or even that they'd been walking.

Ian reached around her and opened the glass and chrome door, and mercifully a cool air-conditioned breeze wrapped around her and lowered her rising temperature.

"Of course, nothing beats picking fruits from your own tree and vegetables from your own garden," Ian was saying as they stepped inside.

"Back home?"

"Hmm, umm. My folks grew all of our vegetables in the yard. We had a mango tree and an orange tree out front. Came in handy when things got tough financially."

Nina frowned as she picked up a cucumber. "How?" She turned to him and ran her thumb along the slick skin.

"We'd sell what we grew at the market. Make ends meet." He looked down at the basket of sweet peaches, picked one up, and took a deep bite. The succulent juice burst in his mouth, slipped over the side, which he licked away with his tongue.

Nina felt her own juices flowing as she watched him tease and suck the tender fruit even as she mindlessly ran her fingers up and down the hard surface of the cucumber and across its bulbous top.

Ian did everything short of saying a Hail Mary to keep his building erection in check. He knew she'd taste just as sweet as the fruit he had in his mouth, and he couldn't wait to sample her and . . .

"Ian? Is that you?"

He turned in the direction of a voice and did a double take. "Cara."

Before he could get in another word, she walked up to him and kissed him full on the lips, looping her arms around his neck like a woman who knew her man.

Whoever this Cara was, she was nothing less than a bronze bombshell. Petite, maybe no more than five foot five, curves from head to toe, arresting gray-green eyes, and layers of strawberry blonde hair that bounced around her shoulders. She was an almost perfect shoo-in for the actress and one-time Miss America Vanessa Williams.

Nina didn't know which way to look. Had this been Brooklyn, she might have said something to the woman who had totally disrespected her presence. But it wasn't her call and Ian wasn't her man and this wasn't Brooklyn.

Ian peeled Cara's arms from around him and held her away from him. He looked her firmly in the eye, then took Nina's hand that still held the cucumber. "Cara Kingston, this is Nina Forbes." He moved closer to Nina so that they became a united front.

Nina's spirits instantly lifted. She could just kiss him. She pressed her hip closer to his and smiled sweetly at Cara. "Nice to meet you."

Cara didn't miss a beat. "And you as well." She turned her full one-hundred-watt voltage attention on Ian, displaying impossibly perfect white teeth. "Imagine running into you here." She made a little face. "I had no idea you'd left Barbados," she said in the delicate mixture of British and Caribbean.

"Should you?"

She wagged a manicured finger at him. "I thought we were friends."

Ian moved closer to Nina and casually put his arm around her waist. "So what brings *you* here?" he asked, diverting her question.

"I came down with friends. We're staying for about two weeks. We have a condo just off the water. You must come by and bring"—she glanced at Nina for a moment—"Dina."

"Nina."

Cara lightly slapped her brow with the heel of her palm. "Forgive me. I'm so terrible with names."

Her deep dimples flashed. "Imagine being a public figure and not able to remember names." She slowly shook her head as if the confession were the saddest thing she'd ever done. "In any event, the invitation is open. We're having a 'thing' this weekend." She dug in her purse, found a business card, and wrote the address and her cell number on the back. She handed it to Ian. "Do drop by. It would be good to have you . . . over." She turned to Nina with wide eyes. "And you as well." She reached up and kissed Ian's cheek this time. "Try to make it, love," she said into his ear. She turned away and strolled off, leaving her flowery scent behind.

Nina pushed out a breath and felt the stiffness in her back begin to relax.

Ian squeezed her hand. "Sorry about that. Cara can be a bit much sometimes."

Nina laughed lightly and continued examining the fruit. She wondered if Cara tasted the sweet peach juice that had certainly lingered on Ian's mouth when she stole that kiss. She was dying to know how well they knew each other, but she would walk barefoot on broken glass before she showed any interest or concern whatsoever.

"I'm going to get a basket. I see already that what I want will be too much to carry."

Nina studied him as he walked down the vegetable aisle. She hadn't had the opportunity before to get the full effect of his confident swagger, a Denzel kind of stroll that made her imagine him just walking right on up inside her and there would be nothing she could do to stop him.

Nina shook her head to scatter the vision as Ian

returned, and the coming-right-at-ya view was equally as stimulating.

"I probably should have gotten one too," Nina said, needing to speak some words to clear her head.

"We can share." He winked.

They walked up and down the aisles, picking up strawberries, bags of bing cherries, peaches, tomatoes, romaine lettuce, baby carrots, and fresh string beans until the basket was near to overflowing.

"Either we check out or get another basket," Nina quipped.

"Is there anything else you see that you want?"

Nina swallowed. Her throat was dry. She was a breath away from him, close enough to feel the steady beat of his heart thumping against his chest. Or was that her heart? "Nothing else from here," she said, coyly.

His brow quirked. "Let's go then." He took their selections to the cashier and was placing them on the counter when Nina began plucking items from the basket.

"What are you doing?"

"These are the things I picked up. I can't have you paying for them."

He took the box of strawberries from her hand and put it back on the counter. "And why not?"

She blinked several times. "Well . . . because it's not right."

The corner of his mouth lifted. "Why?" he probed, enjoying her moment of discomfort even as he continued to unpack the basket.

"'Cause we'll get our stuff all mixed up," she offered.

His smile came full bloom. "I'm looking forward to getting our stuff all mixed up." He bent his head and kissed her until they were interrupted by the throat-clearing of the cashier.

Ian released her lips and turned his attention on the cashier. "How much is that?"

"Forty-two dollars and sixty cents."

He gave her his credit card. Nina picked up one of the smaller bags. Ian took the other two after signing the slip and getting his card back. They walked to his car.

"Thanks. I owe you."

Ian opened the trunk. "Only if you *want* to owe me." He put the packages in the trunk and shut it.

She stood in front of him, looked up into his eyes, let them roam over his face for a moment. "To be quite honest, I don't know what I want to do with you," she said with a husky note of invitation.

He held her chin between his fingers. "Shame . . . I know *exactly* what I want to do with you."

Nina's heart bumped in her chest. Her face was on fire.

Ian opened the passenger door for her and somehow she managed to get in. She wiggled into a comfortable position. If Ian didn't put out the fire that was raging inside of her—and soon—she was sure she would combust.

Chapter 7

It was nearing five o'clock by the time Ian pulled into Nina's driveway. They'd listened to music from the CD player and made small talk about the weather while both of them were on simmer.

Ian compelled himself to concentrate on the winding narrow road and not the silk of Nina's legs, the rise and fall of the swell of her breasts barely held in place by the dipping neckline of her dress, or the sultry scent that wafted off her and had him wondering if he had enough condoms for all the times he was going to make love to her. His erection was so hard that it hurt and there was only so much shifting he could do to hide it from her.

He turned off the engine. He couldn't get out. Not now, at least not yet. Inwardly he groaned.

"Um, if you pop the trunk I can get the bags."

"Why don't I just bring them for you when I come and pick you up later?"

She angled her head to the side. "I really wanted those strawberries," she said in a half pout. Her gaze rolled down his body and she thrilled to realize the effect she was having on him.

Ian turned halfway in his seat to face her. He was tired of the cat and mouse game. It was driving him crazy and either they were going to have mind-blowing sex right now or . . .

"Come inside," she said in a thick whisper. She reached across the gearshift and placed her hand on his muscled thigh, inches away from his throbbing cock.

Ian's jaw clenched. "Make sure this is what you want."

She ran her tongue across her lips. Her eyes grew dark. "I can't think of anything else that I want more at the moment."

Ian released the locks with a metallic pop and they exited the car simultaneously. He went around to the trunk, took out their packages, and followed Nina to her front door.

They were barely across the threshold when Ian set the bags down and shoved the door shut with his free hand, then grabbed Nina from behind with his other and turned her into his waiting body.

His mouth covered hers, stealing her breath away, capturing it and letting it fill his lungs. He breathed her in, made her one with him. The curves and fullness of her body merged with his. He pulled her closer, his fingers massaging the sleek lines of her edible form. His hunger to strip her naked built with the intensity of a hurricane swirling inside him.

The sweetness of her tongue as it sensuously danced with his sent jolts of electricity coursing through his limbs. He gathered the folds of her dress and pushed it up around her hips, then cupped her plump bottom in his palms, thrilled to discover that she was wearing the barest of thongs.

Nina moaned in delight when she finally felt the thrust of his rock-hard erection press between her thighs. She felt dizzy with need and found herself peeling his shirt up and over his head, then tossing it to the floor.

Ian unfastened the snap that held the front of her dress closed, and the treasure of her breasts bloomed before him. He groaned deep in his throat and lowered his head to sample what he'd fantasized about from the moment he'd met her.

When the heat and wetness of his mouth touched down on the swell of Nina's breast, her legs trembled. He pushed aside the cup of her bra and teased a taut nipple into his mouth. Lights went off behind her lids, and when he sucked harder, she was sure she would have crumbled in a heap at his feet had he not been holding her around the waist in the vise grip of his arm.

They moaned and rocked against each other, stroking and pulling at clothes, tossing aside what they could and opening up the rest.

"Upstairs," she urged against the onslaught of his mouth. She grabbed his hand and pulled him willingly behind her up the winding staircase to her bedroom.

Nina walked inside and stepped out of her dress. She reached behind her to unhook her bra.

"Wait."

Her gaze collided with Ian's.

"Let me." He crossed the room to where she stood. With taunting deliberation, he reached around her, dropped hot kisses along her exposed neck, and let his fingers play along the curve of her spine, which caused her to arch her body toward him, just the way he wanted. He took her mouth again, palmed her bottom in his large hand, and urged her to quell the throb that thumped between his muscular thighs.

Nina gasped with pleasure, slid her hand between them, and gently caressed him. The feel of his hardened shaft in her hand set her own juices to flowing.

The snap was released. Ian took down one strap and then the other, slipping the cups down one at a time for his own private strip show before tossing the lacy garment onto the armchair. He inhaled deeply, taking her in. She was beautiful. Perfect in his eyes. He reached out and reverently caressed her breasts, thrilled to hear her soft sighs escalate to moans. He stroked her flat belly and toyed with the elastic band of her thong as he inched down her body, planting fiery kisses along the way. He kissed and suckled the insides of her thighs until she began to tremble and clutch his shoulders for support.

He was on his knees now, kissing and nibbling her thighs, her legs, while he inched off her thong until it was around her ankles, and then he worked his way back up until he reached the epicenter of heat.

Her clit was already slightly swollen and glistening in arousal, peeking out from the folds of her sex, almost begging to be taken care of.

First he teased it with a gentle stroke of his thumb. Her body jerked and she cried out. He did it again, and again, softer, harder, faster, slower, until her gentle whimpers grew into ragged moans and her fingers dug deeper into his shoulders and her body shook with pleasure bolts and his fingers became wet and slick with her essence.

She was ripe for the tasting then, like the sweet peach he'd sampled earlier, so he took a lick and another and another, overcome by the hunger for her that rocked him. She was sweeter, tarter, more succulent than he could have ever imagined. He wanted all of her, to drain her dry, feel her body convulse and shimmy with an orgasm that she would always remember, and remember that he was the one who gave it to her.

So he took her over and over, drank of her until she begged him to stop, to finish, to help her, to make it happen . . . cried out to God for mercy, and to him for fulfillment, yes, yes, over and over, until the shudders stopped, and her knees finally weakened.

Ian was nowhere near finished. He picked her up and put her on the bed. Took off his pants and shorts. He stood over her. "Where are they?" he demanded to know.

She looked up at him and felt like she was trapped in some crazy erotic dream that wouldn't end. Her insides were still on fire. Her breasts ached. Her vagina longed for something to fill it.

"Where are they?" he repeated.

Nina blinked. "In the drawer," she managed to say.

Ian pulled the nightstand drawer open and immediately saw the box of condoms. He pulled the box open, scattering some of the shiny packets to the floor.

Nina watched him as he tore open the packet with his teeth and slowly rolled the lambskin over his pulsing member, which began to look more and more like a lethal weapon that, if not controlled, would do real damage. She bent her knees and spread her legs in welcome.

Ian snatched a pillow from the top of the bed and pushed it under Nina's hips, giving him full and total access, then positioned himself between her thighs.

Nina took a deep breath when she felt the thickness of the head press roughly against her opening. She lifted her hips and spread her legs even farther. She buried her face in his neck to keep from screaming when Ian pushed across her wet threshold and filled her to near bursting, knocking the air out of her lungs and sending her cry to bounce off the walls around them.

Ian kept perfectly still, nestled deep within her, even as his body desperately wanted to move in and out of the heated tunnel. But he could feel her trembling as her body slowly adjusted to accommodate him. He would take his cue from her, and when she was ready, he would love her to the bitter end.

Of its own volition and a need that went back to

the beginning of time, her body loosened and began a steady rhythmic undulation, meeting his long, deep thrusts with a slow three-sixty that had them both groaning in pleasure.

They found each other's beat and devised their own dance that went from quick and short to long and deep and back again, ebbing and flowing in intensity, both wanting the end and satisfaction from this sublime torture, yet not wanting it to be over.

But all at once her spot was hit and her insides squeezed around him, and that thrust that he didn't want to give her took over and they surrendered to the will of their bodies that fought and clawed and gripped and shoved and dipped and rolled until one explosion after the other rocked through them, shaking them like rag dolls in a tornado before tossing them back to the earth.

Chapter 8

Be careful what you wish for, kept running through Nina's head as she willed her body to come back to her. *Oh my God.* Never in all of her life had she had sex like that, had an orgasm like that. She was still having aftershocks, and as difficult as it was to comprehend, Ian was still hard as a wood beam inside of her. She stroked his back. Ian was incredible. Sweet, caring, sensitive to her. And if you added that he was handsome, smart, talented, and doing pretty well for himself, you had a man of every woman's fantasy.

Inwardly, she shook her head. *Get yourself in check, sister. You can't let a good ride get you all mushy in the head.* That's not was this was about. This was two consenting adults who had consented to some mind-blowing sex. That's it. Period. She closed her eyes and silently repeated that mantra over and over. *You can't let a good ride get you all mushy in the head.*

It was just sex, Ian told himself. He kissed her gently on the mouth and her sweet response stiffened him even more. This was not what he expected. He knew she would be wonderful, but nothing like this. He stroked the curve of her hip and his fingertips tingled. He felt as if he'd had a spell cast over him or had been "rooted," as his grandmother would say. By now, under normal circumstances, he'd be ready to get up, take a shower, and figure out what was for dinner. But all he could think about now was how he was going to make this last. The problem was this was not what she signed up for and neither had he.

Besides, no matter how good the sex was, it couldn't sustain a relationship between people thousands of miles apart. Relationship! Now he was getting ahead of himself, but he couldn't help it if her cat kept milking him like that. Damnit. He was going to come again. He needed to pull out and get a fresh condom.

"Nooo," Nina moaned and tried to hold him in place by tightening her thighs around him when he pulled out of her.

"I'm coming back, baby." He sucked her nipple and her body bucked. He reached down to the floor and grabbed a condom packet, pulled off the used one, and gingerly placed it on the dresser. He flipped onto his back to roll on the new one. "Turn on your side," he said.

She looked at him and frowned in confusion.

"Go ahead. You'll love it."

"Okay." She turned onto her side so that her back was to him.

Ian scooted behind her, lifted her leg, and draped it over his hip. He positioned himself and pushed and poked and she wound and wiggled until he slipped up inside home sweet home. Could it possibly be better the second time around? The sensation caught them by surprise and rocked them to their toes. With his free hand, he cupped and kneaded her breasts, then traveled down her quivering stomach to play with her clit while he moved in and out.

Nina was sure she was going to lose her natural mind. The thrills and shockwaves that were relentlessly running through her had her brain on scramble and her body on ignite. She covered Ian's hand, and she not only guided his delivery of pleasure to her, but she could feel him move deep inside her, and the sensation was impossible to describe. She bent halfway forward, so that her lower body angled farther upward toward his thrusts.

Ian took her cue and lifted her leg from his hip up over the curve of his arm, giving him full access and total control. He pumped deeper and her encouraging moans urged him on. Somehow she was able to reach around their entwined bodies and palm his ass, demanding that he give her what she wanted—*all of him.*

Tears sprung from her eyes while Ian grew harder, his thrusts deeper, faster, and more urgent. Their slick bodies slapped and popped against each other like rain pounding and splattering against the window. And finally broke through like lightning breaking through the clouds to the roar and rumble of thunder that shakes the earth to the core.

They lay together spoon-fashioned, with Ian holding Nina as tight as he could without squeezing the air out of her lungs. His skin tingled. Her entire being had yet to land. They both silently marveled at what had happened between them, not once, but twice. Both of them knew that whatever it was could not go beyond the sunshine beaches of Hamptons for this one summer. Neither of them wanted it to end. But it had to; that's just the way it was.

Nina eased out of bed and went to the bathroom, quietly shutting the door behind her. For a moment she squeezed her eyes shut and leaned against the door. If she were alone, she would probably be jumping around the room screaming like a crazy woman. The man had turned her out. She would never tell him that, but he sure enough did.

She shook her head. The plan was that *she* was supposed to have put *him* in check. She walked over to the shower and turned it on full blast. Humph, maybe it was that thing he did with his hips, that thing those island men are famous for—*whining*. Lawdhavemercy. She shook her head again as a shiver of delight ran up her spine.

Nina opened the shower door and stepped inside. Ooooh, everything still tingled, she realized as the water hit her and she slowly lathered her body with shower gel. The nerves beneath her skin were still jumping, her nipples were still hard, and her clit was so swollen that it was fully exposed.

"I'm going to need another vacation just to recover from all this," she murmured. *Rita will never believe this.*

She took her time bathing, paying special attention

to all of her sensitive spots. Finally she shut off the water and wrapped up in a thick, full-length towel. The bathroom was filled with steam so that when she stepped out into the bedroom, Ian would have sworn that she was walking out of his dreams and into his life.

"I didn't want to wake you," she said softly. She crossed to the opposite side of the room, if only to keep from jumping back in the bed with him.

Ian was sitting up with the sheet draped across the lower half of his impressive body. "I was up the moment you left my side."

Her heart thumped. She looked around for something to do. *Get dressed, that's it!* "Hungry?" she asked instead.

He grinned. "Ravenous." He stood and the sheet fell to the floor.

Nina sucked in a breath of alarm. Even at half-mast, his sex was threatening. He bent to pick up the remnants of their sexcapade, and she squeezed her eyes shut to keep her mind from going back into hyperdrive. She ran her tongue across her lips. She was parched.

Ian put on his shorts, then finished getting dressed. "I'm going to run home, shower, and change." He crossed the room to where she stood, transfixed. The vanilla and jasmine smell of her went straight to his head, and for a moment he lost his train of thought.

Nina's breathing escalated. The heady, sticky scent of good old-fashioned, toe-curling sex hung on him like an expensive overcoat. Her clit twitched. If he didn't leave, like right now, she thought, there was no telling what she would do. She clung to the hold she had on her towel.

Ian stepped closer. Her senses clouded. He tugged at the knot in the towel. A half smile flickered on his mouth. He tugged again. The makeshift knot loosened. Nina sucked in a breath. Ian peeled the towel away. Slowly he shook his head, knowing good and well that he shouldn't have done that. He tugged on his bottom lip with his teeth to keep from taking one of those raisin-sweet nipples into his mouth.

He swallowed over the dry knot in his throat. "I'll see you around seven," he said, his voice ragged.

Nina nodded.

He turned to leave, then swung back around and pulled her into the need of his body, taking her mouth in a searing kiss that had them sighing and rocking against each other.

Nina unzipped him and pushed his pants down around his ankles. He lifted her and she wound her legs around his waist while he backed her up against the wall and pushed up inside her with such force that his muffled groans matched hers as she clawed his back and sucked his tongue.

The ship was just about to cast off as Ian and Nina came running and giggling down the gang plank. They were both delirious with happiness as if they'd suddenly been awakened for the first time in their lives. Colors seemed brighter, and noises, voices, and music were crystal clear as if their loving was a psychedelic drug that wouldn't cut them loose.

Ian escorted her on board, and they wound their way around the passengers and climbed the stairs to the upper deck to watch the dock recede as they slowly set sail for the dinner cruise. They fit right in with the well-heeled crowd. This definitely was not a T-shirts and flip-flops gathering.

Nina was glad she'd decided on a flirty white dress that hugged her upper curves and swung around her knees, giving a delectable view of her curvy legs. And from what she could see, she was on the arm of the most handsome, sexiest man on the ship. Ian was bedecked in black linen, with a thin leather belt that defined his physique. She tingled inside.

The evening was perfect. The sun was just beginning to descend, casting a glow across the horizon. The air was warm, with a light breeze that caressed more than blew.

Nina and Ian found an empty spot by the railing and took in the scenery that unfolded. They hadn't talked about the amazing late afternoon into early evening that they'd had. Instead they made small talk about the beautiful weather, the cruise ship, and the throng of people who floated around them. But their minds were on each other and what they wanted but didn't dare say.

"Well, fancy running into you again."

They turned. Cara stood behind them, arm in arm with her companion. She glided over to Ian and only kissed his cheek this time. "Nina, right?"

"Right."

Cara turned to her escort, who looked young enough to be her son. "Troy, this is an old and dear friend, Ian Harrison, and Nina. I didn't catch your last name."

"Forbes," she said woodenly and wondered when Cara would remove her hand from Ian's arm.

"Do join us for a drink," she said, linking her arm through Ian's.

"Maybe later."

She pouted. "All right then. But I'm going to hold you to it." She wagged a thin finger at him before whirling away.

Ian lowered his head for a moment and muttered something that Nina couldn't make out. *The hell with protocol,* she decided.

"Who *is* she?"

Ian pushed out a long breath. "We used to date years ago before she became 'famous.'"

"Oh." A million thoughts ran through her head at once. Did he do to Cara the things he'd done to her? Did he make her scream his name in ecstasy? Did he . . .

"Very short and uneventful," he added, cutting into her racing thoughts.

"What does she do?" *Besides get on my nerves,* she inwardly fumed, not at all mollified by his assessment, as it was clear to her that Cara thought differently.

"She's a news anchor for one of the local stations back home. She fancies herself to be a star." He laughed without humor. He turned his full attention on Nina. "She's not important. Although you could never tell her that." He offered a wry smile.

Nina pressed her lips together. He'd be going

back home at some point and so would Cara. The thought darkened her light mood.

Music from the onboard band started from below deck and floated up to them.

"Come on. Let's go down and get a table. I'm still famished." He gave her a meaningful look and her heart pounded a little faster. He took her hand and led her down the winding staircase.

The lower deck was filling up with passengers. The band was set up on a stage at the far end. An enormous buffet table took up one whole side of the ship, offering everything from salads to lobster and everything in between. The bar, with at least six bartenders, took up the other side.

"Drinks or food?"

"I think I need to put some food in my stomach before I dare take a drink," Nina said.

"Hmmm, you're right. No telling what I might do to you with a belly full of alcohol." He kissed the tip of her nose.

It was the first mention of their romp and Nina didn't know what she should make of it. Was it simply casual to him or did it have any meaning? She knew she shouldn't be thinking that way, but she couldn't help it. Something happened between him and her, and it was more than just sex, at least it was to her, and she felt ridiculous for feeling that way. It wasn't what they'd nonverbally agreed to. She'd come on to him like a woman of the world. Like this was just a fling. But now she was having second thoughts.

Ian handed her a plate. "Are you all right? You seem distracted."

She forced a smile. "No. I'm fine. I was thinking about some calls I need to make."

He looked at her for a moment, hoping to see in her eyes what he was experiencing inside. But she wouldn't meet his gaze and instead focused on filling her plate as she moved down the length of the table.

After the early bumps in the evening, they began to unwind, relax to the music, and enjoy the gentle sway of the ship. The food was fabulous, the drinks top-shelf and strong, and the atmosphere was perfect. To cap everything off, Ian was an incredible dancer, smooth and light on his feet, and he held her just right.

Nina felt like a precious jewel in Ian's embrace. He cooed and whispered in her ear as he moved her around the floor. Told her jokes that made her giggle and misstep, and when the band played the Luther Vandross classic "A House Is Not a Home," he held her close and she rested her head on his chest, and the scary thought settled deep inside her: She wanted this to last.

"Mind if I cut in?"

Nina opened her eyes and lifted her head to find Cara standing beside her with a Cheshire cat grin on her face. The scent of brandy mixed with her perfume.

Nina's brow rose a fraction. She stepped out of Ian's arms. "Be my guest." Before Ian could react, she walked away. The last thing she wanted to see was Cara all hugged up with Ian.

She quickly crossed the room, not daring to look back. She headed for the stairs and went above deck to get some much-needed air.

Finding a semisecluded spot in a small alcove, Nina gripped the rail, lifted her head to the heavens, and drew in the salty night air.

The strains of the music drifted up to her and she envisioned Cara in Ian's arms. Why should it matter whom he danced with? They'd had great sex, no strings attached.

"Hey . . ."

Nina turned halfway.

Ian walked toward her, his gaze burning across her length. Her heart knocked.

"Why did you leave me with that woman?"

But before she could answer, his mouth covered hers. His tongue teased and played hide-and-seek in her mouth as he pulled her fully against him.

Reluctantly he pulled back. He lifted her head with a finger beneath her chin. "We don't have a lot of time, but the time that we do have I want to spend with you." His gazed moved across her face. "Does that work for you?"

Nina swallowed. "Sure," she said and hoped she didn't sound as breathless and shaky as she felt inside.

He lightly pressed his lips to hers. "That's what I wanted to hear. Now, I think you still owe me a dance, love."

"What about Cara?"

He took her hand and led her toward the stairs. "What about her?" he responded without missing a beat, his tone dismissive.

Nina decided to leave it alone and enjoy her evening with her summer fling.

Chapter 9

"I had a fabulous time," Nina said, a bit light-headed from the three drinks and the sea air.

Ian held her securely around her waist as they walked to her front door. She stopped at the entrance and fished around in her purse for the key.

"Coming in?"

"Not tonight." He stroked her cheek. "I think we could both use some rest and that will never happen if I'm in your bed."

"Are you sure?" she purred, running her finger along the opening in his shirt.

He clasped her hand. "Yes."

She turned away, feeling foolish, found her key, and opened the door. "Good night, then."

"Breakfast tomorrow?"

She shrugged. She pushed the door open, turned to give him a parting look at what he was missing, and shut the door.

Ian pushed out a soft laugh, trotted down the two steps, and headed across the space that separated the houses and went inside.

He fixed himself a cup of tea and went out on his back deck in hopes of clearing his head. Nina had a stronger effect on him than he'd allowed himself to admit. The last thing he needed to do was spend the night with her, as much as he wanted to. When was the last time he'd turned down a willing and available woman?

The thing was, he knew deep in his gut that she wasn't like the others. And if he treated her as such, she would be hurt in the end. He couldn't do that to her. The best thing for the both of them was for him to back up, give them some distance and him some perspective. Otherwise . . . well, he simply didn't know.

Nina squinted against the sun. She groaned. Her head pounded. She pulled the sheet up over her head and willed herself back to sleep. It didn't work. She turned onto her side and squeezed her eyes to focus on the digital bedside clock. It was after ten. She never slept that late, but she never drank that much either. One drink was usually her quota for a night, and she'd had three.

"Aggg." She forced herself to sit up and every joint in her body rebelled. Why in the world was she aching . . . And then everything flashed back in blooming, high-speed Technicolor. Yesterday. Ian. In her bed, up against the wall, her body twisting and turning, her legs in positions that defied possibility.

She shut her eyes and flopped back onto the thick pillows. She ran her hands along her naked body, stretching like a cat, remembering what he'd done to her. And how he'd left her at the door. She sat up, covered her face with her hands for a moment, then slowly stood. The room wobbled for an instant or maybe it was her that wobbled. Taking a deep breath to shoot some oxygen to her brain, she walked into the bathroom and looked at her reflection in the mirror.

Her face was a bit puffy and her wild natural curls stood up on her head in a hundred different directions. There was a blooming red spot, the size of a quarter, above her right nipple, where Ian had suckled, and another on her inner thigh. She shut her eyes and shivered, recalling how they'd gotten there.

She shook her head. Ian Harrison was not the first man she'd ever had sex with, for heavensake. She reached for the knobs of the shower and turned on the water. This was crazy, she thought, even as her kitty cat still purred for more.

About an hour later she was finally feeling and looking more like herself. She donned a tank top that came halfway down to her stomach and a pair of old shorts that she'd had since college and padded down to the kitchen. Her tummy growled as she rummaged around in the fridge to fix something to eat, then she remembered that Ian had promised breakfast.

Humph. So much for that. She took out the carton of eggs, some wheat bread for toast, and set up the coffeemaker. She was just beating the eggs in a bowl when she heard a car door slam. She strolled over to the side window that faced Ian's house.

Her pulse began to race. She looked closer. It was Cara, tossing what appeared to be an overnight bag into the backseat of her car. What the . . .

Ian stood shirtless in his doorway. His pajama pants hung low on his hips. Cara blew him a kiss, strutted around to the driver's side, and got behind the wheel.

Nina couldn't move. She was paralyzed with disbelief and outrage and stood rooted in the same spot long after the car was gone.

She sat at the kitchen table staring at her cold eggs and lukewarm coffee. No wonder he didn't want to come in last night; he'd already made plans with Cara to take her place. Is that what they'd talked about when they danced?

She was an idiot! An idiot to give it up to a man she barely knew. Ian and Cara had a history. He'd admitted as much, and obviously it wasn't over, no matter that he'd denied it. What he'd really done was lie to her.

Her throat tightened. She would not cry. She wouldn't. She pressed her lips tightly together and blinked away the burn in her eyes.

Finally she pushed back from the table and stood, tossed her uneaten food in the trash and the coffee down the drain. She drew in a deep breath of resolve.

Fine. They'd made no commitment. He was free to do what he wanted. And so was she. She went upstairs, put on a bathing suit, threw on a sundress in bright orange, and grabbed the sunscreen, a wide floppy straw hat, towel, blanket, the first novel she laid her hands on, ID, and her keys, stuffing the necessities in an oversized tote bag, and marched out.

She didn't dare look in the direction of Ian's house or she was liable to throw something through his window. She got behind the wheel of her car and pulled off, and never saw him stepping out of his house with a breakfast tray topped with a red rose.

Nina made a quick stop at the deli and ordered a sandwich, got several bottles of water and some fruit, got back in the car, and drove for a good twenty minutes, wanting to get as far away as possible. She drove through town, beyond the shops and the docked boats, to the other end of the sandy shore. She drove around until she found a place to park, then hiked down to the beach.

She scanned the expanse of beach and spotted an area not too close to the water and with enough shade that she wouldn't have to move anytime soon or be disturbed by anyone. Spreading out her blanket, she then pulled her dress over her head, shoved it in her tote, and settled down with her book. Much to her dismay, it was a romance novel.

Page after page detailed the blistering romance between a young nurse and a rising star doctor, and the sex scenes had Nina in flashbacks of her liaison with Ian. Finally she couldn't take it anymore and tossed the book aside. In romance novels the heroine always gets her man and they live happily ever after. Yeah, in romance novels. This was no novel. This was her life and she'd messed up big time. There was no happily ever after in her book.

She dug in her bag for the sunscreen and liberally

applied it to all the exposed parts of her body. A big mistake people of color make is thinking that they can't get sunburned or, worse, skin cancer. Melanin or not, she had no intention of being a statistic. Returning the sunscreen to her bag, she removed her sandwich and took a few bites, contemplating the rest of her weeks at the Hamptons. Number one, she would stay the hell away from Ian. Two, she'd find something to do every day. She'd never gone waterskiing. Maybe she would try that. And she had brought the pages of a manuscript she'd been working on for years with her in hopes that the change of environment would inspire her. That would certainly keep her busy.

She'd be fine and before she knew it, her time would be up, and she'd go back home and pretend that none of this ever happened. She pulled the hat down over her eyes, laid back, and closed her eyes. Maybe when she woke up it would all be a bad dream.

After an hour and Nina had not returned, Ian emptied the wasted food into the garbage. He was sure he'd said they would have breakfast together in the morning. Maybe she'd forgotten or changed her mind. He'd been over to her place twice. Her car wasn't in the driveway and there was still no answer when he rang the bell.

When he saw her drive off, he figured maybe she was making a quick run into town. Obviously he was wrong. He didn't have the time to dwell on it or the inclination to uncover the mysteries of a woman's thought process. He had a big day ahead of him. It was opening night and he was already behind schedule waiting on Nina to return.

He gathered his things and headed out to his car, dropped everything in the backseat, then walked across to Nina's front porch. He stuck a note in her door and took one last look at her empty driveway before he pulled off.

A low and distant rumble penetrated Nina's dreams, followed by a splat of water on her belly. She jumped up. Her hat toppled to the sand and her tote bag tumbled on its side. The horizon had turned an ominous gray. Dark clouds raced across the sky. She looked around. The beach was all but deserted save for a few intrepid souls. She tugged her dress over her head and pulled it down. Another drop of water hit her, followed by another. She scrambled to gather up her belongings, shoving what she could in her bag and tucking the rest under her arm. If there was one thing she remembered from her Georgia summers with her grandmother, it was to stay away from trees and beaches during a storm.

She ran off in the direction that she remembered parking her car and the heavens opened. Before she was halfway there, she was drenched. Thunder rumbled and lightning flashed. The rain came down in blinding sheets and her feet sunk into the wet sand, making running nearly impossible. Her hat blew out of her hand and sailed off into the storm. She tried to cover her eyes from the swirling wind and blowing sand as she tripped and stumbled her way to shelter.

Mercifully she reached her car, wiped the water from her face, and searched in her bag for her keys. A crack of lightning lit up the sky. Her dress was stuck to her body, and her feet were caked with sand. She couldn't find her keys. She pushed everything around inside her bag. No keys.

Her heart pounded. They had to be in there. She looked again and came up empty. Oh hell, what was she going to do? It was miles back to her house and there was no way she could make it in this weather. She'd brilliantly decided to find the most secluded spot on the beach and now she was paying the price. There wasn't a soul in the vicinity who she could ask for help, and the only person she knew in the whole town was Ian. She had no intention of having him come to her rescue.

Wait. Lauren. She'd given Nina her phone number the night they'd met. She pushed her wet hair out of her face and took her wallet out of the bag, thumbed through the contents. Her body deflated in defeat. It wasn't there. Why would it be? Nothing had gone right since she'd awakened this morning.

She felt tears stinging her eyes. She slid down the side of the car and dropped her head to her knees. What was she going to do?

Thunder boomed, followed by rapid snaps of lightning, shaking her to her core. She couldn't stay out here. It was dangerous. She looked around at nothing but miles of sand and darkness. Standing and trying to shield her face from the onslaught of mother nature, she tried to determine which way to go. She was so rattled she'd totally lost her sense of direction. Now she did cry.

Ian was busy checking with the chef to ensure that the menu was ready for the evening. They were scheduled to open at seven for dinner. Entertainment would start at nine. According to his hostess, Marissa, they were booked for the night. Reservations had been made weeks in advance in anticipation of opening night. He'd built a solid reputation for quality, exquisite dining, an eclectic blend of entertainment, and professionalism. His customers always returned, and word of mouth had brought people in from far and wide. So the storm didn't bother him. His customers were loyal, and even if a few didn't show up, he would still have a pretty full house.

"Sea bass is the house special tonight. You're sure we have enough?" he asked his chef.

"We have plenty." He patted Ian's shoulder. "Not to worry."

Ian's jaw clenched. He nodded then walked away.

"Ian, there's a call for you," Marissa shouted out, holding up the phone.

Ian crossed the dining area and walked around the bar to where Marissa was at the reception podium reviewing reservations.

"Thanks." He took the phone. "Hello. Hello? I can't hear you. Who is this?"

Static and a muffled voice that sounded as if it

were coming from under water filled the line,
breaking the words into indistinguishable particles.

Ian held one hand to his free ear in the hopes of
blocking out any excess noise. It was definitely a
woman.

"Hello. Who is this?" He frowned, then his pulse
kicked up a notch. "Nina. Nina, is this you? I can
barely hear you. What? Stranded . . . Where? Do
you know where you are?" He strained to make out
what she was saying and the line went dead. He
looked at the phone in disbelief.

The lights flickered. Marissa gasped. An unbe-
lievably loud boom like the earth opening up filled
the air, and the sky lit up for an instant like the
Fourth of July.

Quickly Ian pressed caller ID. Although the
name didn't show up in the dial, the number did.
Accustomed to freak storms, he quickly jotted
down the number in the event that the phone lines
went dead. He dialed the number from his cell
and prayed that the call would go through. His
blood heated as a dozen unpleasant scenarios
played out in his head. The phone rang. *Pick up.*
Pick up. The scratchy sound of the line being answered on the other end allowed him to release
the breath he'd held.

"Ian! I'm stuck." Her words felt as if they were
being whipped into the maelstrom and she had no
idea if he even heard her.

"I'll come for you. Tell me where you are."

"Not sure. At the farthest end of the beach. It's

empty out here." Her voice began to break. "I can't see."

"Can you get to any shelter?" he yelled into the phone.

"No. I'm near my car."

"I'm on my way."

"Sounds serious," Marissa said when he'd disconnected the call.

"A . . . friend is stranded. I don't know how long I'll be. If things get too bad, I want you to lock up. Don't worry about tonight. We'll play it by ear."

Marissa nodded and patted his shoulder, urging him toward the door. "I can handle it. Go to your friend."

He grabbed his jacket from the hook behind the desk, checked for his cell phone and his keys, and pulled the door open, only to be blasted by whipping winds and rain. He tried to shield his face with his arm as he pushed against the wind to get to his car.

The streets were deserted. The sky was black as pitch. The few streetlights that were on flickered limply. He got to his car and struggled against the wind to get the door open. He turned on the car and then the high beams, which reached out and hung in the darkness like two ghosts.

What was she doing way out on the other end of the island? he wondered as he pulled away from the curb and headed toward the beach. Being near all that open water was the last place anyone should be in this kind of weather.

He gripped the wheel. He should have told her

to move a safe distance from her car. Although being inside the car during a lightning storm was safe because the car was grounded, being outside of one was a different story. Everything about a car potentially could attract lightning.

He stepped on the gas, splashing through at least a half foot of water that doused the windows and momentarily blinded him. The wipers were working overtime and almost to no avail. As fast as they pushed the water aside, it was replaced with twice as much.

The trip under ordinary circumstances should take only about twenty minutes. But with virtually no visibility and flash flooding it would easily take twice as long. Twice as long for Nina to wait for him to get to her. Too much time. Anything could happen.

He wouldn't focus on that now. He needed to keep his head in the game and his eyes on the road.

Nina had wrapped her towel and blanket around her and was huddled by the rear tire of her car. Even though it was at least ninety degrees, she'd begun to shiver. She was no longer sure if it was a chill or fear.

She'd never in her life felt so utterly helpless and alone. This was totally unbelievable that she'd found herself in this dangerous, if not ridiculous, situation and needed rescuing of all things.

She hugged herself tighter as a chill rippled through her. Next she'd have pneumonia on top of everything else. Resting her head on her knees, in one hysterical thought she wished she could call for Lassie like Timmy did in the sixties black-and-white television show, and have the rescue collie lead her to safety through the blinding storm, because she certainly felt like she'd been mistakenly cast in the reality television show *Survivor*—her against the elements.

What if Ian never found her? What if something happened to him along the way? It would be her fault. It was crazy to think that this storm would never stop and that she'd never be found, but that was exactly how she was feeling until she thought she spotted headlights piercing through the rain.

Nina pushed herself to a standing position and was quickly knocked against the side of the car, banging her hip. She tried to wave in the hopes that she would be seen as the wind and driving rain whipped the blanket and towel around her, lassoing her legs.

Ian spotted her up ahead. The car rocked back and forth and it struggled for traction. The last thing he needed was for the both of them to get stuck. He turned off the ignition but kept the lights on, got out, and half walked, half trudged to where Nina was huddled.

When he reached her, no words were exchanged between them. She tumbled into his arms and he held her trembling body against the warmth of his. His kisses were quickly washed away with the rain, but he kissed her face anyway.

"Come on," he shouted, draping his arm around her and pulling her close. "Let's get out of here."

Chapter 10

Nina didn't even pay attention to where they were going. She was so tired and weather-beaten that all she wanted was a hot bath and dry clothes.

Ian ushered her into his house, and before she could get her bearings, he'd swooped her up in his arms and carried her upstairs to the bathroom. He turned on the tub while he ordered her to strip out of her saturated clothes. He gave her his robe to put on while the tub filled, then added some sea salt to the water to take out any aches that may be brewing.

Nina pulled down the seat to the toilet and sat down. "Thank you," she murmured.

Ian glanced at her. "I'm just glad you called." He wanted to ask her what she was doing out there, what happened to her car and to their breakfast date, but decided that there would be time enough for that. "Water is ready. Hope it's not too hot."

She shivered and gingerly walked over to the tub. She'd never felt more vulnerable in her life. And the fact that she'd done things with this man and he'd done things to her that should have stripped away any apprehensions didn't matter. She quickly turned her back to him and let the robe fall from her shoulders to the cool sea blue mosaic tiles and stepped into the steamy water.

Her entire body moaned with pleasure as she sunk down into the tub, the water rising up to her neck. She leaned back and closed her eyes, enjoying the first moment of peace since she'd awakened. *This morning.* The reason for her current dilemma came hurtling back. *Cara.* Her eyes flew open and she looked around. Ian was gone. She hadn't heard him leave.

Was the lovely Ms. Cara going to wind up down in his living room, waiting to greet her after her bath? She felt her ire rise along with the steam from the water.

She roughly scrubbed her skin with the cloth he'd given her, reached for the soap, and lathered. His scent immediately filled her nostrils and for a moment she felt lightheaded with the heady memories of him. She drew in a breath. Whatever the situation was between him and Cara didn't really matter. She was in his house, in his tub. He'd come out into a blinding storm to get her. He didn't have to. That had to mean something, a little something—didn't it?

Nina secured the belt of Ian's robe around her waist and padded downstairs to the mouthwatering aroma of simmering chicken and the sound of cool jazz. She found him in the kitchen, chopping vegetables.

He turned at her approach, and the smile he gave her and the light in his eyes warmed her more deeply than a hot bath ever could.

"My mum always said chicken soup was the cure for anything. Don't want you catching cold from being out in the weather. Made you a cup of tea in the meantime. Hope you like apple cinnamon."

Her heart filled. She nodded and came to sit at the table. "My favorite, actually."

He chuckled. "Mine too." He looked at her for a moment, wanted to say what he really felt, but thought better of it. No point in leading her on by trying to make more out of what was only a temporary situation. She'd given him no indication that she wanted more than a summer fling, anyway. He returned his attentions to dicing vegetables and dropping them in the boiling pot.

Nina sipped her tea. There was so much she wanted to say but didn't dare. He'd really think she was a fool if she opened her mouth and the words in her heart tumbled out.

Her gaze slowly rose. Ian was standing above her. Her heart thudded. He reached for the cup and took it out of her hand before gently pulling her to her feet. She held her breath when she witnessed the raw look of desire burning in his eyes.

"When I heard your voice and knew you were out in that storm alone . . . I've never been so . . ." He drew in a breath. "I know that in a few weeks you're going to go back home and so am I. At first

I figured—no problem. But now it is a problem, Nina."

"W-what are you saying?"

"I'm saying that for as long as we have, I want us to spend the time together, really get to know each other . . . in and out of bed."

Nina looked down at their entwined hands then into his eyes. "I need to know why, Ian. Why does it matter?"

He released her hands and turned away, crossed the room to the sink, and turned on the water to give himself something to do. He wasn't going to confess. He wasn't going to break down and tell her that he felt that he could really care for her. That he *did* care for her. That maybe somehow they could work something out when the summer was over. She wasn't going to get him to say that. If what he'd told her wasn't enough . . . well then . . . it just wasn't.

Nina felt as if an eternity had passed and he wouldn't tell her what she wanted to hear. Could she deal with that? Did she want to? Could she spend time with him, make love with him, share parts of herself with him, without knowing if there was an end game? What would be the point of that? She wasn't sure if she could keep her budding feelings from sprouting into full bloom. It was scary. It was risky. It was a chance she was willing to take, and she decided in that instant that if she was going along for the ride, she would give only as much as she got and not an ounce more, and maybe at summer's end she could return to her life with parts of her soul still intact.

"You know what," she said, walking over to him at the sink. She reached over and turned off the faucet. "Forget I asked. I want to get to know you too. Whatever will be, will."

"You sure?"

She hesitated a moment before nodding her head.

He studied her face, looking for any telltale sign of doubt. "Okay, so you want to tell me why you tore out of here this morning when we had a breakfast date?"

"You get right to the point, don't you?" she said, spinning away and returning to her spot at the table.

"Well . . ."

Nina blew out a long breath then looked him straight in the eyes. "I saw Cara leaving your house this morning." There, she'd said it.

He frowned for a moment; then sunshine seemed to break through the clouds. His head snapped slightly back. "Cara! Oh bloody hell." He paced across the room, pulled out a chair, spun it around, and straddled it backward so that he could drape his arms across the top. "She was not invited. She did come by to . . . see if we could resume our relationship. I told her no. I told her not to come back if that was her agenda." He made a noise in his throat. "She asked me if you were the reason."

Nina's nostrils flared as she sucked in air. "What did you tell her?"

The corner of his mouth lifted ever so slightly. "What do you think I told her?" he challenged. "Who's sitting in my kitchen, naked beneath my robe? You or Cara?"

Nina's body flushed. Her temples pounded.

"Does that answer your question?"

Nina lifted her chin. "For the time being."

Ian chuckled and shook his head in bemusement. "Women," he muttered.

"Men," she tossed back with a flirty smirk on her face.

Ian's gaze began to smolder. He pushed back from the chair and stood and walked purposefully toward her. He tugged her to her feet and hard up against his body. "It's going to be at least another hour before that soup is ready." He slid his hand under the folds of her robe and cupped her breast, ran his finger over the nipple until she moaned and turned into putty in his hands. "You think you're up to handling this . . ." He took her hand and placed it on his blooming erection.

Her heart skipped in her chest.

"Until the dinner bell," he added, dipping his head to taste the lush fruit of her breasts.

Nina moaned, arching her body to give him better access as she held his head in place, letting him feast. "I thought you wanted us to get to know each other," she whispered breathlessly.

"I did say that, didn't I?" He pulled the string on his sweatpants and let them pool at his feet. He backed up to a chair and sat down. He tugged on the belt of the robe that Nina wore and it parted. "Humph, umph, umph. Woman . . . you will make a man do some crazy things. Come here."

She offered him a sultry look, dropped the robe to the floor, leaned down so that the weight of her breasts swung like a tantalizing pendulum before him.

He reached for her and she slipped out of his way and strolled naked as the day she was born into the front room, where she'd dropped her bag when she came in. With any luck, she wouldn't have lost her emergency condoms along with her car keys.

Knowing that he was watching, she bent over very slowly to reach for her purse and chuckled to herself when she heard him utter something like "sweet heaven."

One thing was going right so far. She found a lone condom packet in the folds of her wallet. With exaggerated slowness, she returned and held it out to him. "You were saying something about me being able to handle this," she taunted, clasping his member in her palm and stroking him languorously up and down until he gritted his teeth to keep from shouting.

Nina tore it open with her teeth and put the empty foil pouch in the robe pocket. She'd never put a condom on a man before and she wasn't sure if she was right or wrong as she unrolled it over his length. There was something uniquely sensual about what she was doing. It thrilled her in a way she didn't expect. This was a different level of intimacy, and although she would never tell Ian, she was glad that this first experience was with him.

Ian tried to control himself as he watched her sheath him. He gripped the sides of the chair. He knew that if he didn't think about something other than the way her tender hands caressed him with such care, the almost reverent way she covered him that shook him deep down inside, he would explode in her hand.

Mercifully, she finished and then straddled him like a cowgirl ready to ride a bronco, lowered herself down slow and easy, sucking in air with each inch of him that she took until he filled her completely.

And then the fun began.

"This has got to be the best chicken soup I've ever had," Nina said, mouthing another thick spoonful.

Ian threw a lightweight quilt over her as they lay on the floor in front of the fireplace finishing off the soup. "Glad you like it. My mum would be happy to hear it. It's the family recipe."

"I've never been to Barbados, or England either, for that matter. What's it like?" She trailed her finger along his hairline, studied him, committing every feature to memory.

At some point they'd wandered into the living room after ravishing each other and coming to the conclusion that his kitchen chair would never be the same again.

"Hmmm." He rolled onto his back, thankful for the thick quilt beneath them. "Barbados is like paradise on earth. The weather is beautiful. The beaches are white. Fruit hangs low from the trees. On a clear night, the sky is midnight blue like a velvet box with millions of diamonds inside," he said, easily slipping into the musical cadence of his home. "Nothing can compare to growing up on an island. Running barefoot, swimming every day." He laughed lightly at the memories and turned to look at her. "You would love it there."

Her breath caught for a moment, but she refused

to read any more into what he'd said. She'd simply take it at face value that Barbados is a great place to visit. "Sounds wonderful. I can understand why you always go back. When did you go to England?"

"A rite of passage for children of the Caribbean. The islands never really shook off the British influences even after independence. I was shipped off after primary school. I finished secondary school in England, then stayed there and got my degree. What about you?"

"Hmmm, quite uneventful. I'm a product of a Catholic school education. First to twelfth grade. Oldest of two girls. My dad passed when I was fifteen. I suppose I grew up before my time since I had to help my mother. It seemed like I was always working, some part-time job or another." She sputtered a short laugh. "Made it through high school forever traumatized by the nuns and threats of burning in hell."

Ian chuckled and patted her thigh. "Poor thing."

They were quiet for a moment, imagining each other as children in a different life, a different world.

"You hear that?" Ian asked, propping up on his elbow.

"Hear what?"

"Silence." He pushed up from his reclining position and went to the window. "The rain finally stopped."

She pulled his robe on around her and joined him at the window. "Look!" She pointed toward the horizon. "A rainbow."

They watched it in awe, fascinated by beauty in the aftermath of nature's wrath.

"Guess it's safe for me to head home," she said quietly and started to move away.

Ian captured her around the waist. "I meant what I said earlier about us spending time together." He kissed her lightly on the lips. "Why don't you come to the club? I'll be doing my thing, but we can have dinner, and the band that's playing tonight is worth the price of your free admission," he teased.

She looked up at him and her heart skipped around in her chest. "I'd like that."

"And then afterward you can spend the night here. I want to wake up with you in the morning. How does that sound?"

"Sounds like a plan that I can live with."

"I doubt that your clothes are dry. I'll give you something to put on and walk you over."

"You don't have to do that."

"Do what, give you something to wear or walk you over?"

She playfully swatted his arm. "Walk me to my door."

He chuckled. "I know I don't have to; I want to. I had home trainin'," he added in that sexy British and Caribbean blend.

"Fine. If it will make you happy." She spun away.

He watched her sway across the room and had the stirring sensation that he could very easily get used to having Nina around.

Chapter 11

With the storm having passed, the Hamptonites were out for a night on the town. Harrison's was full. The waiters could hardly keep up with the orders. Food was piled high, the wine and spirits flowed, and the music soothed the soul.

Nina was seated near the stage where she had a view of all the comings and goings. Ian had been able to stop by only briefly, but he'd promised as soon as things slowed down he would join her.

The waitress brought her dinner, and as delicious as it looked, she wished she didn't have to eat alone.

"Nina?"

She glanced up and it was as if her silent wish had been answered. "Lauren. Keith."

The couple came over. "So good to see you again," Lauren said. "Are you here alone?"

"Hmmm. Not exactly. I came with Ian, but as you can tell, he's busy tonight."

Lauren looked around. "Definitely a full house.

We have a table, but you seem to have the best seat in the house. Mind if we join you?"

"I'd love it. Please. Sit."

"Why don't you ladies chat? I'm going to hang out at the bar. When you're ready to order, babe, get my usual." He kissed his wife's cheek and wound his way around the tables and people in route to the bar.

"That was easy," Lauren joked as she sat down opposite Nina. She put her purse on the table. "So how do you like the place?"

"It's great. Ian gave me the tour the other day when it was empty. I had no idea it could hold this many people."

Lauren smiled. "Even though Harrison's is relatively new to the Hamptons, Ian has done a fabulous job building his clientele."

"So I see."

"Tell me what you've been up to, getting settled?"

"I had a bit of a scare today," she confessed.

"Really? What happened?"

Nina told her about her trip to the secluded end of the beach and getting caught in the storm with no way of getting back.

"Oh my goodness. You must have been terrified. That storm was vicious. I'm surprised there isn't more damage."

"I know. Believe me, I realize how lucky I am."

"What did you do about your car?"

"Ian called a tow company and it's at the shop. Fortunately I had a spare key at the house. I'll pick it up tomorrow."

Lauren slowly shook her head. "I'm glad that you were able to reach Ian. Even if you had been able to get me on the phone, we were miles away. We drove out last night to visit Keith's parents in Hempstead."

The waitress stopped at their table. "What can I get for you, ma'am?"

"A glass of white wine. Can you give me a few minutes to look over the menu?"

"Of course. I'll be right back with your wine. Is everything all right with your dinner?" she asked Nina.

"Oh, yes. It's fine. Thanks."

Lauren turned her attention to Nina. She angled her head to the side. "So . . . how are you and Ian getting along?"

Nina blushed and was thankful for the dim lighting. "Fine. He's a great guy." She cut into her salmon. "Do you know Cara, by any chance?" She kept her eyes on her plate.

Lauren made a sucking noise with her teeth. "That hoochie," she said with disgust. "Trouble. From the day she came into his life." She shook her head. "I tried to tell him to steer clear of her. But she got her hooks in him good." She blew out a breath. "I'm glad it's all behind him now. He finally saw the light." She leaned toward Nina and lowered her voice. "I hear she's in town."

"She is. We've met." Nina gave a quick rundown of their encounters.

"Hmmm." Lauren was thoughtful for a moment. "I'm assuming that if you asked about her that you have a more than casual interest in Ian."

Nina had no idea Lauren would be so bold, but then again, Nina opened the door by asking about Cara. She took a breath and put down her fork. "I like Ian. I like him a lot. But we can't get all wrapped up in each other. We live hundreds of miles apart. It could never work." Her last words were more of a question than a statement.

"Ridiculous. Let me tell you one thing. Me and Keith . . . I lived in Barbados and he lived in England. For five years." She held up her hand to emphasize her point then slapped her palm on the table. "But he finally woke up and realized that if he wanted all this"—she ran her hand dramatically down her body—"then he was going to have to make a decision . . . live with me or without me." She tossed her hand in the air. "Girl, I got tired of flying back and forth and of phone bills that were as large as the national debt."

They laughed.

The waitress returned with her wine and Lauren put in the dinner order for her and Keith. They both wanted the sea bass. The waitress picked up the menu and asked Nina if she needed anything.

"Not right now. Thanks."

Lauren lifted her glass toward Nina. "To going after what you want."

Nina lifted her glass before taking a sip. Keith and Lauren obviously wanted the same thing. She couldn't say the same for her and Ian. She had no idea what he really wanted. All she could go by was what he told her.

* * *

Keith had stopped by the table when the food arrived and just as quickly returned to the bar, where he'd struck up a friendship with two other men. Ian dropped by several times but couldn't stay long, promising to come back as soon as he could. Lauren and Nina spent the better part of the evening getting better acquainted, sharing stories about their respective careers, Nina's love of vintage clothing, and Lauren's abhorrence of the cold and her overwhelming desire to have a baby.

"We've been trying," she said, looking off into the distance. "I'm scared of the fertility drugs. I mean, look at Octomom." She gave a little shiver. "And Keith isn't thrilled about adoption." She slowly turned her glass around in a circle.

Nina hadn't thought much about children, at least not in the immediate sense. Her days were filled with them in the classroom, and she didn't hear her biological clock ticking in the distance.

She caught a glimpse of Ian talking with one of the staff members and she thought that maybe the reason children weren't on her radar was because she'd never found anyone that she wanted to have children with. One that made her feel so strongly that she wanted to share the joy of creating something with them.

"Everyone says when the time is right," Lauren said, cutting into Nina's thoughts.

Nina focused on Lauren and saw the sadness that hung in her eyes. She reached across the table and covered her hand with her own. "I'm sure your friends are right," she said gently. "You need to believe that too. It'll happen."

Lauren looked at Nina with so much hope in her eyes, as if Nina held the secrets of the universe in the palm of her hand and could somehow make dreams come true. And then just as quickly, she was back to her fun-loving, sometimes snarky self as she began a running commentary on the couples in the club, the outfits, how the sax player held his sax, and, of course, the gossip that had Nina in stitches.

Ian did manage to sweep her onto the dance floor during one of the band's slow numbers and whispered hot and deep in her ear that if she let him, he'd make up his absence to her until the sun came up.

It was well after two in the morning by the time they pulled into Ian's driveway. Once inside, he poured them a glass of wine and they snuggled together on the couch, talking about the successful opening and some of the upcoming entertainment he'd planned, including his signature Spoken Word evening.

By silent agreement they made their way up to Ian's bedroom, and he was good at his word. They made slow, crazy love until they were too weak, too satisfied to do anything more than curl up in each other's arms and dream of the impossible.

Chapter 12

Nina stretched catlike beneath the silky-soft cotton sheets. The morning sun was high in the sky. The air conditioner was on just right. Even though her body ached in all the right places, she felt incredible. Happy. Almost giddy. Who would have thought that a house-sitting gig could turn into every girl's fantasy—getting busy with a man to die for.

She sat up. Where was Ian? She got out of bed and went to the door and walked out into the hallway. Downstairs was quiet. She returned to the bedroom and looked out the back window that opened onto the deck.

Ian had set up his easel and was busy painting. A warm feeling of comfort and stability filled her as if this was the way things were supposed to be.

She shook her head and stepped away from the window. *Don't go there,* she warned herself. In a few weeks this fantasy would be over and reality would resume. She went downstairs and recovered her clothing that had been washed and dried after the storm, then went back upstairs, showered, and joined Ian on the deck.

"Good morning."

"Hey." He put down his brush and wiped his hands on his paint-splattered jeans. "You were sleeping so peacefully, I didn't want to wake you." He walked over to her, threaded his fingers through her hair in back, and pulled her into a deep, sweet kiss.

"Hmm, good morning," she whispered against his mouth.

"I could get used to this," he said, then turned back to his painting.

Nina blinked away her surprise. No. She would not read anything into what he just said. "What are you painting?" She walked down the last step and came up next to him. Her mouth opened, but no words came out.

It was her! And not. The image of her was there, with the body type, the wild hair, pouty lips, and wide eyes, all superimposed on bursts of colors, splashed behind the woman, through, and around her. It was as if she were stepping out of a rainbow of color.

"Ian . . ." It was all she could say. She stepped closer.

Ian gauged her reaction. It was a mixture of surprise and awe.

"It's . . . it's me."

"I started it shortly after we met. I wanted to make a present of it to you."

Her throat clenched. Her hand went to her mouth. She'd never seen anything like it. It was sexy and understated and bold and surreal all at once.

"I . . . I don't know what to say."

"You can tell me if you like it," he hedged, with a lift of his right brow.

She turned to him and he was stunned to see tears welling in her eyes.

"You hate it."

"No, no," she croaked. "It's . . . beautiful. I . . ." She shook her head, at a total loss for words. A tear rolled down her cheek.

Ian came closer. He wiped away the tear with the pad of his thumb. "Why the tears, luv?"

Nina tried to swallow over the knot in her throat. "No one has ever done anything like this for me before . . . made me feel . . . so special." She sniffed.

"You are special. Don't you know that?"

She lowered her gaze.

Ian tipped up her head and held her chin in his palm. "Do you?"

She blinked back the tears that threatened to fall. "You make me feel special," she admitted on a choked whisper, against all her good sense.

"That's what I intend to do. For every day that we have together I plan to make you feel special."

Nina's stomach pitched then settled. *The days that they had together.* There wasn't enough time. Not enough time. She forced a smile and sniffed back her tears.

"Hungry?"

She nodded.

"Why don't you relax and I'll fix us something."

"I'll help you."

"You're sure?"

"Yep." She nodded, pushing cheer into her voice and not the inevitability that she felt.

"Well, come on then. Do you know how to make crepes?"

"Um . . . no. I'm a scrambled eggs and bacon kind of girl."

Ian tossed his head back and laughed. "It will be my pleasure to teach you and then I can see if you're as skilled in the kitchen as you are in the bedroom." He hooked an arm around her waist and they headed back into the house.

Just a fling, she kept telling herself. *Just a fling.*

"Okay." Ian clapped his hands. "Today you learn how to make crepes. When you're back home on the cold winter New York mornings, it is the perfect breakfast."

He took out the flour, eggs, milk, salt, and butter and set them out on the counter. "All of this gets mixed in a big bowl."

Nina opened the cabinet above the oven and took out a glass mixing bowl.

"The butter needs to be melted."

Nina put the two tablespoons of butter in a small pot on a low flame.

"First, we blend the flour and the two eggs." He took a whisk from the cutlery draw. "While I mix this, you can pour in, hmmm, a half cup of milk and half a cup of water."

Nina measured the milk and the water and slowly poured them over the eggs and flour.

"And just a pinch of salt."

She sprinkled a bit of salt into the mix.

Ian leaned over and lightly kissed her lips. "I knew you would be a good student." He turned and bent down to get a frying pan out from the lower cabinet and put it on the stove, then some cooking oil, just a little of which he poured in the pan. "Now for the million-dollar question." He ran his finger along the curved opening of her top and pulled her close, then lightly dragged his lips along the lines of her neck. He felt her tremble. "What would you like inside . . . your crepe?" he said into her ear.

Nina's lids fluttered. Making crepes shouldn't be a turn-on, but Ian made it an erotic affair; stroking her hip while she poured, whispering in her ear when he stirred, dropping kisses on her lips, her cheeks, her ears as he explained what he was doing.

The frying pan began to heat.

"Cherries," she said on a breath while he suckled her neck.

He stepped back. A dark and dangerous smile moved slowly across his mouth. He opened the fridge and took out a box of bright red, plump cherries and dropped it on the counter.

Nina snatched it up, opened the clear plastic, and took them to the sink to run them under water. She lifted one, slowly opened her mouth, and took a bite, the sweet juice running over her lips. She ran her tongue across her mouth, never taking her eyes off Ian.

He came to her, reached into the sink, took one of the cherries, and bit into it. Nina drew in a sharp breath. He withdrew the seed, tossed it in the sink.

"Those have to come out," he said, his voice

reaching down to her center. "I'll spoon the mix onto the hot oil, and you pluck the cherries."

Nina's body tingled. He sure knew how to turn a girl on, she thought, as she slit open the cherries and removed the seeds.

They sat on the deck eating cherry crepes, sipping mimosas, watching the waves and the early-morning swimmers.

"I have to go to the club later."

"And I need to pick up my car."

"I'll drop you off on my way."

She stretched out on the lawn chair and crossed her legs at the ankles.

"Is all your family still in Barbados?"

Ian took the last sip of his mimosa. "My mother, brother, and a sister, two nieces, and a nephew."

"Do they ever come to the states?"

"My mother refuses to leave. I've been trying for years." He gave a short laugh. "My brother came over when I first opened the club."

"And where do you fall in the mix? Oldest? Youngest?"

"Oldest."

"We have that in common too."

He reached across the short space that separated them and took her hand. "We have a lot in common." He ran his finger along the inside of her palm. "Music, movies, hard work, good conversation, sandy beaches . . . each other." He leaned over, raised her hand to his lips.

"What happens when you go back home?" She

knew she shouldn't have asked the instant the question was out of her mouth.

Ian looked at her for a moment, released her hand, and gazed off toward the water. "Let's make the most of what we know." He stood. "What we know is right here. Now."

She looked up at him. "Live for the moment, is that what you're saying?"

"It's the way it is, Nina. What other way can it be?"

She lowered her head, released a sigh, then pushed up from the chair. She stood in front of him. "You're right," she said softly. "What other way could it be?" She kissed him lightly. "I'm going to run home, take care of a few things. Swing by when you're ready." She started to move away.

Ian held her arm. His dark eyes narrowed in concern. "What is it?"

Nina looked at him from over her shoulder and smiled. "Nothing." She kissed him on the cheek. "See you when you're ready."

Chapter 13

Nina closed the door behind her and squeezed her eyes shut. How was she going to get through the next few weeks knowing that what she wanted was never going to happen? She sighed heavily and walked slowly up the stairs to the bedroom.

She plopped down on the side of the bed and stretched out, staring up at the ceiling. She threw her arm across her eyes just as her cell phone rang. She pushed up on her elbows, reached for her purse, and dug out her phone.

"Hello? Rita! How is Hawaii? It's about time you called," she gently admonished.

"I know. I know. But we've been having such a ball. Everything is fabulous. Girl, this place is truly paradise. But how are things going with you? Is everything okay? Isn't the house great?"

"The house is absolutely wonderful. You were right." She curled on her side.

"See, I told you. Oh, I'm so glad. Have you been out to the beach, shopping, restaurants?"

"Yes," she said, giggling, as she was barely able to get a word in with Rita firing questions at her.

"And did you get to meet my handsome next-door neighborhood, Ian?"

"Um, yeah, I did."

"And? Isn't he gorgeous?"

"He's definitely easy on the eyes."

"You don't sound too enthused. Did something happen?"

Nina didn't respond.

"Nina. Did he do something?"

"It's a long story," she finally said.

"What does that mean?"

"Well, let's just say . . . we've gotten to know each other."

"Girl!" she screeched. "You and Ian. Stop. For real? OMG. Leave you alone for a minute and you hook Mr. Fabulous. So, come on, tell, tell. And don't leave anything out. Don't you just love his accent?" she asked on a wistful note. "It's just so reserved and sexy at the same time. I've seen him with his shirt off. Lawd give me strength. Have you?"

Nina couldn't help but laugh. "Do you want to hear my story or not?"

"Yes, girl. What are you waiting for?"

Nina shook her head. "Well, we met . . ."

More than a half hour later Nina had emptied her soul, only skimming over some of the really personal details, right up to just before Rita called.

"Damn," was all Rita could say.

"Yeah. Damn."

"Sounds like you really have a thing for him."

"I do."

"It wouldn't be the first long-distance relationship," Rita feebly offered.

"Long distance to me is a fifteen-minute car ride with traffic," she said drolly, then sighed. "It is what it is, Rita."

Rita paused for a moment. "Is this really about Randy?"

"What! Randy," she sputtered. "Of course not. Why would you even think that?" she said, jumping up from the bed and pacing the room.

"Ever since . . . well, since the breakup, you've had a hard time trusting a man any further than you could see him."

Nina didn't want to accept what Rita said. But if she thought about her abbreviated relationships since Randy, she knew in her soul that what Rita said was true. Her trust factor had been shaken to the core. Even before she got to know Ian, she assumed that he probably had a woman stashed away somewhere, and then meeting Cara only fueled her fears. Both of them lived in Barbados. What was to say that they wouldn't get back together once they were both back home?

"Want my advice?"

"Sure."

"Make the most of it. Enjoy him. Have fun. I know you, and I know it's hard for you to keep your emotions beneath the surface. But in another few weeks, you'll be back home and so will he, and both of you will have wonderful memories and maybe—"

"There's no maybe."

They were both quiet for a moment.

"You'll be fine. Think of this as a summer fever. You're hot for each other and going back to your lives is like . . . aspirin. After a few doses you'll be fine."

"Hmmm, summer fever." She'd wished it were that cut and dry.

In the ensuing days, Nina forced herself to put her apprehensions aside and simply try to enjoy their time together. Each morning they shared breakfast on the deck and walks on the beach. She talked with him about her students while he painted, and Ian taught her new recipes. Some evenings she went to the lounge and had dinner with Lauren and Keith, and at night, she and Ian played heads or tails on which house they would share.

Ian was attentive and loving, funny and knowledgeable about so many things. He made her feel like a queen every moment that they were together. Their lovemaking had taken on new dimensions. It was sensuous and slow, tender and passionate. It wasn't just sex anymore. They talked and loved long into the night, often until the sun came up. It was magical. She'd never been so happy. And if she did have a summer fever like Rita said, she didn't want a cure.

Nina had stolen a couple of hours to clean up around the house and get some laundry done while Ian went into town to do some shopping and stop by the lounge. She was putting in the last load when the house phone rang. The sound was so new to her that she initially ignored it until it kept ringing and she realized what it was. This was the first time in all the weeks she'd been there that the phone had rung.

She picked up the phone in the kitchen. "Hello?"

"Yes. Hello. You must be Nina Forbes."

Nina frowned. "Who is this?"

"Carlos. I own the place." He laughed lightly.

"Oh. I'm terribly sorry. Yes, this is Nina."

"I'm calling with some bad news."

She hugged her waist with her arm and waited.

"I've had a change in plans and I'll be coming to the Hamptons at the end of the week. I know you were to stay for the entire summer . . ."

Nina shook her head in confusion. "You're coming back? Here?"

"Yes. I know this may be an inconvenience, but it can't be helped."

She swallowed, tried to think. "Um. Of course. I mean, this is your house." She forced a laugh. "What day will you be coming in?"

"Thursday afternoon."

Thursday! That was the day after tomorrow. "No problem. I'll start getting my things together."

"How has your stay been?"

"Wonderful. You have a beautiful home and everything"—she swallowed—"has been more than I could ever imagine."

"Glad to hear it. Well, again, my apologies for the short notice."

"Safe travels."

"Thank you and you as well."

He disconnected the call. Nina stood there with the phone in her hand until the computerized voice of the operator telling her that the phone was off the hook snapped her back to her troubling reality.

Slowly she hung up the phone. The dryer buzzed. She had to leave. Two weeks early. Two weeks that she could have been with Ian. She leaned against the counter and lowered her head. The cure for her summer fever was coming much too soon.

She took the clothes out of the dryer and put them in the basket, then filled the dryer with the last batch of clothes from the washing machine.

Mindlessly she went upstairs, dumped the clothes on the bed, and started folding. She had today and tomorrow to make sure that the house was in order and the fridge and cabinets stocked the way she'd found them before heading back to Brooklyn.

Chapter 14

On the drive back from town, Ian's thoughts revolved around Nina. In the weeks that they'd been together, he knew that the dynamics of their relationship had changed, shifted somehow. Of course he'd been physically attracted to her from the moment he saw her, but that was then. It was more than just a physical thing now. He looked forward to spending time with her, listening to her laughter and her awful singing in the shower. He relished the times they shared in the kitchen when she tried out a new recipe he'd taught her, or the walks on the beach together as the sun was coming up.

When they made love now, it wasn't just raw, unquenchable sex; it was truly lovemaking, and that realization scared him. When he was inside of her, it was as if their souls were connected. He was transported to another place, and all he wanted was to stay there, with her. But there was no room in his life for commitment. That was the truth of it. Running his company, looking after his family, and fulfilling his goal of putting his artistic stamp on his island home was the real dream, his life. He'd tried the whole commitment thing with Cara, and that had been a disaster. Although now she claimed that she was wrong for treating their relationship the way she had and didn't realize how much of a mistake she'd made until he was out of her life. She wanted to try again. She wanted to work things out. That's what she'd come to his house that morning to talk to him about, and to tell him that she would be willing and waiting when he came back home to Barbados.

Nina. He turned onto the lane that led to his house. They'd agreed that it was just for the summer. No commitment, no strings attached. He drew in a breath and pulled into the driveway. But was that what he really wanted?

Nina had all but finished packing up her belongings, checking drawers and the closet and under the bed to make sure that she didn't leave anything behind. She'd called the grocer and put in an order for delivery for all of the basics that she'd used during her stay, and they'd promised to be there within two hours. She simply didn't have the will or the heart for one last shopping jaunt.

She cleaned the bathrooms and kitchen, emptied the dishwasher, and tied up the garbage, then went out back to check on the deck.

She hadn't heard his car pull in, but he was back. She saw him moving around in the kitchen unpacking his bags. Her stomach seesawed. She turned away and went back inside. She had the fleeting thought of just leaving to avoid what she knew would be a painful good-bye—at least for her. But that wouldn't be fair. He did deserve to know. Besides, the next few hours would be their last together. She wasn't going to drag this out and wait until Carlos showed up at the door. She was going home tonight.

Ian wanted to surprise Nina with a late brunch. He had margaritas chilling in the fridge while he was preparing soft tacos and salsa dip. Although he was an island man at heart and loved his seafood, Mexican was also at the top of his list.

The doorbell rang as he was heating up the pan to cook the ground beef.

"Open!" he called out.

Nina came in and found him in the kitchen. "Hey," she said softly, her heart lifting at the sight of him.

"Hey yourself." He came over to her, pulled her close, and took a long, sweet kiss that left them both with their pulses racing. "Hmmm, guess I missed you," he said against her mouth, his fingers moving up and down her spine.

Nina eased out of his embrace. "Something smells good," she said.

Ian looked at her for a moment, sensing a strange vibe coming from her, but she wouldn't meet his gaze. "What's wrong?"

She looked everywhere but at him and finally leaned her hip against the island counter. "I'm leaving."

He blinked back his surprise and confusion. "What are you talking about?"

"Tonight. I'm leaving tonight." She pushed out a breath. "Carlos, the owner, he called earlier and told me that he was coming back early."

"I . . . so what's early, right this minute?" His voice rose, hard and fast.

Nina flinched, the sudden anger in his voice taking her by surprise. "He'll be here the day after tomorrow. I didn't see the point in hanging around. I've already cleaned up, ordered groceries, and packed my bags . . . they're in the trunk."

His broad shoulders reared back a bit. *Didn't see the point*. He stood there, looking at her in disbelief. Her cavalier attitude threw him off center. He'd expect her to be a little upset, maybe even ask him if they could figure something out temporarily.

"Is the engine running, or do you have time for a margarita?" he asked, trying to make light of everything.

"No. The engine's not running."

"I was trying out a new taco recipe," he said, turning away from her and back to the stove. "Want to try some before you go?"

He wasn't going to ask her to stay. She shouldn't have thought otherwise, not even for a minute. "Sure. Sounds delicious."

They worked side by side as they'd done on so many other occasions, and slowly, as they mixed and stirred and simmered, the tension that had them in emotional knots began to loosen. And the laughter was back and the little intimate touches, the intentional bumps, the looks and soft smiles.

They dined in back and sipped margaritas until the sun had cooled and their heads were light, and by tacit agreement, they found themselves in Ian's bedroom.

Ian began his conquest of her body the moment they crossed the threshold of his room. He stripped her naked to the tune of some erotic beat that thrummed through his veins, lifting a piece of clothing here, running his fingers, his mouth, his tongue along thin straps and tiny elastic bands, tasting and teasing her through her barely there lingerie before removing it completely.

Nina's body vibrated, heating from the inside out as Ian paid homage to her, stretching her out on the bed and beginning at the top of her head and working his way downward, not leaving an inch of baby-soft skin unattended. Her soft whimpers of delight bloomed to moans of need as his tongue brushed and brushed across her hardened nipple before taking it fully into his mouth, gently sucking and pulling until the dew of passion made her slick and ready, which he found when he slid a finger slowly inside of her.

Nina's hips instinctively rose and her thighs widened. Ian groaned in her ear, her reaction to him a turn-on in itself. He relished igniting her passions, seeing her writhe and moan, open and give herself to him without any inhibitions. And because of her uncompromising gift of giving herself to him, he had no other choice but to do the same and more.

"I'm going to make this last," he moaned in her ear, slipping his finger in and out and using the pad of his thumb to gently play with her swelling clit.

Nina's belly quivered as a tremor ran along the inside of her thighs while Ian moved downward with maddening slowness, taunting and teasing her, heating the blood in her veins. She thought she would go out of her mind when his mouth covered her sex. She gripped the sheet in her fists, and Ian's large hands clamped down on her hips to mold her to his will.

His expert tongue dipped in and out of her, stimulated the swollen nub, over and over as she writhed and moaned, crying out, "Please . . . please . . ." as her hips rotated against the onslaught of his mouth and tongue.

Her body shuddered from the inside out as the intensity grew and grew and her toes suddenly curled. A jolt of electric energy shot up the backs of her legs. Her body grew so hot that sweat popped along her hairline. Her heart thundered.

Ian slid two fingers inside of her, found the soft, spongy epicenter, aptly named G for *gratify,* and gently pressed.

Nina's ragged scream punctuated the air. Every muscle contracted. He pressed again and the dam broke as one explosive sensation after the other ran over the one before. Her body shook and her cries of ecstasy were trapped in her throat. Her head spun and white lights burst behind her lids, and still the pleasure grew and grew. She felt faint, weightless, as the most powerful orgasm she'd ever experienced seized her and would not let go.

Tears sprung from her eyes as she thrashed her head back and forth against the pillow.

Ian gripped the round orbs of her ass, raised her hips even higher as if the very essence of her were on an altar of offering.

As much as he wanted to continue to take her back and forth to heaven, he knew his own want of her could not hold out any longer. He needed to be deep inside her, surrounded by her wet heat that closed in around him like a perfect-fitting glove. He waited for her orgasm to ebb before he entered her so that he could take her back there again.

Ian cried out in a sound so deep, so full of emotion, when he pushed past her willing opening, that for a moment he couldn't move. The sensation was so overwhelming he wouldn't risk losing it.

But Nina wanted him. Wanted him to move hard and deep and fast within her. She wanted to make him come so hard that he would never forget this night no matter how far away he went. She wanted him to dream of her, to keep her under his skin, to remember her scent and the way she tossed her cat at him, made it talk, and made him moan.

Ian rose up on his knees, took her legs, and draped them over his shoulders. He held on to the headboard and moved in and out of her, steady and long, sucking in air through his teeth as he teetered on the brink of exploding. He wanted it to last. He tried to hold out. But he could feel it coming, like a storm on the horizon. He knew it was on its way and there was nothing he could do to stop it.

Nina knew it too. She felt him harden even more inside of her, growing in width, stretching her even farther. The muscles of his body tightened, his breathing grew more ragged, his thrusts faster. She reached down between their pumping bodies and cupped his jewels, gently massaging them.

Ian's head went back. He jammed himself inside her as she milked him with her inner muscles, and he shook as if he was being electrocuted as the climax he'd been holding at bay was released with indescribable force.

For a long time afterward they lay entwined, damp and weak and plagued by their separate thoughts. Neither of them talked about what the next few hours would mean, as if not talking about it would make it less real.

Ian curled closer to her, pressing her back to his chest so that he could still fondle her breasts, make her nipples rise again. He wanted to remember how they felt on his fingertips, on his palm, and in his mouth. His jaw clenched as the suddenness of another erection pushed against her.

Nina moaned softly and pressed herself closer, took his hand, and put it between her legs. He found her wet and ready, which only intensified his arousal.

Without a word of warning, he turned her on her stomach, lifted her hips to meet him, and plunged into her slick cavern for the last time.

Chapter 15

Ian stood beside Nina's car as she put her purse on the passenger seat and then turned to him.

She drew in a long breath and made herself smile. "Well, guess this is it."

Ian opened her car door for her. "We'll stay in touch."

She pressed her lips together to keep the cry in her throat from escaping. She nodded her head and got into the car. She looked up at him. "Take care."

"You too. Drive safely."

She fastened her seat belt and stuck the key in the ignition.

Ian stepped back from the car. She turned the car on, backed out of the driveway and onto the road. She refused to look in her rearview mirror and see him standing there or, worse, not see him. Tears burned her eyes, but she promised herself she would not cry. She had a two-and-a-half-hour drive ahead of her. She didn't have time for tears.

* * *

"Oh, Nina, I'm so sorry about everything," Rita was saying three weeks later over lunch at Two Steps Down, one of their favorite restaurants in Fort Greene, Brooklyn.

Nina sighed. Every day since she'd been home, she thought and hoped that she would hear from Ian, at least a phone call, but it never came. On more occasions than she could count, she'd picked up her phone, started to press in his phone number, and stopped halfway. His silence was a clear indication that he had no intention of continuing beyond their time together in the Hamptons.

Still, when she thought of their brief and fiery romance she couldn't help but smile, remembering the times they shared and how happy she felt, how he made her feel. Whoever came into her life now would have big shoes to fill.

But as time moved on and classes started again, she wanted to believe that her real life was the aspirin that Rita said it would be. But the fever still coursed through her veins.

Classes had been in session for about two weeks and she'd gotten back into a routine—go to class, engage the students, go home and grade papers. She was finishing up her last class for the day and thinking about heating up leftovers for dinner. The students were filing out and she was gathering her things when all of her senses went on alert.

She looked toward the classroom door and, like

an apparition, Ian was standing there. The air hung and caught in her chest. She shook her head to dispel the vision, but he was still there. She didn't move, but he did. He was coming right to her.

Her heart was thundering so rapidly in her chest she couldn't catch her breath.

"Hello, Nina."

She stared at him, taking him in, and her soul filled.

"I stopped at the office and they said it was okay," he said, as if that could simply explain what he was doing there, miles away from his home.

"I . . . What are you doing here?"

He stepped up to her and lifted what he had in his hand. She hadn't noticed anything but him.

"You left without this." He held up the portrait he'd done of her. But now another image was in the background—a man. "I looked at this every day," he began. "Ridiculously hoping that you would step out of the picture and back into my life. I found myself adding my own image, the one who longed for you, missed you . . . loves you." He knew the moment that she was gone that going back home to Barbados, maybe even trying to work things out again with Cara, wasn't what he wanted. So he'd spent his time on the island getting things settled, and hoping that when he came for her, she would want him as much as he wanted her.

Nina's chest pounded.

"When it was done, it told me the story of two people who were destined to be together, in one place, Nina, working things out." He reached out and stroked her cheek, his eyes doing a slow dance over her face. "I came to be here with you. If that's what you want."

"Ian . . . here . . . What about your work, the lounge, the business?"

"That's one of the perks of running your own business, love; you get other people to do what needs to be done."

Was he saying what she thought he was saying, or were her own desires playing tricks on her?

"I'm crazy in love with you, Nina. I love you enough to leave everything I know behind to make a life with you. If you don't feel the same way . . . I'll catch the next plane and be out of your life."

She looped her arm around his neck and pressed her lips against his—the feel, the taste so familiar, like coming home.

Ian melted against her. The fear that had clenched his gut eased.

"I love you," she whispered against his mouth. "Love you from the bottom of my soul."

He lifted her in his arms and spun her around until she burst into fits of laughter.

"You think you can put up a homeless bloke until he finds accommodations?" he asked before setting her on her feet.

"I'm sure I can think of something." She looked up at him, delirious with happiness. "And I have the perfect place for our painting."

"Where?"

"Right above our bed."

Ian took her in his arms and made love to her lips with his own.

The painting, bursting with color, life, and vibrancy, sizzling with heat between the man and woman who'd found each other, was an eternal reminder of the summer fever that brought them together and would forever burn in their veins.

One Hot Summer

Niobia Bryant

Prologue

It's amazing how pain—that deep, searing, emotionally based heartache—can eventually lead to feeling completely numb. The line between the two is way thinner and flimsier than the one floating between love and hate. The jacked-up part was, Nylah Lovely knew about each line very well, and in that moment, she drifted across both.

Bzzz . . . bzzz . . . bzzz . . .

Her body was stiff with shock, afraid to move, afraid to do anything to intensify the pain that felt as if she had been shot by a bullet and not shocked by the truth. And so nothing but her pain-filled eyes shifted from the computer to take in the vibrating cell phone on the edge of her desk.

"Do you want me to get it?"

Her eyes shifted to the concerned face of her best friend, Tashi Oyoni. "No. It's either Byron with more lies or the press with more questions and speculations," she said softly, barely above a whisper, before she sighed as she forced her body to lean back against the leather sofa in her office. "I don't have it in me for either."

Falling in love and getting married was risky no matter what the circumstances. Everyone took a chance on placing their heart into someone else's hands and could only hope not to have it crushed within their grasp. Love under the spotlight was even more tenuous. It felt like groupies, bloggers, and the entertainment news media were drooling, waiting to hear about one of the mighty falling. Like her husband, multiplatinum R & B star Byron Bilton.

Their entire relationship had been chronicled, from the first spotting of them trying to have a low-key dinner at a tucked-away restaurant to their two-year relationship and subsequent fairy-tale marriage at a castle—and everything in between. They knew her name, they took her picture, but truly they forgot about the person out of the limelight—the noncelebrity—just trying to be happy in her relationship, just trying to make it work, just trying to enjoy being in love. That person became a casualty of something they simply considered news.

They cared nothing about her shame, her pain, her heartbreak. Her embarrassment. And yes, yes, she was woman enough to admit that having his infidelity exposed to the world before she even knew and could process it made the pain all the more hurtful. All the more haunting. All the more difficult to forgive . . . or forget.

What woman—what person at all—would want to discover that her husband had cheated via some blog post showing the crappy cell phone video of him, his privates, and some faceless woman?

Bzzz . . . Bzzz . . . Bzzz . . .

Tashi looked down at the BlackBerry. "It's Byron again. Do you want me to answer it?"

Love said nothing. She had nothing to say.

She had nothing to say to him. She had so much to say to him.

Another line to swing back and forth over.

"Byron, hold on, Love's right here."

Her eyes widened as she looked up at Tashi setting the cell phone on the table in front of her.

"Love," he said, his deep voice echoing.

"You put him on speaker?" Love mouthed, her face incredulous.

Tashi immediately looked apologetic. "I'm sorry," she mouthed back, before biting her bottom lip.

"Love, I know you don't believe that bullshit."

Love's eyes shifted again to take in the photo. "I know that I am looking at a picture of your privates snuggled deeply in a woman's mouth . . . in our condo . . . on our couch . . . during the weekend I went home to Holtsville," she said, her voice hollow.

"Love—"

"I know that we were supposed to celebrate our anniversary in another week. Celebrate *our* love. *Our* devotion." She laughed bitterly. "But you never were ready for this. You are not the one for me. You are not going to be my husband. Or my lover. Or in my life anymore. *That* I know."

"Love—"

"And I know that you need to give me fifty feet, because I didn't need to find out in a fucking blog that the man I love ain't shit," she finished in a harsh whisper, tears filling her eyes before she closed them as a sharp and piercing pain radiated across her chest.

One solitary tear filled with the weight of her pain raced down her cheek.

"I love you—"

Love laughed bitterly before she picked up her BlackBerry and threw it away from her. It hit the mirror over the brick fireplace, shattering the glass.

"Oh, Love." Tashi sighed, coming around the table to wrap her arms around her shoulders and hug her up in some sistah-friend love that she needed.

The act of friendship and support shook her to her core and the dam broke from the act of compassion. The tears raced down her cheeks like an endless relay race to soak Tashi's cinnamon brown shoulder.

"Girl, what are you going to do?" her friend asked as she patted her back like a mother belching a newborn.

The question made Love weary deep in her soul. Everything about her life and the path she was on—with love and marriage and family—was just shattered into a billion pieces and blown away by imaginary winds, never to be reclaimed. Her life with Byron was over. It was way more than she wanted to tackle at the moment.

Chapter 1

"Summer Lady"—Santana

Three Years Later
May

"If my lover could be the summer sun, I would lay naked beneath him, exposed and waiting for him to reach out to kiss and caress my skin as his heat would fill my body and his light would elevate my moods," Love said in a husky voice with just a tinge of her South Carolina accent slipping through as she stretched her long and slender limbs up as if she could touch the clear blue skies from where she stood on the rooftop of her brownstone. "If only my lover could be the summer sun, I would have no regrets and our love would last a lifetime. I would even share his brilliance with millions as long as he stayed available for me upon request."

She fought the urge to slip her silk robe from

her body and truly let the sun bronze her already cinnamon brown complexion. Even though she owned the two-story brownstone and, thus, exclusive rights to its spacious rooftop, she had no desire to give her neighbors a peep show. Instead she wrapped her arms around her body and looked out at the city landscape as the sun rose in the sky. Harlem.

Once the mecca for African-American art and culture, the city was now known for more than just its historic Renaissance.

Love flew to its warmth and character in the months following the end of her marriage to Byron. It was the place that embraced a wounded sistah needing to flee the flashing lights of the paparazzi as she tried to recover from the hurt and embarrassment from where she lived on the Upper East Side. Harlem's warmth nurtured her. The sense of community embraced her. The success of its revitalization revived her. The beauty of the brownstones intrigued her. The history healed her.

Duke. Langston. Billie. Ella.

And now Love.

There was nothing better than sitting on the rooftop just as the sun began to rise and writing about her day in her leather-bound journal. Knowing she was in the city that nurtured art and culture, and maybe even sitting on the same roof as a famous Renaissance writer, made her feel more connected to her words and their composition.

She smiled softly as she picked up her sweating glass of peach tea from the ledge of the roof. Only the hint of summer was in the air, but she could feel it coming. And she couldn't wait. Love had a jones for the summer season. There was a whole new life and vibrancy to Harlem during the summer months. Everything got kicked up a notch.

The entertaining on rooftops.

The summer festivals in the park.

The sounds of music of many genres mingling in the air.

Gospel brunches.

Lovers strolling down the tree-lined streets at a pace that could be considered lazy by those who just didn't understand how to relax and enjoy the moment.

It was only May, but summer was almost home in Harlem.

She smoothed the edges of her shoulder-length hair pulled up into a loose chignon and took a deep sip of her home-brewed peach tea before she tilted her head back and allowed the rays to kiss her neck and the soft brown skin exposed in the vee of her robe. She hated to leave the sun, but other duties called for the day.

With one last soft release of air, Love turned and padded barefoot across the brick-paved rooftop to the large black metal door. "If my lover could be the summer sun," Love said, with one last look at the sun over her shoulder before she walked through the door, and down the flight of stairs.

She loved her brownstone. It was a mix of the building's original 1900s architecture, with moldings, a fireplace, and hardwood floors, and plenty of contemporary upgrades and modern design.

The entire building could fit inside the living room of the apartment she had shared with Byron on the Upper East Side, but this felt more like home than any of the three residences she walked away from. Everything about the warm décor with small hints of fuchsia was her. She never regretted her decision two years ago to move to the Hamilton Heights section of Harlem.

It was a different pace—one that she desperately needed.

Trying to heal her broken heart under the lights of paparazzi and bloggers had nearly broken her. She felt like she didn't want to leave the house. She got tired of the hoopla. She got frustrated with the fame.

True, her event-planning and design company, Lovely Events, had a celebrity client list filled with athletes, musicians, and actors, but she had found the balance between promoting them and their events while staying in their shadow.

Unlike celebrity wives before her who had been done wrong, she had no comment to release, no publicist to tell her side to, no wish to grace the pages of *Essence*, *Vibe*, or *Vanity Fair* to sing her sad song. She had a life to rebuild and a thriving business as an event planner on which to place her focus.

Like the wedding today she had been planning.

Although she planned out every minute detail to the likes of her clients —and to ensure that her signature taste level was achieved—there still was a lot to do.

She rushed across the living room and down the short hall to her master bedroom. Her cell phone was vibrating on the center of her unmade all-white bed. She never took it or her house phone onto the roof. She considered that her time to unwind and get her thoughts clear for the day ahead or to sit under the stars and reflect on the day behind her.

Slipping out of her robe, she grabbed up her cell just long enough to answer the call and put it on speakerphone before placing it on her ebony dresser. "Hey, Tashi," she said, reaching into the long drawer to remove undergarments. She selected a deep purple sheer bra and matching thong.

"You haven't changed your mind about letting me slip into the wedding today?"

Love rolled her eyes and smiled as she sprayed her favorite perfume, Lovely by Sarah Jessica Parker, all over her body. "Tashi, you know I am not letting you crash these people's wedding. You can forget about it."

"That's what friends are for," Tashi sang through the line, very off-key.

"I offered to let you work for me and you turned me down," Love said, walking across the room to her closet—the one complaint of the apartment. It was more of a step-in than a walk-in.

"Work? It's Saturday! I did my forty hours for the man this week," she balked.

Love just laughed as she shook her head. "Talk to you later, Tashi," she said, grabbing a tailored black satin skirt and a top with sheer blouson sleeves.

"Guess I'll have a spa day or something . . . but

you . . . uhm, you take care. I know how weddings get to you."

Love paused in pulling the skirt up over her hips to lock eyes with her reflection in the mirror hanging on the inside of the door. Tashi was her best friend and she had been there through all the mess and stress of Byron's betrayal. "I'm good . . . but thanks, girl," she said, before moving over to pick up her cell. "I'll call you later."

She ended the call and forced herself not to think about the past as she finished getting dressed.

"Girl, you were born to fulfill dreams."

"I'm glad we were able to bring your vision to life." Love smiled warmly as she eyed the look of pleasure on the bride's and groom's faces. She always could tell if she truly hit the mark with her event planning and design by the look on a client's face. *Another satisfied customer,* Love thought, as she rubbed her slender hands together in front of her.

When she moved from small-town Holtsville, South Carolina to New York to attend college, her plan was to take the city by storm. She loved her down-home raising, but she always felt that there was so much more of the world to explore out of the small-town limits. Ever since she could remember, she knew she was headed up north first chance she got. College was her way out.

And it was the best four years of her life, living on campus, studying, exploring the city, and planning small events for friends, on-campus clubs, and some of the faculty. Once she graduated, she was filled with big dreams, a huge sense of style, and a head for business. She eventually set up her own event-planning business on the side, and within a few years, her business began to grow through word of mouth and press for her uniquely planned events.

But then she met Byron at one of her charity events and everything changed. Everything. Love happened. Big time. His jet-set life and powerful friends became hers as well. Two years later they wed. Their contacts helped her expand her brand and her business. She never thought she would go from being a small-town girl just making it in NYC to being both the wife of an R & B superstar and one of the premiere event planners in New York, catering to celebrities, athletes, and the wealthy elite.

In their marriage, her career had thrived; unfortunately, her heart hadn't fared that well.

Love pushed away any sad thoughts of love lost—or rather crushed—as she guided the couple out of the elaborately decorated ballroom to an outer room designed with subtle hints of their chocolate and ivory wedding colors, a bottle of their favorite Veuve Clicquot champagne, and light appetizers.

"Just relax and enjoy the moment as we finish up the cocktail hour and then get all of your guests seated," Love told them, her soft voice very calming and relaxing. "We should be ready to announce you in about ten to fifteen minutes, and again, congratulations, here's to the rest of your lives together."

With one final reassuring smile, Love slid her slender figure out the door just as the multimillionaire football quarterback and his new bride shared a deep kiss. As soon as the door closed, her smile faded just a bit. It wasn't that she wasn't happy for her clients, she just wasn't disillusioned about how long the happiness would last.

Been there. Done that.

As an event planner, it was Love's job to plot, plan, and execute every detail for charity events, awards galas, dinner parties, and red-carpet events . . . but weddings were the worst for her since her divorce a few years back. Everyone focused on the wedding and not many gave a bootie-toot about the marriage. And with him being a high-profile athlete, the battle was going to be even tougher for them with the world's focus on celebrity and fame.

But her job was to focus on the wedding day, not warn them about how tenuous love could be under the spotlight.

Love paused at the entrance to the ballroom and placed a hand to her chest as she took a moment to get herself together. This day—and any day she was at an event for a client—wasn't about her. Her issues. Her problems. Her drama.

She let nothing affect her professionalism.

Love always stayed cool, calm, and totally collected.

Always.

After a quick walkthrough of the cocktail hour in the spacious library, Love quickly checked in with her staff to ensure they were following her strict instructions. She took a moment to look out the large floor-to-ceiling windows of the semicircle foyer. It was a beautiful day out, but she was glad they opted against any outdoor activities. That would've meant more work and more challenges for her. More planning. More—

Love did a double take, locking her wide expressive eyes on the tall and slender man climbing out of the back of a huge SUV with blacked-out windows. Her heart pounded as he turned, but she didn't need to see his face or his two burly bodyguards to know it was her ex-husband. They began to walk up the steps together toward the front door.

"Shit," she swore.

Flustered, she made an un-Love move and clumsily backed away from the window before she turned and fled into the guest bathroom off the foyer. She pressed the button on her wireless headset. "Faryn, uhm . . . is . . . is . . . my ex-husband on the guest list for the reception? I know he wasn't at the wedding. Was he?" she asked, nearly slipping on a wet spot in four-inch vintage Gucci heels.

"No, Ms. Lovely. Let me check something. One sec."

Love paced.

"It had to happen, Love," she advised herself. "You couldn't avoid him forever."

Love hadn't been alone with her ex since the day the story broke about his cheating. She stayed with Tashi until he moved out of their penthouse, and anytime after that, they were accompanied by their lawyers hammering out their divorce. He was always busy touring or in the studio, and she always made sure to steer clear of any red-carpet events, parties, or premieres that she knew he would attend.

"Shit," she swore again, hating the unexpected. The unplanned. The sudden pothole in the road.

The press would have a week or two worth of speculations about the awkward meeting between Byron Bilton and his done-wrong ex-wife. Love *hated* to be in the press outside of mentions or blurbs about her events. She wanted her personal life to be . . . personal.

She turned on the gold faucets and lightly dampened a hand towel to moisten her neck and behind her ears. Now she wished Tashi was there with her. They met when Love hired her as her personal assistant just a little over three years ago. After just four short months, Tashi moved on to a less stressful job, but their friendship had lasted. Her friend was the bold one with the quick wit and snappy comebacks for days. Tashi would know what to say. What to do.

Love licked the peach-tinted lip gloss on her full heart-shaped mouth before releasing a stream of air through pursed lips. There was the slightest tinge of warmth and color around her long slender neck and high cheekbones. She used her fingertips to smooth her shaped brows and the soft edges of her jet-black hair pulled up into a loose topknot. "Okay. Alright. No biggie, Love," she said to her reflection, smoothing her satin skirt over her hips before she turned and left the restroom.

Beep.

"Go, Faryn," she instructed, closing the door behind her.

"Mr. Bilton was the last-minute plus one for one of the bride's guests . . . a Sasha Kilmore."

Love's steps faltered as she caught sight of her ex, and a woman she presumed to be Sasha, in the corner enjoying an impassioned embrace while his bodyguards pretended not to watch.

"Yes, I see that, Faryn," she dryly told her assistant. "Thanks."

Everyone turned at the sound of her voice, and all of the men's faces shaped with surprise.

Love locked eyes with her ex and then shifted them away. She took some pleasure in knowing the desire to slap the taste out of his mouth was gone. She hadn't known if she would ever get over that. "Excuse me," she said, polite and reserved.

Byron stepped away from his date. "Nylah, you're the event planner?" he asked, his voice just as husky and soulful as when he sang.

Byron was the only person to call her Nylah. The only one. All her family and friends back in Holtsville called her Love. The tradition continued once she went to school in New York. Back then, she thought it was endearing that he called her by her given name, but now she, ironically, realized that *love*—her name or the emotion—was no way in his vocabulary. She had loved and trusted this man with her heart, her soul, and her body. Hindsight is twenty-twenty.

She spotted the dark-skinned beauty trying to step forward, but both the guards blocked her path. Love rolled her eyes heavenward before she turned to walk down the hall.

"I don't want you to be uncomfortable, Nylah," Byron said from behind her.

Love paused, her back still to him.

"So I'll leave. Okay?" he said.

Surprise and relief washed over her. She nodded. "Thank you," she said over her shoulder, before hurrying forward, away from her past.

Chapter 2

"Summertime"—DJ Jazzy Jeff and The Fresh Prince

"One last shot, Maleek. Make it money."

Maleek Trenton formed his face into the stern look of a Zulu warrior as he fixed his tall and broad muscular frame into a relaxed pose in the black towel he wore low-slung on his hips. Like it would drop to the floor in the blink of an eye and expose his semihardness to the world. He didn't care. He was a professional athlete who worked hard on the build of his six-foot-ten-inch frame. Plus . . . his inches below the waist were nothing for any man to be ashamed of.

He maintained his sexy and aloof composure as the photographer from *Total Fitness Magazine* eased her camera to her face and the flashes began to lightly explode around him.

"That's a wrap," she said, finally lowering the camera. "Unfortunately."

Maleek looked up at the six-foot-tall woman, whose features were not classically beautiful but gave her an interesting angular look that would have dominated on the runways. Their eyes locked as she flipped her waist-length bone-straight blond hair over her shoulder. He slipped on the thick robe her assistant handed him as he allowed his eyes to peruse her.

After a long NBA season and a shocking loss in the post season, the last thing Maleek was looking for was a fling. If there was one thing he knew better than basketball, it was women, and he could tell from the predatory look in her eyes that Mali Gonzalez wanted to suck him bone dry for the night and then hypothetically bite his head off (i.e., kick him out of her bed) when she was done with him.

He broke the gaze and gave her a cool nod. "I can't wait to see the photos."

She gave him a hint of a smile. Her eyes showed a moment of regret, but then she moved on.

Maleek didn't doubt that she was hell in bed. Most older and more confident women were. He'd been schooled by the best. Ever since he entered the NBA at the tender age of eighteen, he had made enough money and experienced enough women to not be fazed by either anymore.

He hurried into his dressing room to change back into his loose V-neck tee and plaid shorts. His publicist, Brad Ferrell, was standing outside the door of the studio, busy talking in clipped tones on his cell phone. Maleek breezed past him and motioned for his driver to pull up in his blacked-out Tahoe. "We're out, Brad," he called over his shoulder before climbing into the back of the SUV.

Maleek shaped his defined lips into a smile as he watched the short and portly white man whirl around, nearly dropping his cell phone as he rushed to climb into the SUV behind his client.

"You're done?" Brad asked rapidly, talking a mile a minute as always. "I was sure Mali would keep you . . . occupied for a minute."

Maleek made a face. "Nah, I'm good," he said, pulling his iPhone out of his pocket and using his thumb to tap the touch screen.

"From what I hear, she is too," Brad said with a chuckle.

Maleek frowned. "I'm not up for groupie love," he said, listening to the phone ring in his ear.

"*She* has the groupies, playa."

Maleek cut his eyes at his publicist. He had told his long-time publicist that it wasn't necessary for him to "act black" when he was around him, but Brad persisted with his random use of slang. He made *playa* sound like *playheeeeer*. "Sounds like you're one of them," he drawled.

Yuri, his driver and bodyguard, barked out in laughter.

Brad nodded. "I'd give away a kick in my right nut and everything in my pocket just to smell it."

"That good?" Maleek asked, ending the call when his sister's cell went to voice mail. He didn't do messages.

"Right nut. Empty pockets. That's all I have to say."

Maleek leaned forward and rubbed his slanted

eyes with his fingertips even as he laughed. Since he had entered the league, Paul had been his publicist and his sidekick. He was good for laughs and even better for business. Whenever his client was in New York, he loaded Maleek's plate with TV appearances, interviews, photo shoots, and business meetings.

Maleek was a dominant force in the league, consistently being named to the All-Star team as he led his team to division titles and the playoffs. He was just as popular off the courts with endorsement deals that made his life even more lavish.

The thing was, Maleek was tired as hell and wanted nothing more than to get to his sister and brother-in-law's estate and crash.

It was his routine for the last eight years. As soon as the regular season and playoffs were over, he went back to his penthouse in Colorado and locked it up for the summer before he hopped on the first plane heading toward New York. He was born and raised on the East Coast and he made sure to get back home for at least a part of the summer and stay connected with his family and friends.

"Long day ahead, dawg," Brad said, looking down at his BlackBerry. "Next stop is a taping of this new sports talk show. Olive is meeting us at the studio with a change of clothes for you."

Maleek nodded and cast his eyes out the window as Brad laid out the rest of his plans for the day. He barely heard him. His mind was elsewhere.

Maleek was a planner. Always had been. Always would be.

When most people thought two steps ahead, he

was plotting four steps. And right now, his focus was on business. He had minority ownership in several commercial ventures, but this desire was different. He wanted to begin to plan his life outside of basketball and entertainment. His worst fear was being sixty and having to do commercials for bullshit Viagra or hair dye or cleaning supplies just to make it.

He was a multimillionaire with a locked-in contract guaranteeing him millions more . . . but there had been many wealthy athletes and celebrities before him who ended up broke.

Bzzz . . . bzzz . . . bzzz.

His iPhone vibrated in his hand. He flipped it over and eyed the picture of his sister filling the screen. He answered the call.

"Whaddup, Ayannah?" he asked, a smile already spreading across his handsome face.

"Is my little big brother home?" she asked.

"Your little big brother is a grown-ass man," Maleek teased, his dimples deepening in his mocha cheeks. "And, yeah, I landed a couple of hours ago, but Brad got me stretched out pretty much all day."

Ayannah let out a little grunt of disappointment. "I'm still the oldest and you tell Brad slavery's been over and to set you free."

"I heard that, shawtie," Brad said, loudly. "And slaves didn't sign ten-million-dollar endorsement deals, so I personally think they'd be offended by your comments."

Ayannah just chuckled. "Love you, Brad, with your wannabe my-brother-from-another-mother ass."

"Deuces, Ayannah," Brad said, mimicking the

Chris Brown chorus, focusing his attention back on his BlackBerry.

"No. He. Did. Not."

Maleek shook his head. "You know how that go," he said, using his thumb to turn the volume down. "As soon as I get done, I'll be there."

"Okay. See you then."

Maleek ended the call just as the Tahoe slowed to a stop among a small crowd of photographers ready with their cameras posed. He pulled on a pair of aviator shades before he locked his phone and slid it into the side pocket of his athletic bag.

He waited for Yuri to climb out of the driver's seat and walk around to open the passenger door for him. He climbed out among the flashing lights of more than a hundred cameras going off around him. The questions were just as rapid as Yuri escorted him to the metal door leading into the production studio. Out of the roar of shouting voices mingling into background noise, a few questions reached him.

"Maleek, are you disappointed that you will not be playing in the NBA Finals . . . again?"

"Is it true your dream is to play for the Knicks since you're from New York?"

"Mr. Trenton, are the rumors about you dating Kim Kardashian true?"

"After eight seasons and no ring, are you interested in being traded to another team?"

Maleek was glad when the heavy metal door finally closed behind him and the noise was cut off. He glanced down at his Gucci sports watch. Not even two o'clock.

"Hey, Maleek, when you fart, does it stink?" Brad joked, holding his fist up to Maleek as if it were a mic.

"Shut up, Brad," he said, holding back a laugh as a production assistant led them into his dressing room. "Especially since you tipped them off about us being here."

Brad tried to look offended . . . and failed.

It was close to midnight when Maleek and Yuri finally arrived at his sister's estate in Saddle River. Yuri went to his room in the guest house—as he did every summer he worked as Maleek's bodyguard—and Maleek made his way into the mansion, not at all surprised when Ayannah walked out of the kitchen.

"Leek," Ayannah exclaimed, using her child-hood nickname for him as she ran across the hard-wood floors to jump and hug him around his neck.

He hugged her back, thinking about how important they were to each other. Their mother had raised them alone and when she passed away four years ago, their bond had only tightened. They were siblings and best friends. Thick as thieves since childhood.

Maleek had schooled Ayannah on boys and pro-tected her from everything and everyone. Ayannah taught him how to woo girls, and Maleek had been a master at it ever since. Although he towered over her by nearly a foot, she had two years on him.

"Where's Lance?" he asked, setting her down on her slippered feet.

"In bed," she said, pulling him into the kitchen

behind her. "He tried to wait up, but he just got in from overseas and was tired as hell."

Ayannah's husband of the last three years was an entertainment host of a nationally syndicated show. They'd met at one of Maleek's away games and had hit it off immediately.

Maleek slid his tall frame onto one of the twelve stools surrounding the island in the center of the kitchen. "I'm ready to catch some z's myself."

Ayannah shook her head. "No, no, no. All your boys are going to grab you up from me in the morning and I want to be able to look at my little brother—who is twice my height—and have him tell me that he is okay," she said, reaching across the table to touch the back of his hand.

What she said was true. All of his childhood friends knew he was in town and his phone had been ringing nonstop all day.

"You worry too much," he said, rubbing his large hands over his eyes and then his closely faded hair. "I'm good."

"Mama would be so proud of you. Championship ring or not," Ayannah said softly.

Maleek looked at her, thinking she was a slightly slimmer and younger version of their mother. "She would be proud of both of us," he said, smiling a little to fight off the sadness that still clung to him at the thought of her.

"She cut our behinds enough to keep us *both* on the right path," Ayannah joked, rising to pour them both a glass of lemonade.

"Like that time I cut school and our neighbor, Miss Clarke, told her that she saw me in the park."

Maleek shook his head at the memory of just how his mom convinced him to never skip school again.

"Or like the time I took that nasty book about the pimps to school and my teacher caught me with it," Ayannah added. "Mama was no joke."

They laughed as she set the drink next to him along with the ceramic rooster cookie jar filled with the pecan sandies he loved.

"I miss her at all my games wearing any and everything with my number on it," Maleek admitted, feeling an actual pang of loss in his chest as he took a deep sip from his glass.

Ayannah bumped her hip against his back as she passed him to reclaim her seat. "Trust me, she's still there," she said softly.

They fell into a comfortable silence as Maleek stared off into the distance.

"I . . . uhm . . . I saw Monique last week," she said gently, reaching into the cookie jar.

Maleek tensed. "Oh, yeah?" he said nonchalantly, pretending like hearing her name again meant nothing to him.

Faking it, like an image of her didn't fill his head. Like his dick didn't jump to life at the memory of her hot enthusiasm in bed. She was built for amazing sex, with one of the best bodies ever. She worked out five days a week, and not only was she thick, but she was solid and well toned—and she knew it. She was soft where she needed to be soft and firm where she needed to be firm.

"She was working the *Vanity Fair* party last week," Ayannah added, casting a sidelong glance at him.

Maleek grunted in scorn. "Probably on the lookout for her next sponsor," he drawled sarcastically.

Ayannah made a mockingly painful face. "Ouch, Leek. Be nice."

He just shrugged. Two years ago, Monique Landing had swooped into his life. The aspiring publicist was immediately supportive, an independent woman not overly impressed by his riches and fame. She was a chocolate beauty, with skin so smooth he used to dream of kissing every inch of her. She was everything he ever wanted a woman to be. She was his savior from a lifetime of groupie sexpots and one-night stands freaky enough to make a whore blush.

In time though, he discovered that Monique was the worst of the lot. She was a false image seeming to be perfect because she showed him only what he wanted to see. She was a better actress than Halle, a better liar than Job, and a better illusionist than Houdini. She was a husband hunter determined to marry well, determined to be a wealthy Mrs. . . . by any means necessary.

It took him a year to discover that everything about her and their life together had been penned, planned, and plotted by her.

Everything.

"You can't let her have you afraid to fall in love again," Ayannah said gently.

Maleek froze from biting into a cookie as he looked at her like she was crazy. "Monique schooled me, she didn't change me. Trust," he said.

"Good," Ayannah said with a satisfied smile.

Maleek was over Monique, and thankfully he had come out of the experience well schooled but not changed. He hated that he let a big butt, a smile, and some lies fool him, but thankfully by having women like his mother and his sister in his life, he knew there were plenty of good women in the world. He couldn't wait to find the one meant for just him. He was more than ready to get married and spoil his wife for the rest of their lives.

So to hell with Monique and good luck to her next mark.

"I was thinking about throwing a big end-of-the-summer, start-of-the-NBA-season party," Maleek said, wanting to change the subject and not caring one bit how obvious that was.

Suddenly Ayannah sat up straight, her eyes excited. "You're going to be so busy this summer, you really should hire an event planner. Right?"

Maleek leaned back from her enthusiasm a little. *Ayannah really wants to party.* "You and Lance need to get out more," he joked.

Ayannah sucked air between her teeth. "Boy, shut up."

"So I guess you have a planner in mind?" he asked, rising from the stool with a stretch and a yawn.

"Yes, Love," she said, rising to set their glasses in the sink.

"Okay, what's her name?" Maleek asked.

"*Love,*" Ayannah stressed. "Actually it's Nylah Lovely of Lovely Events. Everyone calls her Love. Remember, she planned my wedding?"

Maleek frowned. "Uh . . . no."

Ayannah chuckled and shook her head as she followed him out of the kitchen. "That's funny because I'd bet any other man not getting cha-cha thrown at him night and day would find her pretty damn unforgettable."

Maleek shrugged as he climbed the stairs. "I don't care if she makes Monique look like a man, I just need her to plan my party," he said over his shoulder before entering his bedroom and closing the door.

Chapter 3

"Summertime"—Billie Holiday

Love pulled her Range Rover to a stop in front of the three-story brownstone, feeling lucky to have found a spot right in front of the building. The tree-lined streets. The concrete sidewalks. The historic brownstones lined up and down the street with an odd mix of regality and a certain down-home charm. The community garden on the corner brimming with colorful spring flowers. Lights beginning to flicker on as the sun began to set. Children making their way inside to prepare for the final days of school. Neighbors waving to each other or just offering a smile in acknowledgment.

It reminded her of home. Holtsville, South Carolina. The epitome of small-town America. Maybe that's another reason that Harlem called out to her after her divorce. The similarities were clear. That familiarity between neighbors. That charm that southerners had. None of the briskness and cold-ness of rushed living to be found in the city. This was a community. This was more than a place to stay. It was home. A place to raise families and move at a slightly slower pace in life than the hustle and bustle of Manhattan.

Grabbing her briefcase and oversized Coach duffel, she climbed out of the vehicle and activated the alarm. She stepped up on the sidewalk and re-moved her shades as she looked up at her next-door neighbor, Mrs. Greenville, sitting on the porch bouncing her one-year-old baby daughter, Kiley, on her knee. "Hi, Camille," Love said, pausing by the steps long enough to stroke one of Kiley's brown chubby cheeks.

"Hey, Love," she said, smiling down at her daugh-ter, who giggled as Love jiggled her cheek lightly.

A sad pang of regret hit Love because she wanted nothing more than to have children, but Byron had requested they wait until he wasn't traveling and touring as much because he didn't want to miss any of it. At the time, Love had agreed because she was busy with her business and she also wanted a more stable home environment for a child.

But now her marriage was over.

She dated, but there were no serious relation-ships in the works.

One-night stands were a definite no-no.

Love frowned at the image of a sperm bank in her future.

She gave Camille and Kiley one last smile, leaving them to their nightly ritual of greeting Camille's husband, Aaron, on the porch when he arrived home from work. Love walked to her own home, her stomach instantly grumbling from the scent of cooked food filling the air from the home of her other neighbor, Ms. Lopez.

As soon as Love unlocked her door and stepped inside her home, she hit the switch to bask the living room with light and used the remote from the small foyer table to turn on her high-definition sound system. Soon the sounds of Chrisette Michelle filled the air as she kicked off her red-soled alligator shoes and quickly shuffled through her mail.

Love had just set all of her things onto the travertine counter of the kitchen when her doorbell rang. Summer was her busiest season and she had had three separate bridal appointments that day. But zoning out in the tub before reading on the roof would have to wait. Her book club meeting was tonight.

Moments later Tashi strolled in carrying a bottle of wine and a bag filled with containers of takeout. Love could tell from the smell that it was sushi and tapas. Her stomach grumbled. She hadn't eaten since her last cake tasting at Sylvia Weinstock's.

"Girl, I am starving, so Oran and June need to get it moving," Tashi said, making quick steps into the kitchen to place everything on the round wooden table by the wrought iron windows.

Love's cell phone rang. She retrieved it from her purse and then smiled in surprise and pleasure at the name on the caller ID. "Hey, I'm going to take this in my bedroom," she said over her shoulder as she made her way up the stairs to her bedroom.

"Excuse me, Miss Secrecy."

Love ignored Tashi's bemused drawl and answered the call. "Hi, Ayannah."

"Hey, Love. I hope I'm not catching you in the middle of an event," she said.

She tucked her cell between her ear and her shoulder as she untied her fuchsia cotton sundress. "No, not at all. So what's up?"

"You know my brother, Maleek?" she began.

Love scrunched up her face as she moved about the room gathering a more casual outfit. "Uhm, who doesn't?" she asked, visualizing the smiling face that endorsed a dozen different brands and kept him on the television in a nonstop rotation.

Ayannah laughed. "Well, he wants to throw this big, fabulous end-of-the-summer party in August before preseason, and I suggested that he hire you to plan it out."

Love paused in pulling on a pair of black lounge pants, nearly toppling over onto the bed. "Ayannah, I would really love to, but I am booked for the whole summer for larger events. Really, I'm not accepting anything new without at least six to nine months' notice. I'm sorry," she said, actually feeling remorseful.

"The budget is bananas, you know the press he gets, so the PR for you would be huge, and I know you could really pull this together for him."

Love was shaking her head before she even spoke again. "Ayannah, I can recommend someone else. I would never half step on any event, regardless of who the client is. I hope you understand."

Ayannah sighed. "I understand, Love. But do me a favor. Just think about it overnight? For me?"

Love shifted her expressive eyes up to the ceiling as she bit her glossed full bottom lip. "I'll tell you what. I will call in the morning with a yes or with a list of event planners that I highly recommend. Okay?"

"Okay. Thanks, Love."

Love pushed all thoughts of work away as she pulled a sports tank top over her head. For one moment she allowed herself a second glance at her less-than-buxom breasts in the mirror before she left the room.

"Ooooh, I love these shoes," Tashi was saying.

"My bride surprised me with those this weekend as a bonus," Love said, walking up to take them from Tashi's hand. "She's opening a boutique."

"Dammit! Why do I have such small feet!"

"Hell, why do I have such small titties?" Love joked. "It's the luck of the draw."

She kissed the cheeks of her friends, Oran, a plump Afro-wearing sister whose confidence drew men to her like flies to honey, and June, a short and petite woman with fine features and a quiet sensibility who owned a cat named Garfield.

She rolled her eyes as she spotted one of those entertainment gossip shows on the television. "Nobody but Tashi watching this," she said, thinking the host, Guiliana Rancic, *did* look cute in the strapless metallic dress she wore.

"And you know it," Tashi called out from the kitchen.

For a moment, Love flashed back to the day she saw the video evidence of her husband's adultery. It had been Tashi who saw the blog posts and gently broke the news to her.

"Even though I'm tired, I am looking forward to hearing what you all thought about the scene in the barn," Love said, plopping down onto the corner of one of the three love seats positioned around the huge fireplace.

Oran laid back on the couch and fanned herself. "This is one city girl curious as hell about a barn!"

June frowned. "Wouldn't the hay scratch up your ass from all the . . . motion?"

"Shit, who cares?" Tashi exclaimed.

The ladies all laughed as they took turns passing the containers and filling their plates with heavy appetizers.

"Next on *E! News* we have exclusive footage of the basketball superstar, Maleek Trenton, and his entourage, all over New York . . . including this shot of him enjoying lunch at The Veranda in New York with pop superstar Gigi."

Love's eyes locked on the face of Maleek Trenton. Hearing his name drew her attention to the television as her friends continued to socialize around her. He really was as handsome as everyone proclaimed and she could tell from the look in his eyes that he knew it. The mix of his exotic-looking eyes and his deeply browned skin with his low-cut fade and full brows all combined to form one beautiful man. The sculpting of his body was sick. Not an ounce of fat in sight. He was one amazing total package, there was no doubt about that. And his looks and his skills on the court combined to create an endorsement monster.

Ayannah was right that his every move was chronicled by the press, and Lovely Events would garner some amazing press for a successful event . . . but she was booked solid and so she knew in the morning her answer to Ayannah would still be no.

Maleek sighed as he tilted his head back under the shower spray and let the water course over his body. The feel of the water combined with the heat of the steam was loosening his tight muscles. With his daily two-hour practice session, the shower felt damn good. Summer didn't mean the end of working on his game and taking himself to another level with each passing season. Sleep was not for the driven. And every morning at five AM, he pushed himself to rise out of bed and drill himself physically. He had been doing this since his middle school days. Working harder. Pushing himself further.

He wished it worked as well to free his mind of the coulda, woulda, shoulda of the playoff games replaying in his head. Missed shots. Failed free throws. Bad passes. Holes in the defense. Ineffective plays. Fouls. Fuck ups.

It was always like this after any loss. It always hit him the hardest when he was alone. Truth: He wanted to win the division title and go on to win the finals.

Maleek Trenton hated to lose. He wanted a championship ring. He wanted his spot in the Basketball Hall of Fame in Springfield, Massachusetts.

With one last stretch, he grabbed his washcloth and soap and lathered every inch of his body, smiling at how his sister kept his bedroom at her home supplied with all of his favorites. She made sure that he felt at home and even supplied his bodyguard and friend, Yuri, with free usage of their guest house.

Foregoing a towel drying, Maleek strode naked and damp from his adjoining bathroom, his long member swinging back and forth across his defined thighs. Kicking the boxers he left on the floor earlier out of his path, he climbed back onto his king-sized bed and used the remote to turn up the volume on CNN as he slid on his glasses. Usually he wore contacts, but when he was alone or reading, he preferred his spectacles.

Grabbing his laptop, he logged on to his Twitter account and sent a general update to his million followers. He hadn't posted since they lost and brought their postseason to an end.

Maleek shifted his eyes to the flat screen over the fireplace as the highlights from last night's playoff games played. Beyond being an athlete, he was an avid sports fan with an interest in the series.

Soon the sun rose in the sky and Maleek turned his head to look through his glasses out the wall of windows that framed the towering trees of the backyard. For him, there was nothing better than waking up to the sun's rays across his face. He never closed his curtains in the summer. There was too much of the sunlight to enjoy in just a few months.

Ayannah knew how much he loved the summer season and gave him a room where he could experience it.

Beep.

"I know you're awake, Maleek Ali Trenton," Ayannah said through the intercom system. "Come on down and tell me about this date with Gigi . . . and I *might* feed you breakfast."

Maleek shook his head with a charming one-sided grin, his stomach growling as he removed his glasses and placed them in their hard case. Quickly he put in his contacts before he finished his morning rituals, including applying his favorite warm and spicy cologne that *always* drew a woman's attention. He pulled on a crisp navy and white striped shirt, dark stiff denims, and a pair of two-tone Kenneth Cole leather loafers with a matching belt. His platinum watch and jewelry accessories finished him off nicely.

"So fresh, so clean, boy," Maleek jokingly told his reflection before leaving his bedroom.

He jogged down the stairs, the smell of breakfast reaching him. He found everyone in the octagon-shaped glass sunroom off the kitchen. "Morning, morning, family."

His brother-in-law, Lance, and his bodyguard shared a long glance before they both gave him a look filled with warning before turning their attention back to their heaping plates. Maleek knew his sister had already grilled both of them about their knowledge of him and Gigi. Lance for his industry contacts and Yuri for his close contact with Maleek daily. They both were glad he was there for his turn and their freedom.

"A little birdie told me that you were spotted at The Veranda with Gigi," Ayannah said, her short auburn hair already curled and spiked like she just stepped out of the hair salon.

"A little birdie?" Lance drawled from behind his open paper.

Ayannah rolled her eyes as she handed him one plate with fresh fruit and croissants and another plate with poached eggs and ham.

"This little birdie wasn't our competitor's show, was it . . . because we didn't report on the Maleek and Gigi spotting," Lance added, folding his paper and eyeing his wife.

Ayannah waved her hand dismissively. "I like Guiliana Rancic. Sue me!" she snapped, before smoothing her hand over her shortly cropped hair on her nape and cutting her eyes at her brother with a fake grin. "Now, Maleek—"

"I'm not dating Gigi," he said around a big bite of honey-buttered croissant. "She wants me to play her man in her next video. I agreed. We celebrated with dinner."

Lance sat up. "On the record?"

Maleek shrugged. "They didn't ask me to keep it quiet," he said.

"Good looking out." Lance made a fist and tapped it to Maleek's.

"Oh," Ayannah said, sounding disappointed as she sat, her slender face in her hand, and halfheartedly stirred her tea.

"You want me to date Gigi?" Maleek asked, more than surprised.

"No," Ayannah stressed. "I hate that I wasted a whole night worrying about you dating Gigi. A flippin' video. What the hell ever."

Maleek chuckled.

Ayannah glared at him. "Don't you get sick of your name being linked to every random celeb-chick or groupie within a foot of you? Do you understand how sickening it is for me as your sister to have to verify your love life against the press . . . *especially* when some of the rumors are true, Mr. Single, Sexy, and hopefully Safe?"

Maleek held his hands up as he chewed a bite of cantaloupe. "What do you want me to do?"

"Settle your black ass down with a good woman," she countered quickly.

"I'm not against that, just having a hard time finding one."

"I can only imagine what you have to sift through, brother-in-law," Lance added.

"Exactly," Maleek stressed, pouring himself a cup of coffee.

Ayannah made a face like she smelled a fresh pile of horse manure. "Sift . . . through? Okay, gentlemen, women are not ashes, and matter of fact, they are more than asses."

Lance opened his paper to hide behind.

Yuri focused on his plate.

Ayannah turned in her chair to face her brother. "Listen, take yourself out of the running for the Golden Penis Award, Cassanova, and you will meet a better caliber of woman. Your problem is quantity and not quality. The women love you and you love the women. We get it. Now get over it."

Yuri laughed but then wiped his mouth with a beefy hand when Maleek eyed him with a hard stare. His sister's words were hitting too close to home for him, but she also had no idea how it was to be a wealthy man afraid to fall in love.

Ayannah sighed, rising to her feet and dropping her napkin onto her plate. "You know what, forget it. Just make it your life's goal to keep your penis wet, Maleek." She made a childish face and walked away.

"TMI, baby. TMI," Lance said with a deep frown.

"Did you book my event planner?" Maleek asked.

Ayannah froze and turned on her heels. "Yes, she called this morning and declined," she said, crossing her arms over her chest. "I guess you ran into the first woman to turn you down, little big brother. See if them dimples will change *her* mind."

Maleek slowly let his best, most charming, most teeth-baring, dimple-deepening smile spread across his face.

Chapter 4

"Summertime"—Fantasia

"Are you Nylah Lovely?"

Nylah sat back in her chair and her eyes widened a bit as they traveled from the feet and up to the divinely handsome face of Maleek Trenton. The full effect of him, with his tall athletic build, the tailored fit of his clothing, and his sharp features with those incredibly unique eyes was overwhelming.

Especially when it was completely unexpected.

Nylah pretended to remove her reading glasses, giving herself a moment to steady her trembling hands and calm her racing pulse. "Uhm, yes, I am, Mr. Trenton. How are you?" she said, just the hint of a quiver in her tone as she rose to extend her hand.

He took a long step forward. The warm and spicy scent of his cologne reached her. Not overpowering and annoying to the senses. It was a subtle, sexy scent of a confident man. Just enough to tease a woman when he was walking by.

"So you know me?" he asked, enveloping her hand in his while removing his shades with his free hand.

Nylah's mouth fell open even as she lost her breath.

Was it the moment that he removed his shades and gave her the full effect of his handsomeness?

Was it the current of electricity—that sharp awareness of a woman for a man—that coursed over her body at the simple pressing of their hands together?

Or . . . was it both? A lethal combination that was wreaking total havoc on her senses. The sight of him. The smell of him.

Forcing herself to exhale, she pulled her hand from his and reclaimed her seat. "Don't be cute, Mr. Trenton—"

"Maleek," he asserted, folding his tall frame into one of the three club chairs before her massive antique desk.

"Everyone knows you, *Mr. Trenton*," she said, fighting to compose herself as she settled back in her chair, crossing her legs and folding her hands in her lap.

Maleek's eyes dropped down to take in her legs exposed in the fitted straight skirt she wore with a crisp white button-up shirt.

Nylah cleared her throat. "How can I help you, Mr. Trenton?" she asked politely.

He bit back a smile as his eyes finally shifted back up to her face. "My sister let me know that you

weren't able to take on my end-of-the-summer party,"
he began, folding his shades and sliding them into
the front pocket of his shirt.

Thank God he didn't slide them on the top of
his head, she thought, knowing it was completely
random. "That's right. I'm booked solid, but I did
send Ayannah a list of three planners in the area
that I highly recommend."

"I want you."

Her heart hammered hard even though she
knew that wasn't what he meant. *What in the hot hell
below is wrong with me?*

"That's understandable," she said, not missing
the amused glint in his eyes. "I'm good at what I
do . . . but I'm not available, Mr. Trenton. You have
to understand that this is my busiest season and—"

"I'll double your fee," he said with ease.

Love knew the look on her face was akin to
Scooby Doo's when he scratched his canine head
and said, "Huh?"

"And I will compromise with you and select an
event date that fits your schedule," Maleek added,
sitting back in the chair and crossing one Gucci-
covered ankle over his knee with a satisfied look on
his handsome face. "Now, come on, Ms. Lovely.
What more you want me to do? Get on my knees
and beg?"

She'd bet her jewelry collection that he didn't
have to beg . . . for *anything*. "I'm sure a man like
you doesn't beg very often, Mr. Trenton," she said,
hating that his innocent words flustered her so.

He held up his hands and shrugged.

Lovely smiled as she uncrossed her legs and

grasped the edges of her desk to pull her chair forward. "Mr. Trenton. Why?"

His brows dipped a bit. "Why what?"

"Why me?"

He opened his mouth but then closed it like he changed his mind about saying whatever thought or question popped into his head.

Love's eyes locked with his, and it took everything in her not to break the stare. Not to feel so aware of him. His eyes. His scent. His confidence. His sexiness.

"Any event planner on your level will be just as busy, and since my sister preferred you, I decided my buck stops here," Maleek said, his eyes filled with an intensity. "I like everything that you did for my sister's wedding. The eye for details. The décor. No glitches that we saw. But mostly I like that you made your presence known without making your presence overwhelming."

Love brought her hand up to press against the pulse racing at the base of her neck. Her face filled with confusion.

"You were there to plan the event and not attend the event," he explained. "I don't remember even seeing you or your staff there."

Love nodded in understanding. "Pretty forgettable, huh?" she joked lightly.

Maleek sat up a bit straighter in his chair. "You could never be forgettable," he said, his voice sounding like a Teddy Pendergrass song—soulful and filled with meaning.

Love shifted her eyes from his as she pretended to shift papers and folders on her neat and uncluttered desktop, not wanting to reveal the awareness she had of him. She didn't want her own surprise of her responsiveness to change to embarrassment.

A man like Maleek Trenton had women flocking to him in droves; she didn't want him to think she was another to be added to the list.

And she didn't want to be either.

He was the epitome of everything she had carefully avoided since her scandalous divorce. His good looks coupled with fame and celebrity was a mix for disaster for any woman in his life. And Love had heard the rumors and seen the headlines. She thought about how his date with Gigi broadcasted over *E! News* just last night.

No. Her body was naturally responding to an attractive man, but her days in the spotlight because of whom she dated or married were so over. *So* over.

You're acting like he's interested, Love, she chastised herself, even as her pulse continued to race and a cloud of awareness surrounded her body like a warm blanket on a cold winter night.

Maleek felt like a fool.

When he strolled in the renovated Tribeca warehouse offices of Lovely Event, he thought he would breeze in, flash his dimples, and get Ms. Nylah Lovely to change her mind. Just like that. He would lock in an event planner and irk his sister all at once. No biggie.

He never thought the first sight of the slender beauty would hit him like a sledgehammer. Behind his shades, his eyes had not missed one single detail about her. From her sophisticated air, with her hair twisted up loosely, exposing her long neck, to her proper outfit that was just short of high society by the lack of pearls. And then there was the way that skirt and seemingly innocent white shirt were so well tailored to her curves, in addition to her shoes, with heels that seemed so high she would topple. It was an odd mix of sophistication and sass that led to a level of sexy most women could not comprehend.

And then there were other things he noticed in just a few fleeting seconds.

Her expressive eyes.

A mouth made to be kissed.

The type of quiet beauty that was not seeking attention—but received it, nonetheless.

And so her eyes and her mouth and the way her shirt clung lightly to the curve of her breasts had him wanting her to reconsider with an intensity he felt only on the courts. He wanted her to want to do this for him. With him.

The more she formed her luscious lips to say no, the more he yearned to have them say yes. When he told her he wanted her, it was not about the event he was speaking of. He did want her. He wanted to loosen her hair, pull her proper shirt apart, and hitch her knee-length pencil skirt up to her hips to expose her body to his eyes. His hands. His mouth.

Forgettable?

Never.

He couldn't explain it or even define it; he felt a loss at the thought that these could be the last moments he spent in her presence. She was calming. She was classy. She was composed. She was comforting.

And all without trying.

"I will triple your fee," he said, still not believing how the tables had turned on him or how he was not fighting it one bit.

"I am not one to do things just for the money, Mr. Trenton," she told him.

Maleek didn't miss the way she pressed her hand to her throat. Even that subtle move stirred movement behind his zipper. "How about for charity?" he asked.

Love paused, arching a brow as she looked at him in question across the wide expanse of her desk.

The look made his pulse beat hard.

Maleek sat up on the edge of the seat. "I will triple your fee, but a third will be donated to a charity of your choosing," he said. "Now, I'm not saying it has to be my own foundation that fights illiteracy and helps kids discover the arts—"

Love started in surprise. "The arts and illiteracy? I would think an athlete would have his focus on different endeavors."

Maleek nodded his head. "Every child who dreams like I did to be a professional athlete won't fulfill that ambition. It's just reality. We have to encourage children to have other dreams. To have another focus. Musicians, poets, writers, teachers, doctors. All of it is important."

Love was impressed. He could tell from the look in her clear eyes. He'd bet there wasn't much of her emotions that didn't show in her eyes.

She pressed her gaping mouth closed as she opened the large leather planner on her desk. "Uhm, like I was saying . . . I'm, uhm . . . not easily moved by money, so I will do the event for twice my normal rate . . ."

Money makes the world go around, he thought, unable to keep the smugness from filling his face.

"With one half going to a charity," she added, looking up from her planner.

He quickly made his face expressionless.

Love's eyebrow arched just a millimeter. "So I am in fact working for my regular fee, but of course, Love loves the kids," she joked softly, picking up a pen. "Again, I am booked on the date you originally wanted, but is the . . . last weekend in August good for you?"

Maleek's eyes dropped to her mouth as the words "good for you" seemed to echo inside his head.

"Mr. Trenton, is the last weekend in August good for you?" she repeated.

Wiping his hand over his mouth, Maleek nodded. "That's perfect," he said. He didn't know if he was more surprised that she turned down the offer for extra money or that this subtly sexy woman had him thrown off kilter so quickly . . . without even trying.

"It'll be nice to plan another event with Ayannah," Love said with a smile that filled her eyes.

Maleek's gut clenched. "Actually, I'll be handling this, so you'll be working with me," he said, again surprising himself and going completely against his own plans.

Love looked surprised. "Of course. My apologies.

We have a lot to do in a short amount of time, but luckily I have some great vendor relationships and that will help a lot."

Maleek's eyes fell to her left hand. Her ring finger was free of a ring. His eyes darted to her desk. The photos there were of her and a group of ladies. No man or any children in sight.

"Unfortunately, I do have another appointment today," she said, rising to her feet.

Maleek felt a deep pang of disappointment that his time in her presence was coming to an end.

Knock, knock.

They both turned as her office door suddenly opened and the room filled with three men. Maleek closed his eyes and shook his head at the sight of his three childhood friends.

Love's assistant pushed through them. "I'm so sorry, Ms. Lovely," she stammered. "I asked them to *please* wait."

They all began speaking at once as Faryn attempted to push the men back out the door.

It was a scene out of a bad comedy. He looked over his shoulder, and the look of shock on Love's face pushed him into action. He stepped forward. "Hey, hey, man. Y'all chill out. I'll be right out—"

"Excuse me," Love said in a voice filled with reprimand.

Everyone stopped and turned to look over their shoulder as she came around the desk like a teacher about to scold pupils.

"This is a business. *My* business. Respect that *and* yourselves," she said, walking up to them slowly as she eyed each one. "You are in public. And regardless of what anyone tells you, *gentlemen*, there is a time and a place for everything, and I can promise you that this is not the time nor the place for this type of immature foolishness. You are grown-ass men."

As he watched her calmly but efficiently chastise his friends without even raising her voice and her eyes gleaming with fire, Maleek wanted to pull her into his arms and kiss her.

"Now, Faryn, you can go back to work, please, because these grown men are going to remember where they are and how they should act—even if they're pretending—and quietly leave my establishment so that we can continue to conduct our workday in peace. Have a good day, gentlemen." She walked to the door and touched the doorknob with a stiff smile.

Maleek sneaked a "kill it" motion with his hands across his neck for good measure.

Soon his friends were gone and Faryn pulled the door closed behind her with another apologetic look at her boss.

"I apologize, my friends only get to see me once a year, really, and we had plans for today," he began, walking up to stand before her.

Love sidestepped him and wrapped her hand around the door knob. "Mr. Trenton, are you sure you have the time available to take on such a large event?" she asked, sounding doubtful.

He pushed his hands into his pockets and turned his head sideways to lock eyes with her. "I will make the time to be available to you whenever you need me," he said, serious.

She licked her full lips.

The sight of the tip of her tongue stroking across her bottom lip caused his dick to swell with life.

"I have to request that you leave your entourage at the playhouse whenever we have business to tend to," she suggested softly, stepping back as she pulled the door open.

Maleek chuckled as he took the few steps out the door. He paused and turned, bending down to press his lips to her cheek. "I'll have my assistant call you with all my contact information."

He felt her stiffen.

"And I'll have Faryn draw up a contract, and let's meet tomorrow to discuss your vision for the event," she said.

His eyes searched her face, but she avoided his eyes. "We can make it a lunch appointment at The Veranda."

"That seems to be a favorite place of yours," she said quickly, and then looked like she regretted it immediately. "Here is fine. I have some other appointments tomorrow."

Maleek paused at her polite turndown. "See you tomorrow, then," he said, walking out of the office without looking back.

Maybe it's for the best, he thought. His initial reaction to her had been visceral, but in hindsight, he could tell that there probably was very little he had in common with Nylah Lovely.

Love woke up with a start, her feet kicking the covers from her body. She released a deep breath through pursed lips and hitched her cotton nightgown over her head to fling it to the floor. She felt sweaty and damp. Her heart was racing and she felt like she couldn't swallow down enough air. Her nipples were hard and the bud nestled between her thick lips literally pulsed with life.

Love reached for the glass of ice water that she'd set on her nightstand earlier. She took deep sips, enjoying the still cool feel of it going down her throat before setting the empty glass back on the wooden coaster.

She closed her eyes as she eased her knees up to her chest and wrapped her slender arms around her legs. When she dropped her head to the groove between her knees, she could smell the scent of her heat. The ceiling fan did absolutely nothing to cool her. The water did nothing to quench her thirst.

All of it from a dream.

Her second that night.

And both seemed all too real.

"Come on, Love, get your shit together," she warned herself, eyeing the digital clock and groaning as 2:32 AM glared back at her.

With one last deep and steadying breath, she snuggled back down on the queen-sized bed and pulled just the crisp cotton sheet over her nudity. Closing her eyes as she snuggled her face deeper into her down pillow, Love said a silent prayer that *this* time her dreams would be sex free.

But minutes later, just as she felt her body relax as she succumbed to sleep, Maleek Trenton stood there waiting for her, naked and hard, with his hands already reaching out to stroke her . . .

* * *

After signaling Yuri not to follow, Maleek eased out of the front door of the guest house, leaving behind the raucous nature of his friends. He was enjoying their company, reminiscing on their days growing up and the adventures they shared as horny teens.

Random thoughts claimed his attention, pulling him away from stories of three fifteen-year-old boys chipping in to buy time with New York prostitutes or being chased out of unfamiliar neighborhoods in their attempts to visit some cute girl with a smile. Instead, his thoughts were filled with memories of Love.

He had seen women more luscious, more beautiful, more vibrant. All races, shapes, and sizes. But not once in his adult life could he remember a woman affecting him so quickly. So deeply.

Her mouth. Her eyes. Her scent.

A desire to see her again. To be in her presence again.

Even after he made his way into the main house and up the stairs to his bedroom, he lay in bed naked and unable to sleep as he inhaled the scent of summer wafting through the open windows and wishing it were the smell of Love instead.

"Damn," he swore, releasing a heavy breath.

In an instant, Nylah Lovely had gotten under his skin.

Chapter 5

"Summer Soft"—Stevie Wonder

One Week Later

Love was with Faryn in the outer office reviewing the final guest list for a charity luncheon in two weeks. When the elevator slid open, she looked up over the rim of her square-framed glasses as Maleek stepped off.

She thought of her dreams and felt warmth flood her neck. She removed her glasses and rose to her stilettos. "I wasn't expecting you today, Mr. Trenton," she said, hating that her heart pounded so hard at the first sight of him. She stepped toward her door to open it wide.

Maleek nodded at Faryn as he walked up to Love.

Overwhelmed by the sight of him, devastatingly handsome even in a V-neck T-shirt and shorts, she instinctively stepped back against the wooden door of her office as she looked up at this man who made her five foot ten inch height seem like she was a dwarf. "How can I help you?"

"I was headed out of town for a last-minute weekend trip and wanted to check on things before I left," he said, stepping past her into the office.

Love entered and closed the door behind them. With him in it, her spacious office seemed like a cubicle. While his back was turned, she pressed her hand to her heart. It was beating wildly.

She hadn't seen him since the day he signed the contracts and paid his deposit. Nearly a week. She thought her reaction to him would have faded. No such luck.

Just as she passed him, he lightly touched her shoulder, and Love turned by the bookcase to look up at him.

Maleek reached down to brush his fingers against her cheek.

Love gasped a little, completely taken by surprise by his touch.

"You had glitter on your cheek," Maleek offered, smiling and showing off his even white teeth and deep dimples, which made his strong and angular, handsome face totally adorable.

"It's on some of the decorations for events," she offered, stepping back again and finding nothing but the unrelenting hardness of the bookcase pressing into her back. "Sometimes I find it in the oddest places, trust me."

Maleek's smile widened and Love felt her neck and cheeks warm with embarrassment. She could have crawled into a hole and died. *Oh, God, why in the hell did I just say that?*

His eyes—those smoky and all too sexy slanted eyes—traveled over every point of interest on her face before landing on her lips.

Love was aware of his eyes on her and her mouth parted just a bit.

"I really like the shape of your mouth, Love," Maleek said huskily, low in his throat.

Love hated that she shivered and took joy in his compliment. It unnerved a woman fighting ever so hard to resist his charms.

"Thanks," she mumbled, shifting to the side to gain freedom from his aura surrounding her and luring her in to everything she didn't want.

Maleek laughed, low and husky and slightly mocking.

Love looked at him over her thin shoulder. "Something funny, Mr. Trenton?" she asked, her southern accent coming through.

His smile dropped a bit as he met her eyes with humor. "Whenever you say 'Mr. Trenton,' you sound just like this mean old school teacher I had back in sixth grade. Old Miss Lemons. She was just as sour as her name."

Love smiled a bit as she thought that over before she came back around her desk to face him. "And you remind me of every bad little boy—or egotistical wealthy man—that thinks what his heart desires is his for the taking."

Maleek nodded. "You really do look like a school teacher," he said, crossing his arms over his chest and showing a tattoo of a panther on the back of his forearm.

Another dig. "Oh, and why's that?"

He shrugged. "Nothing."

"Oh, no, you wrote the check, now cash it," she told him, tilting her head up to lock her wide eyes with his.

"Okay," Maleek agreed, circling her fully as he eyed her up and down. "The hair up in a bun–"

"It's a chignon, *Mr.* Trenton."

"The no-fuss makeup—"

"I'm a busy working woman. Not sure how many of those you run into," she quipped, looking over her shoulder to keep her eyes on him as he continued to circle her. "What else?"

"The slacks and dresses with your prissy little shirt *and* pearls . . . you have teacher written all over you," he finished with satisfaction, lightly touching the double-strand necklace she wore.

"First, let me say thank you. I will take it as a compliment that I 'look' like a teacher." Love crossed her arms over her own chest and then circled him fully. "Second, you can dish it, but can you take it?"

"I'm straight," Maleek said with confidence, sliding his hands into his pockets.

She lifted one tweezed and shaped brow, pausing in front of him. "And you call a grown man wandering the streets dressed like a twelve-year-old . . . straight?"

Maleek pretended to look wounded. "A twelve-year-old?" he balked.

"Better still, like one of those forty-year-old rappers. Uhm, yo, yo, yo, this MC Grandpa in this house, foshizzle, my nizzle." Love did a classic Run-DMC stance, actually enjoying their banter.

"Oh, you got jokes?"

"You do know they sell suits in your size?"

"And you assume I don't own one."

"Did you not assume that I don't own anything but conservative clothing?"

"A'ight, you got me," he said, smiling as he held his hand to his chest with a grin.

Love forced herself to look away from him. "Can we discuss your event really quickly before you head off?" she asked, bending down to pull a large leather-bound portfolio from beneath her desk.

"Of course."

During the next thirty minutes, she updated Maleek on ideas she had for the event, getting his approval for each item on her list. Many times she looked up from her design board of swatches of colors to find his eyes on her. And always—*always*—her heart swelled. She was a mature, observant woman who knew damn well when a man found her desirable, and the look in Maleek's eyes hinted at nothing less. That and the way he kept focusing on her mouth.

"Okay. You know what? Stop doing that!" she finally said, slapping her hand down on the desktop.

Maleek looked confused. "Stop doing what?" he asked, holding up his hands.

Love rose to her feet, shaking her head. "Never mind," she muttered, feeling foolish. "So this should do it for now. I have your cell number if I have any other questions. Monday we will go and view the locations I have in mind. Okay? Alright. Enjoy your weekend."

Maleek rose as well. "Did I do something?" he asked.

Love brought her hand up to play in the soft tendrils at her nape. "No, nothing at all," she rushed to assure him, just wanting him gone. Wanting her body to ease back to normalcy.

Maleek hung his head, and then cut his eyes up to look at her as he licked his lips. "I better get going," he said, his eyes dipping again to watch as she nervously licked her lips.

Love's heart raced, but she was learning well to hide how he made her feel. And he made her feel hot. Very hot. Nervous. Anxious. Dizzy. "Good-bye," she told him, turning on her heel to walk away from him.

She held her breath until the door closed quietly behind him.

Maleek took three steps before he turned and strode back into Love's office. She looked up, obviously startled by his return.

He was just as surprised.

"Listen," Maleek began, closing the door behind himself.

"Yes, Mr. Trenton?" she asked, all too politely, leaning back in her chair.

The nerves he suddenly felt shocked him. He had ten women on speed dial, but it was this woman dominating his everything. It was Love he wanted to make smile. It was Love he wanted to know more about. It was Love he wanted to see sitting across a candlelit table. "I have a charity dinner to attend next week and I wanted to—"

Brrrnnnggg.

"Excuse me," she said, leaning forward to answer her phone. "I've been waiting on a call from one of my vendors."

Maleek licked his lips as he turned from her. *Am I making a mistake asking Love out?* he wondered. *What do I even know about her?*

Love rose to her feet, covering the phone with her hand. "I'll be right back," she mouthed before coming around the desk and crossing the floor.

Maleek's eyes dipped to take in the subtle back and forth motion of her hips until she passed him. He smiled before he dropped his head. He was curious as hell about what was hidden beneath her pencil skirts and sophisticated blouses.

But if that was all that intrigued him about Love, then it would be easy to ask her out, show her a good time, and wait for her to show him a better one . . . and then eventually go their separate ways.

But it wasn't just the hint of sexy contained beneath her sophisticated garb. Maleek found himself wondering what made her curve her luscious lips into a smile or just what would put a mischievous glint in the depth of her bright eyes. He would catch himself wondering what she was doing throughout the day. He wondered what she liked to do outside of work.

Maleek wanted to know more about her than just what sweetness was hidden between her thighs . . . and that reminded him of the fall he took for Monique.

But he knew if he wanted that bigger picture—the happily ever after—then he had to take a chance on falling in love again.

But . . .

Rubbing his hand over his mouth, he pulled his iPhone from the pocket of his crisp short-sleeved T-shirt. He opened the browser and quickly typed her name in the search engine. After quickly scrolling through the results for her professional Web site and some newspaper articles on her business, his eyes lit on the ex-wife of R & B superstar Byron Bilton is now taking the entertainment world by storm in her own right . . .

His stomach tightened as if he'd been gut punched. Love had been married to Byron Bilton.

The office door opened.

Maleek looked up as he exited out of the screen with his thumb.

"Okay, sorry about that. What were you saying?" she asked, lightly touching his arm as she came around to reclaim her seat behind her desk.

Maleek looked down at her and suddenly everything looked and felt different. All of his internal alarms were ringing, even as he felt his desire for her still stirring. He had to think with his bigger head.

With his wealth and celebrity status, he had run into many types of women. Some were intelligent, hard-working women filled with independence. Then there were the groupies, handing out random sex acts to collect in their mental scrapbooks; the ones looking for a relationship with celebrities as their own claim to fame; and the worst of the worst—the ones looking to wed a celebrity to live in the lap of luxury. It was the husband hunters who faked their love. It made him feel like a walking bank account and not a man with blood and flesh and feelings.

At least the groupies kept it real.

Love's face filled with confusion as she picked up a gold pen. "Mr. Trenton?" she said.

His eyes shifted to her face. "Uhm . . . never mind," Maleek said. "Don't worry about it."

Love lifted one shoulder in a semishrug. "Okay," she said simply. "Enjoy your weekend."

Maleek said nothing else, wishing he didn't feel so disappointed, as he turned and walked out of the office. He rode the elevator down and met up with Yuri, who was dutifully waiting in all black in the lobby. After they climbed into the SUV, he slid down in the seat and covered his mouth with his hand as he peered out the window at nothing.

"You a'ight?" Yuri asked as he drove them toward the Newark Liberty International Airport.

Maleek nodded even as the word *no* formed on his lips.

Chapter 6

"Hot Fun in the Summertime"
—Sly & the Family Stone

Two Weeks Later
June

As an event planner, Love was so busy organizing and executing the events of others that she rarely had time to entertain or be entertained. So as busy as she was, she couldn't turn down Ayannah's offer to attend a dinner party. She needed a break from work and a chance to enjoy the beginning of summer. Especially a nice laid-back evening of good food and great conversation at someone's private home. No press.

Lance didn't count. He had a strict rule that whatever went on in his home stayed there. Ayannah made sure Love knew that.

"You came."

Love turned on her straw-stacked wedges to find Maleek standing beside the front of her parked Range Rover. She took an inadvertent step back from the sight of him dressed in a white linen suit and a pale blue silk shirt. She swallowed hard and fought the urge to hum in pleasure. The sight of him, tall and strong and handsome in white as the summer sun just began to set in the skies behind him, truly was a majestic vision.

"Yes, I needed a night out of my own house," she told him, closing her door after slipping her floral satin clutch under her arm. "And how are you doing this evening, Mr. Trenton?"

"Damn good, seeing you in that dress, Ms. Lovely," he said, his voice filled with warmth and unabashed praise.

Love knew that she had great style. She paid attention to fit and form and the latest trends. The strapless empire maxi dress was a beautiful shade of blue that accentuated the deep bronze of her skin and pushed her plump breasts high up on her chest while flowing around the curves of her hips and her long legs. She wore her hair in a side-swept ponytail and went just a bit heavier with her blusher, bronzer, and lip gloss. "I see you got the memo on the color," she joked lightly, coming to stand in front of him. She had to tilt her head back to look at him.

"Looks better on you," Maleek said, his eyes moving back and forth over her face and down the length of her body before resting on her mouth.

Love arched a brow and tilted her head to the side. "Do I get to go inside or are you going to trap me by my car all night?" she joked, admitting to herself that she was actually quite comfortable in the shadow his body made against hers.

Maleek opened his mouth but then closed it as if changing his mind. He offered his arm instead. "You're alone?" he asked, a seemingly obvious question.

Love slipped her arm through his, instantly noticing the way the side of her breast was cushioned against it. Her nipple hardened in a rush from his touch, his scent. Their chemistry. "I am single and loving it," she told him as they slowly strolled across the garden. "Just like someone else I know."

Maleek smiled. His teeth were as bright as his suit. "Single isn't all it's caught up to be," he countered.

"Neither is marriage," she said softly in return, noticing that he had led her to a small rose-filled garden . . . and not toward the party.

"With the wrong person, you're right. But if you're lucky enough to find the one you're meant to be with, then marriage should and can be the best thing ever."

Love slipped away from his arm to bend down and press her face against a large yellow rose with bright red tips. "So you believe in 'the one' and destiny and all of that, Mr. Superstar?"

"I used to . . . and I'm starting to again."

Love looked over her shoulder to find his eyes on her. She rose to her full height and turned to fully face him, never taking her eyes off him. "I used to . . . and I never will again," she finished softly.

Maleek nodded in understanding before turning

to tear two long-stemmed white roses in full bloom. Careful of the thorns, he discarded the stems before stepping forward to lightly push the roses into her ponytail.

Love allowed herself to take a deep inhale of his cologne as he tended to her. "I love the summer," she admitted, fighting the urge to rub her cheek against his inner wrist.

He paused and looked down at her with a smile. "So do I," he said.

"Perfect weather."

"Vacations," Maleek offered.

"People are friendlier," Love countered with a smile.

"Longer days."

"Outdoor concerts."

"Chillin' on the beach."

"Amusement parks."

"Picnics in the parks," Maleek said.

Love started in surprise. "That was *my* next one," she said, playfully nudging his rock-hard abdomen with her forefinger.

"Maybe we should have a picnic in the park together," Maleek offered, his voice deep as his hands slid down to lightly grasp the sides of her face and raise it gently as he lowered his head to hers.

Yes! Love thought, feeling every emotion that could only be quenched by the taste of his lips. But as badly as she wanted to live out just a small part of her nightly dreams, Love couldn't forget everything that came along with him. The fame. The celebrity. The women. The life.

She wanted him, but the rest could be damned to hell.

"I can't," she whispered brokenly just a millisecond before his mouth touched down on hers. She inhaled the breath he exhaled as their eyes locked for a few hot seconds.

His eyes searched hers before he nodded in agreement and released her face. "You're right," he agreed with a breath.

Love was both relieved and disappointed when he stepped back from her. They both were playing with fire.

The thing was, every moment she spent in Maleek's presence over the last two weeks made her all the more aware of the passion she lacked in her life. There was this vibe between them that she knew he felt too. The truth was in an extra-long stare between them . . . or the way they both rushed away from an innocent touch . . . or one catching the other staring when they thought they were unseen.

The vibe was there. Thick and heavy and almost palpable.

But they never ever came this close to crossing the line from business to pleasure.

"I hope the thorns didn't prick you," Love said, pulling a compact out of her clutch to check the roses in her hair. She still couldn't believe the suave and sexy sports star had done something so sweet.

"It was worth it."

Love refused to look at him. She knew his eyes would draw her in and she would be lost. They couldn't keep playing with fire. "We better get to the party."

Maleek offered her his arm again, but Love declined, walking quietly beside him instead.

"You can't take your eyes off her, little big brother."

Maleek shifted his eyes from watching Love across the patio as she animatedly talked to Ayannah's hairstylist, Raoul. He looked down at his sister standing by his side. "Don't you have something else to do but watch me all night?" he asked, only feigning any real irritation.

"Don't you have anything else to do but eye-stalk Love all night?" Ayannah stopped a passing waiter and grabbed two mojito shots from his tray.

"You know I don't drink," Maleek said with a frown, crossing his muscled arms over his chest.

"Who said one was for you?" she asked with her usual sass before tipping one back.

Maleek chuckled. "I feel sorry for your husband."

"Trust me, he ain't sorry," she said with a little belch.

"TMI."

Ayannah nudged him with her shoulder. "Listen, why don't you ask her——"

"She turned me down," he said, shifting his unique eyes back to Love to find her eyes already on him. She licked her lips nervously before looking away.

"Nooo." Ayannah gasped in shock.

Maleek took the other mojito from her hand gently, tossing the contents over his shoulder into the flora surrounding the patio area.

"You know I haven't bought a Byron Bilton album since that freaky bastard embarrassed her like that," Ayannah said.

Maleek's eyes squinted deeply until his brows nearly touched. "Like what?" he asked, watching Love reach up to lightly touch the roses behind her ear.

As Ayannah filled him in on Love's rocky marriage and tumultuous divorce playing out in the press, he finally understood her aversion to press and celebrity.

"It's always been rumored that she found out about Byron's cheating via a sex tape posted on some blog. The press hounded her bad in the days following the divorce. She pretty much stays out of the spotlight."

The pain and shame he knew she must have endured filled him with a desire to protect her . . . and to beat the hell out of Byron Bilton!

Every time he was in her presence, he had to fight like hell not to just wrap her body in his arms and feast on her mouth. And he knew she felt it. He knew that everything brewing inside of him was gathering in her as well.

"She's better than me."

Maleek looked at his sister in question.

"When we were planning my wedding, I made this blasé comment about taking Lance's ass to the cleaners if we divorced, and she told me with all this pride in her chin that she didn't take a dime from her ex. She just wanted out. She didn't want nothing from—"

Maleek didn't hear the rest of his sister's praise

for Love. He was already striding across the patio in Love's direction with his eyes locked on her. She looked up suddenly as if she felt his eyes on her, and then her pretty face filled with surprise and then question.

He smiled politely at the hairdresser. "Can I steal my event planner for a minute? I just had the greatest idea I want to run by her," he said, already wrapping his arm around her waist and pulling her away.

"Oh, okay. Alright then, I guess," Love stammered.

Maleek led her to the dance floor, his hand pressed against her lower back, and he led her in a nice slow drag to the band's serenade. "Since the first time I walked in your office, I've wanted to kiss you . . . and hold you . . . and get to know you better," he admitted, looking down into eyes filled with the moon's light and surprise. "I have thought about you every day . . . and every night. I can't explain it and I don't want to understand it anymore. All I know is there is something there between us that we both feel, that neither of us can ignore."

Love's steps faltered even as her hand tightened on his shoulder and his arm. "Mr. Trenton—"

"Tell me you don't feel it," Maleek insisted, feeling exhilarated by the truth of his words and the feel of her body against his as they danced beneath the summer moon.

"I . . . I . . . don't date my clients," she insisted.

"Then you're fired, because this shit I feel for you is bigger than a dumb-ass party, Love," he persisted as the slow song ended and an up-tempo melody took prominence.

"Hey!" she protested in alarm.

Maleek lightly grasped her wrist and led her off the dance floor and into the shadows and seclusion of tall hedges.

"Maleek," she said softly, stepping away from him, lightly touching the racing pulse at the base of her neck. She turned just as he stepped up behind her and she held up her hand.

He stopped with a nod, his face pensive. "I'm sorry. I'm acting crazy as hell and I apologize—"

"I feel it too," Love admitted softly, looking over at him with eyes filled with her emotions.

In one long step, he had her in his arms and lifted her up easily until her face was leveled with his. Her hands lightly grasped his shoulders. Her heart pounded against his own just as fast and hard. Her eyes were soft and glistening as she gazed back at him.

Maleek moaned deep in his soul before he brought one hand up the length of her back to grasp her neck and draw her face closer to him. He felt her own gasp in the heated air between their lips just before lightly flicking his tongue against her mouth. Once and then twice.

Love captured it between her supple lips and suckled it with a whimper filled with all of the un-released passion that he understood so well.

Maleek's dick hardened as his heart pounded.

The chemistry they both felt for weeks surrounded them as their kiss deepened and their limbs tight-ened around each other hungrily. Her breasts against his chest. Her mouth against his mouth. Her hands lifted to grasp the back of his head, and one of his hands dipped to massage the soft curve of her buttocks.

"Love," he moaned into her mouth, fighting the urge to raise her dress above her hips and press her body down into the soft grass to fill her with every bit of the hardness she created.

But Love deserved more than that . . . no matter how heated and pleasurable he knew it would be for them both.

She rested her forehead against his, her eyes closed as she breathed deeply against his open mouth. "Damn," she swore.

Maleek's heart plummeted before the next words even escaped her lips.

"In a different time and place, this right here would have been everything I was looking for," she said softly, raising her head to look into his eyes. "But I can't change who I am or what I've been through to accept who you are and what your life outside of this moment would mean. I'm sorry . . . I'm so sorry . . . but I can't. I can't."

She broke away from his hold and softly landed on her feet.

He reached out for her. "Love."

She dodged him. "Please, Maleek. Let this go. Please."

He stepped forward, wanting to embrace her again and taste her again and convince her that there was something special between them. Something bigger than either of their pasts or futures.

But the tears and torture in her eyes stilled him.

He let his hands drop to his sides as he watched her turn and walk away from him.

Chapter 7

"Summer Madness"
—Kool & The Gang

One Week Later

What to do, Love?

Love sighed, closing her eyes as the sounds of John Coltrane floated in through the open door of the rooftop. For her, relaxation equaled a hot bubble bath and then slipping into silk men-style pajamas, followed by sipping on a martini while listening to John Coltrane playing as she lounged on the rooftop. The heavy scent of summer was in the air, mingling with the scent of the flowers blooming on the trees in the backyard.

Of course, Maleek's passionate lovemaking would be hotter than the tub, his skin would be smoother than silk, his kisses would drug her more than the liquor, and the touch of that man would draw out sounds way sweeter than even the strains of classic Coltrane.

She had stopped counting the days—no months—since she had a man in her life. In her bed. At least the frustration was good for her creativity and her business. What else did she have to focus on?

Not that she *needed* a man, but she certainly was independent, smart, and forward-thinking enough to admit that she wanted a man in her life. She wanted the whole picture that she never quite accomplished with Byron. The dreams he destroyed with his infidelity.

Then again, maybe the reality was never there in her marriage. Maybe the fading of her dreams happened before his affair. They had the time put in, the dream wedding, and the perfect homes. But no children. No family portraits. No remake of the Huxtables—the perfect upper-middle-class black family.

Love sighed as she looked up to the Harlem sun, loving the feel of it on her skin. She longed for time to get away for even a mini-vacation to somewhere tropical where she could lounge on the white sand beaches in a bikini and do absolutely nothing. It was so ironic that she loved summer so much, but she was too busy grinding for her business to truly enjoy it. She knew, just like every other year, that it would rush to an end and she would be left with nothing but regrets. The coulda, woulda, shouldas.

The day was gone. Her workday complete. Her personal life unfulfilled. She turned on the rooftop and looked out at it. Decorated like an upscale spa and ready for entertainment. Promises unfulfilled of parties and gatherings for her friends. Days missed of lounging topless in the sun and even pretending to be at peace.

Her summer oasis. All of it going to waste.

What to do, Love?

She allowed herself one last glance up at the sun before she left the rooftop and made her way down the stairs. The sound of the music playing from her living room got louder with each step. She took a deep sip of her wine as she eyed the dozens upon dozens of roses filling her living room. All varieties. Various states of bloom. The scents mingling to fill her apartment with the aroma of sweet summer.

Love was being wooed.

Maleek hadn't called or even come by her office. He even had his publicist call to reschedule their last appointment. But the flowers and the candies and the little gifts were constant. Along with the notes.

She sat down on the piano bench and picked up the polished wooden box where she kept the hand-written notes that came with each and every delivery. She read them aloud.

"Let's enjoy the summer together."

"I've never had a picnic in the park. Be my first?"

"Let's forget the past and create a better future . . . together."

There were more. Many more. Some funny. Some not. Most completely and utterly romantic. Baring a side to the millionaire athlete that intrigued Love.

She lightly touched her lips, still remembering their kiss that night. Nothing in the world had ever felt so complete to her. So right.

Love shivered at the memory.

Hungered for a replay.

Felt saddened for the loss.

What to do, Love? What to do?

Her mind said no. Her soul said yes.

She dug out the pale peach note card, even though she knew the words by heart: "What if we were meant to be?" she read softly, thinking of the bejeweled iPod she received filled with love songs, including Dondria's "You're the One."

If only life could be that simple.

A relationship with Maleek meant a drastic change in her life. It meant stepping into a world she had sworn to leave behind. It was like choosing passion over privacy.

Was it worth it?

She had just closed the box and set it back on the piano when her doorbell rang.

"Coming," she called out as she rose to her feet. As she made her way back across the living room, she briefly envisioned Maleek standing on the other side of the door with a smile sexy enough to make her climb right out of her PJs and into his arms. Her cheeks warmed as she bit back a smile.

"A little daydreaming between me, myself, and I is no one's business but mine," she mused as she opened the door. Because daydreaming was as far as she was willing to let it go.

"Cute PJs."

Love leaned against the open door as her best friend, Tashi, strolled in, carrying yet another bottle of wine. "Come in," she said dryly before closing the door.

Love watched as Tashi, a tall and svelte beauty

with skin as smooth and light as butter, kicked off her Escada stilettos and slipped into the comfortable corner of Love's sofa. "Everything okay with you, girl?" Love asked as she moved over to the piano to reclaim her merlot.

Tashi pierced Love with her eyes. "Yes, I'm good. I decided to check on you since I haven't heard from you this week," she said, smoothing her perfectly coiffed bob. "And then I find you in your pajamas at six in the afternoon. No way."

Love poured her friend a goblet of wine and handed it to her. "This is the first early day I've had this week. I'm just glad to be home. I'm so busy with two events this weekend, and I have the bridezilla to top all bridezillas on my ass until her wedding in two weeks."

"Anyone I know?" Tashi asked, leaning forward conspiratorially.

Love shook her head to keep herself from actually voicing the lie as she took a seat on the opposite end of the couch. Many times Love never revealed her clients to anyone and, upon request, even kept them off the list of clients on her Web site. The most important thing to her was a successful event.

Tashi shrugged.

Love traced her fingertip around the cool tip of the goblet. "I never thought I would be single again," she admitted with a touch of sadness.

Tashi smiled and reached over to lightly pat her knee. "It's never too late, but you ain't gone find him in here."

Love laughed with just a touch of bitterness. "Yeah, but I'm so busy working that the only men I tend to come across are celebrities, and you know how I feel about that kind of exposure of my privacy again," she said, thoughts of Maleek filling her head. "I like my life here in Harlem. I don't need the spotlight . . . or to be in the shadow of someone else in it."

Tashi gave her a long look over the rim of her goblet. "I understand your hesitancy . . . especially after your divorce," she said as delicately as she could. "I feel for women having to have all their business out on the street like that. The good, the bad, and the ugly."

Love nodded, bolstering her spunkiness with another deep swallow of her wine. "Maybe a one-night stand with a sexy man is just what I need. No commitments. No promises. Just one night to quench a thirst, you know?"

Tashi gasped scandalously.

Love tilted her head back and finished off the last of her wine. Seconds later, they both fell into a fit of childish giggles.

"Oh, God, I can't believe I said that out loud," Love moaned as she dropped her head into her hands.

Tashi rose from the sofa, taking Love's empty goblet from her hand as she moved over to the bar to refill their glasses. "Me either," she drawled with a delighted chuckle.

Love thought of Maleek. His energy. His vibe. His hardness. His looks. All of it was such a contrast to every other man she ever dated. Somehow, she knew that in Maleek's bed she would find pure, raw, unadulterated sexual satisfaction. "God, sometimes

I just want to get wild. You know?" she said aloud as she envisioned Maleek and the way his hands and his lips felt on her.

She moaned a little in the back of her throat as she felt her nature rise. The silk of her pajamas rubbed softly against her suddenly aching and taut nipples. "For him to just tear off my clothes and have his way with me. No questions. Just pure . . . animal . . . instinct."

Love frowned as her last sentence flew out of her in an agitated rush. She bit her bottom lip before she cut her eyes up to see Tashi looking at her with the oddest expression.

"Alrighty then," Tashi joked with a cuckoo whistle as she handed Love her drink and retook her seat on the sofa. "Exactly who is *he*?"

Maleek.

"No one." Love sighed as she tucked her feet beneath her bottom on the sofa. Her desire for him, coupled with his pursuit—his full-court press for a relationship—was weakening her. Tearing away at her reservations. Breaking through the emotional wall she carefully placed around herself.

What to do, Love?

Fire, passion, and attraction were good things— hell, *great* things—but in the end, she was way too smart and way too together to let the chemistry between her and Maleek manifest. He might fill up her dreams, but she refused to let his overwhelming presence, life, and stardom fill up the world she had carved out for herself.

* * *

"Your destination is on the right."

Maleek slowed the SUV as he lowered his head to peer out the window at the row of brownstones. He double-parked next to Love's Range Rover, his heart hammering in his chest. He still couldn't believe he was at her home.

Love. The mere mention of her name filled his head with images of her. A dozen of them. Love smiling. Love peering at him over the rim of her glasses. Love's moan of pleasure. The look of desire in her eyes.

Was this a romantic move or some weirdo stalker shit?

Was he crazy?

This week it took everything in him not to call or to try to see her. But he couldn't give up on her. On them. He couldn't define or explain the way she affected him. His thoughts. His actions. His reactions. Everything. He couldn't name it, but he didn't want to fight it. He wanted to take a chance with his heart. He wanted to take a chance on Love.

Maleek looked up the street and saw an empty parking spot. He eased the vehicle forward and quickly parallel parked. Before he could change his mind, he slipped on shades and pulled his brim down low on his head before hopping out to walk back up the street to her brownstone.

Yuri hated that Maleek decided to venture out alone, but at worst, Maleek figured he would run into fans wanting autographs. It was Love he worried about, knowing how her ex's fame had affected her life. He understood. He got it. At times, his fame was a mixed blessing. There had been private moments of his own life played out in the press, but he asked for the fame. He stepped into the spotlight.

Maleek knew he had to show Love that he could protect her. He would protect her.

Maleek jogged up the stairs and released a heavy breath before he rang her doorbell.

Minutes later the door opened and he was looking at Love in a pair of oversized silk pajamas. Her face free of makeup. Her hair in a loose ponytail. The scent of a clean and fresh soap clung to the air around her.

He thought she never looked prettier.

Her face was filled with surprise as she peeked her head out to look up and down the street. "Where's Yuri?" she asked, reaching out to grab his hand and pull him into the brownstone's foyer.

"I'm a grown-ass man," Maleek balked. "I don't need Yuri to babysit me."

Love rolled her eyes as she crossed her arms over her chest, leaned against the wall, and looked up at him. "Why and how are you here?" she asked.

"Well, I'll be damned."

Maleek and Love looked over at Tashi standing there with her mouth open.

Maleek slid his hands into the pockets of his pants as she circled him like he was a sideshow act. "Good Lord, how tall are you?" she asked, tilting her head back.

"Six-ten," he answered with a smile.

"Is Love planning an event for you?"

He watched as Love slipped deeper into her stylishly decorated living room and returned with a large designer tote. He bit back a smile.

"Hey, uhm, Tashi. Girl, I forgot I had a business meeting this evening, so let's get together tomorrow. Okay. Alright," Love said with a smile as she pressed the tote into Tashi's hands and opened the front door.

"Girl, you never meet with clients at your house," Tashi protested.

Love gave her a hard and meaningful stare and a frozen smile. "I will call you later. O-kay?"

Tashi smiled and took her bag, slipping it up onto her shoulder as she stepped out onto the porch. She grabbed Love's hand tightly. "I hope you know what you're doing, Love," she said with a soft smile.

"I'll call you." Love closed the door and then turned to Maleek.

He had been quietly sitting back, watching their comical exchange.

"What are you doing here, Maleek?" she asked, sounding agitated, crossing her arms over her chest.

Maleek frowned. "I thought we should finally talk about what happened the other night. What has been happening between us since we met."

Love shrugged. "Nothing happened. You asked me out on a date and I exercised my God-given right to decline."

Her anger surprised him. "Look, I'm sorry I got your address from Ayannah, and I should have called first."

Love snorted in derision. "Exactly," she snapped.

Maleek made a face like "Huh." "Okay, this is turning out to be the biggest mistake of my life."

"Then why did you do it?" she balked as she glared at him. "I certainly didn't want you to."

"Just like you didn't want me to kiss you, right?" he countered, feeling dumped upon.

Love arched a brow. "Puh-leeze."

Maleek threw his head back and laughed. "Don't pretend you don't want me," he told her with the utmost confidence.

Love joined him in his mocking laughter as she leaned toward him. "You are so full of yourself or shit or whatever."

Maleek had to admit he liked the feistier side of Love—it surprised and fascinated him. His eyes darted down to the fire burning in her eyes and her chest heaving in anger. Her cheeks were flushed and she looked absolutely beautiful. Behind the reserved and quiet appearance was a fire that had lit a spark within him. "Did you forget that I'm your client?" he tossed at her. "Do you tell all your clients they're full of shit?"

"Just the ones who randomly come by my house and invade my personal space."

Maleek threw his hands up. "This is not going like I thought, so I'm out, Ms. Lovely," he said, turning to the door.

"I'm curious, just what did you hope would happen?" she asked.

Maleek paused in the open doorway and then turned to look down at her. "I thought you would be happy to see me. I thought you would agree to go to dinner with me. I thought we would talk like two mature adults about our feelings and our reservations about getting involved. And I thought I could convince you that having you in my life is important to me, Love, and that I would move heaven and earth to make you happy. That's what I thought."

He saw the shift of emotions in her wide, expressive eyes, and it pleased him to know his words had affected her, because they were the truth. "I don't know where a relationship may go. In my position, Love, I'm taking a chance on you just like you would take a chance on me. It may last the summer. It may last a lifetime. All I know is you make me feel things that no other woman has ever made me feel, and that has to mean something."

Love closed her eyes and released a heavy breath. A tear raced down her cheek as she dropped her head to her chest.

Maleek's heart tugged and he closed the door to wrap her in his arms. It felt like home. It felt like a victory. It felt like winning the finals. It felt like seeing his mother's smile. It felt like everything that was right in the world.

"I wish I could make you feel what I feel," he told her in a low and thick voice.

Love leaned back in his embrace and looked up at him. "I do feel it," she admitted, her eyes shifting around his face quickly before landing on his mouth and then moving back up to his eyes.

A current seemed to fill his body, and he wondered if he had ever wanted a woman so much in his life.

Chapter 8

"Long Hot Summer Night"
—Jimi Hendrix

Love took a deep breath to steady herself and inadvertently inhaled the heat and spiciness of Maleek's cologne. She licked suddenly dry lips as her heart raced dangerously fast.

Yes, he was right. He did have her wide open.

He must have seen that blatant hunger in her face because the look on his face changed just seconds before he grabbed her face with his sizzling hands. She gasped from the feel of him. Her whole soul was shaken from his touch. She shivered as she closed her eyes.

She didn't know he was bending his handsome head to kiss her until she felt the very first touch of his soft lips against her own. She moaned in sweet release as she brought her hands up to lightly grasp his and press their bodies together.

She shivered as her aching and hard nipples pressed against his chest just as he deepened the kiss with a moan. The feel of his tongue circling her own made everything around them seem to fade to black.

Finally, *finally*, here was the passion she craved and dreamed about for what seemed like forever.

As his lips moved down her cheek to sweetly suckle the base of her throat, Love let out a strangled cry that came from deep within her soul.

"Damn right," he whispered against her ear as he placed gentle kisses from her chin up to her forehead. "Don't hold back. Let it out."

Love shivered as she felt the bud between her legs throb. "Maleek," she whispered into the heat between them.

He touched his forehead down upon hers and their eyes met. "I know we are as different as night and day, but this feels real. And I've never felt like this before," he admitted in a heated rush as she lowered her hands to his narrow waist.

"God knows . . . me either." Love sought his lips with her own and initiated a kiss that shook them both to their feet.

Love took his hand and guided him into her bedroom. As soon as the door closed, Maleek used his strong hands to lift her up by her waist and carry her to the bed. She instinctively spread her legs wider to wrap around his waist. Strong and hot hands pressed to her shoulders until she lay back on the bed before him. She arched her back like a feline being stroked as he brought his hands up to massage and caress her hard nipples.

Love said not one word as he ground his hips against hers, causing the long and hard length of his erection to press against her moist and swollen bud. She locked her eyes with his as she brought her hands up to cover his. She moved them to her pajama top, and as if he read her thoughts, he grabbed the front and snatched it open. She cried out and circled her hips against him as the buttons flew and hit odd spots against the walls.

His eyes flamed with intensity.

Love swallowed over a lump in her throat as she thrust her naked breasts higher. Her aching nipples lightly rubbed against warm skin as they poked through his fingers. She squirmed beneath his stare and his touch.

Maleek cupped her breasts, lightly tweaking her nipples with his thumbs. As he bent low, guiding his open and anxious mouth to the dark chocolate peak, Love arched her back higher. He was just about to stroke his fleshy tongue against the tip when the sudden jarring ring of his cell phone caused them both to freeze.

"Forget it," he whispered against her hot skin.

"Uhm . . . you really should lock your phone . . ."

Love pressed her face into his neck as she nearly died from shame at the sound of Ayannah's voice echoing through his cell's speakerphone. "Oh my God . . . ohmigod, ohmigod, ohmigod, ohmigod," she said like a chant.

Maleek kissed her cheek before his shoulders began to shake.

Love popped one eye open and pulled back a bit to look up at him. He was laughing or at least failing at trying not to laugh. She playfully swatted his shoulder. "Oh, what if we had . . . you know . . . ?"

Maleek laughed even harder as he rose to take his phone from the pocket of his shorts and turn it off. Maleek stood there with his strong and capable hands now on his hips as his hardness strained against the confines of his shorts, seeking to be free and deeply implanted within her walls.

Love bit her bottom lip as she covered her exposed breasts with her slender forearm. In those few heated moments she shared with Maleek, nothing at all had mattered but being in that moment . . . and enjoying every single bit of it. Her cheeks warmed as she remembered guiding his hands to tear her pajama top. She knew it would be that good with him. She *knew* it.

Love felt that now familiar hum of awareness as he walked back to lay beside her on the bed. At the feel of his hands on her forearms, she trembled. He began to massage deep circles in her flesh, and she moaned in the back of her throat as her body involuntarily reacted to his strength and his heat.

What to do, Love?

Enjoy myself.

The thought made Love float on air.

Maleek bent his head down closer to hers so that their eyes were level and locked. He took her hand and pressed it to his chest. Love's mouth gaped at the hard and pounding beat of his heart. She wanted to feel passion. She wanted to feel more alive than ever. She wanted to feel like she was free-falling through air. With one tiny lick of her lips, Love tilted her head up to press her lips to his.

He was right. There was something between them and it was much bigger than all of the things that made her afraid to live with love.

Maleek deepened the kiss and Love brought her hands up to clutch desperately at his back as she kissed him back. As Maleek placed one arm around her waist, it was her who brought her hands around to his chest and pushed him roughly back against the bed, straddling his hips. She saw the look of surprise and desire in his face as she broke the kiss to look down at him.

Love backed off him and the bed and stepped out of her pajama bottoms, naked and exposed before him without a care. She arched a brow as she pulled him to his feet to grab the bottom of his shirt to roughly jerk upward. Maleek paused for a second before his face filled with understanding . . . and agreement. "Yes?" he asked.

Love nodded urgently as she began to unbutton his pants.

"Now?" he asked.

She needed *this*.

She wanted *this*.

She was going to have *this*.

Love reached up on the tips of her toes just as his pants fell around his ankles with a *whoosh*. "Now," she ordered in a whisper against his lips.

He captured her lips in another kiss. Inhibitions were lost. Pure unbridled passion was found.

Love gasped in pleasure as his hands found and massaged places on her body that she had forgotten existed. She couldn't believe she was doing it. She was putting passion before logic . . . and it felt damn good. She had no regrets. Not now. This was the stuff romance books were written about.

Her eyes rolled up into her head and she bit his shoulder as he roughly turned and pushed her back against the wall. Her hair had loosened from its ponytail and flowed up around her head on the wall. He lowered his open mouth just above hers, and they breathed in each other's essence for a few fiery seconds as pure electricity crackled around them like a thunderous lightning storm.

Maleek kissed her lips briefly and roughly before he turned their bodies again to back her against the edge of her bed. They fell onto it, locked, and their limbs entangled. She kicked her feet to the sky as he used his hand to press the tip of his sheathed hardness between the lips of her core.

With one thrust of his narrow hips, Maleek entered her quickly and deeply. Completely. Love bit her bottom lip to keep from releasing a guttural cry. Even as he moved within her tightness with force, she held back the part of her that wanted to really be free. They mated fast and furious as if this was their last day on earth.

As if they would never see each other again.

As if they had found a passion that made anything and everything outside of their physical union insignificant.

As if they were meant to be this way with each other.

Everything about their sex seemed to move in a flash.

Bodies pressed.

Hearts racing.

Sweat pouring.

Limbs tightly clutching.

Hips thrusting.

Moans.

Kisses.

Bites.

Suckles.

Love pulled Maleek's body down above her and she bit his shoulder to keep from crying out as she felt her body fill with small quivers. *So this is what it feels like,* she thought, so desperately craving that feeling . . . that explosion from deep within her soul. Tears fell from her eyes, and she felt Maleek's muscled arms snake around her waist to hold her tightly. Securely. Protectively. Passionately.

Maleek pressed his mouth down upon hers and suckled her tongue deeply as his face twisted and contorted with each explosive spasm of his seemingly infinite release.

Long after, they lay with their intimacies still joined and their hearts slowed from a thunderous roar. They both were completely and totally moved by it all.

Love kissed his shoulder as she stroked his back. "Wow," she whispered.

Maleek leaned up a bit to look down at her face. He smiled broadly before his head dipped to briefly taste her lips again. "Wow is right."

Love looked into his eyes and allowed herself to get lost. "I needed that," she admitted shyly.

"Oh, you did?"

She nodded and then they laughed together softly.

Maleek nuzzled his nose against her chin. "So what do we do now, Miss Lovely?" he asked in a husky voice.

"What do you suggest, Mr. Trenton?" she asked softly. Her tone was as relaxed and content as her body.

"How 'bout putting the cart back behind the horse?"

Love's face became a mask of confusion. "Meaning?"

"Meaning we skipped all around the bases and headed straight to home base." Maleek eyes took in her fine facial features, which were a complete contrast to the current wildness of her unrestrained hair. "You hungry?"

Love looked up at him, her eyes filling with alarm. "I'll cook something. I'm not looking for our date to be all over the blogs and shit tomorrow. Superstar athlete dating ex-wife of R & B icon. Nada."

Maleek nuzzled her cheek. "So you wanna stay in?"

She nodded. "I'll cook you a good down-home southern meal like my grandmamma taught me, and we'll go up on the rooftop and listen to the sounds of Harlem. Just talk. Just chill. Just me and you."

Maleek kissed a trail from one shoulder to the next before he rose to his feet. "You know what? That does sound better than flying my private plane to Turks and Caicos for paella and margaritas."

Love felt no regrets at the change of plans. She lived the jet-set life before. She wasn't impressed. "Intrigue me with your thoughts. Seduce me with your words. Spoil me with your attention. Your money is no good here," she told him huskily, reciting a verse from a poem she wrote ages ago after her divorce.

Maleek nodded before he licked his lips and kissed her deeply, passionately, like there was nothing else in the world he'd rather do.

Chapter 9

"Picnic in the Summertime"—
Deee-Lite

Six Weeks Later
July

Love adjusted the bright orange bikini she wore, untying the straps to be sure not to mar her smooth tan. "If the summer sun were my lover," she began, stretching her long limbs on the beach blanket stretched out across one of her dark wicker chaises.

She couldn't recite her ode to summer because her lover was real now and his name was Maleek. His touch was more heated and amazing than the rays of the sun. She shivered in memory of him making fierce love to her atop her piano after serenading her with the piano keys. His musical talent was both a surprise and yet another layer to the man that deepened her feelings for him.

He was a true Renaissance man. An athlete. A musician. An artist in the bedroom. A thinker. A giver. Maleek Trenton continued to amaze her in a million different ways every day.

He insisted that she still plan his end-of-summer event, but most times the decisions that needed to be made were set aside when he stroked her thigh or commented on the scent of her intimacy.

The last six weeks had been a true whirlwind courtship. Maleek was pulling out all the stops, and Love knew if she had the time available that his surprises would have no bounds. Her weekends were booked, but the weeknights and some days were filled with adventures. Lounging on the beach. Picnics in the parks. Playing in the pools. Fulfilling their own little summer bucket list. Enjoying the heat of the sun and creating even more fire between the sheets.

More and more he was urging her to join him at some of the events he attended around town, but Love declined. She was more than satisfied to have Yuri drop him off at her home as soon as he was able to slip away from the events. Even his promises that she didn't have to walk the red carpet with him didn't ease her concerns.

Everything was so amazing between them, but what future did they have beyond the summer when he would leave New York to begin the basketball season and she would be left with nothing but memories? She didn't like to think about the end of summer.

Her cell phone vibrated on the ground and she instantly reached down for it. She was disappointed not to see Maleek's number. He'd attended church with his family—another invite she had politely refused.

"Hey, Tashi."

"You home? I was going to come over and hang with you, stranger."

"Actually, Maleek is headed straight over after church," Love said, making a face because she knew once Maleek took residence in her world, she had put some restrictions on Tashi and her other friends.

"I ain't mad at you. I'm just glad you're enjoying yourself."

Love smiled, lifting one leg high into the air to inspect her neatly manicured toes. "I am, girl. It's really nice. You know. But he wants to take it a little more public and I'm nervous. You know that."

"Listen, I am all over the celeb press, and I haven't heard a bleep about you two, so whatever you two are doing is working," she advised.

Love squinted her eyes. "I know, but I understand him wanting me at his side . . . and hell, if he didn't, I would think he was up to no good, you know?"

"Hey, last week I tried to drop off the shoes I borrowed from you, but your spare keys aren't in the pot anymore."

"No offense, but there's a lot of things going on in here that you *don't* need to walk in on. O-*kay*?" Love teased.

"Point made," Tashi drawled.

They laughed.

"Okay, I got to find something for me to get into since you're all boo'ed up."

"Let's meet for lunch sometime this week," Love offered, standing when she heard footsteps behind her. "My treat."

"I don't turn down nothing that's free. Call me."

Love barely heard her as Maleek strolled up to her looking so good in his gray and white pin-striped suit with a double-knotted yellow paisley tie. Whether casual in shorts or decked out in a suit, her man looked hella fine.

My man, she thought with an inner smile as she stood up.

"Damn, I shouldn't be thinking what I'm think-ing since I just left church," he said, wrapping his arm around her to lightly grasp her buttocks and pull her close for a kiss.

"Hey, you," she breathed into his mouth.

The spare keys she used to hide on the porch were comfortably in his hand like a man coming home.

As he broke the kiss, Love could tell something was troubling him. She hated the bit of alarm she felt. Had their summer together come to an early end? She turned and bent down to retrieve her oversized shades, quickly sliding them on her face like a shield.

"These last two months have been everything I hoped for," he began, loosening his tie as he squinted his feline-shaped eyes against the glaring sun.

Love tightened the strings of her bikini around her neck, saying nothing.

"Sitting up talking. Playing chess. Banging out music together. Able to talk about anything. Everything."

Love licked her lips as she turned to peer up at him as he strode to the edge of the rooftop and looked down on the city.

"But . . ."

Love's gut clenched.

"If we are going to survive beyond this summer, then we can't keep playing like the rest of the world doesn't exist," he said, turning his head to look over at her.

Love took a sip of her peach tea to stall for time.

"What am I to you, Love?" he asked. "Because, straight up? You are everything to me."

Love gasped a little and her hand tightened on her glass.

"Who am I to you, Love?" Maleek asked again, walking over to take the glass from her hand and lift her face up.

"Everything that you feel, I feel. You know that," she admitted.

Maleek nodded and licked his lips before he released her face and turned away from her. "Do you think we can't survive out there?"

"Out where, Maleek?" she asked.

"Outside of Harlem. In *my* world," he said, raising his voice as he stretched his arm out.

Love shook her head. "Why can't things stay the way they are?"

"Because being hidden in your house and only doing things together in Harlem or wherever there is no press is not gonna last," Maleek said, coming over to stand beside her. "So when the summer ends, it's over and we just pretend like none of this happened? Like *we* didn't happen, Love?"

That could never be. She could never forget him. Never.

"I am sorry that you went through all that bullshit with your ex, but that's not me."

Love looked over at him.

"I'm doing time for his crime."

Love shifted her eyes away.

"And that's not the type of man I am, Love. I would never do that to you."

She hated that tears filled her eyes. She blinked them away, glad for the protection of her shades.

Maleek turned to look out at the tops of the other brownstones lining the street. "If we are going to see if we can last past the summer, then we have to see if we can survive outside of this brownstone."

"I just don't want to go through what I went through the last time," she insisted.

Maleek rose to his feet again. "That wasn't the press or the blogs, that was your ex. It's messed up that they ran with it, but he left it wide open for that. He cheated. He disrespected you. Whether he was famous or not, what he did was some real foul shit . . . but all they did was report it. They didn't lie about it."

True.

"You can't live your life worrying about what people think or say." Maleek removed his blazer and rolled up the cuffs of his tailored shirt.

"I know you're right and you're making sense," she admitted, feeling amused as sweat glistened off his forehead like he had just stepped out of the shower. His shirt clung to the dampness of his torso.

It was every bit of a hundred degrees.

In a bathing suit, that was lovely. A suit? Not so much.

"I'm not asking you to do interviews about our relationship or release a press statement—just claim me. Be proud to say I'm your man." Maleek pointed to himself, every last tooth in his head gleaming between his deep dimples as he smiled.

I love him.

Love's thought surprised her, but she knew it was the truth. She loved Maleek Trenton. Not the deep and profound love built over time, but the kind of sustaining love that she knew could grow and build roots that would keep them together forever. In time.

Somewhere in the last two months, maybe even before then, Maleek Trenton had captured a piece of her heart with his body, with his mind, with his soul.

Although she bit her full bottom lip to keep from yelling it from the rooftop, Love sashayed sexily over to her man to wrap herself around his sweat-soaked body. "Okay," she agreed, reaching up to swipe some of the sweat from his handsome face.

Maleek nodded and bent his knees to level his face with hers. "I won't ask for too much," he told her.

She smiled. "And I'll give all I can."

Maleek kissed her. First sweetly. Then deeply. Then ravenously.

Soon there was nothing but the sound of clothes being peeled from their bodies before their mingled moans filled the summer air with the sounds of their rooftop passion.

Love didn't know that Maleek was ready to test her agreement so soon when he invited her to some huge blockbuster movie premiere not more than a week later. She was quiet in the back of the SUV as Maleek, his publicist, Brad, and Yuri talked and cracked jokes like they were clueless to the battle she was in the midst of.

Maleek reached over and grabbed her hand tightly.

It was a little help for her nerves, especially as the car pulled into the procession of vehicles stopping just long enough for their passengers to exit directly onto the red carpet. With every roll of the tires, the bright lights and the roar of the crowds got closer and louder.

When the SUV came to a stop and the rear door opened, Maleek stepped out looking so handsome and casual in his linen slacks and V-neck tee. As soon as he stepped down, he turned and reached his hand in for her with a reassuring smile.

Love accepted his hand and stepped down out of the vehicle amidst rapidly flashing cameras, grateful for the fitted dark denims she wore with heels. *Any woman with a skirt better beware,* she thought, eyeing a few cameramen taking shots from kneeling positions.

Brad led them to the red carpet, but when Love tried to hold back and ask him how she could meet Maleek on the other end, Maleek held her hand tighter and pulled her forward with him.

The questions being flung at them began to blur together. Some about his disappointing postseason. Others about rumored flings with other celebs. Most questioning him about her.

Love tried her best to grin and bear it, but as the questions continued to be fired at them as if from a semiautomatic rifle and the hundred cameras flashed away, she couldn't help but wonder just what lay ahead.

Chapter 10

"Farewell My Summer Love"
—Michael Jackson

One Month Later
August

Swoosh.

Maleek never really thought it would end. Especially the day that it did. He was shaken to his core. He felt some anger, but mostly he felt helpless. He felt like all of his control was lost.

His heart was broken.

Blinking the sweat from his eyes, he shook Yuri, went to the left, and faded away for an easy jump shot.

Swoosh.

He didn't let up, jumping up to roar as he grabbed the rebound and spiraled his tall frame easily into a dunk that shattered the backboard, sending glass raining down around them like rain.

"Shit, man, you happy now?" Yuri snapped, brushing the little squares of glass from his beefy shoulders.

Maleek kicked the ball away from him with force.

People say hindsight is twenty-twenty. He never saw any of this bullshit coming.

Love wished like hell she could blink her eyes, wiggle her nose, or click some heels to get the hell away from the liquor-induced male-bashing party that had invited itself to her home.

"Girl, at least you had fun while it lasted," Oran said. "A man that fine, with all that money, and all that sexy body is worth the try . . . but men ain't shit!"

Tashi and June toasted to that.

Love couldn't say the same, and it was *her* pity party.

Even through her fears about getting involved with him, when that man looked at her and said, "Trust me" . . . she did.

So why in the hell was she blindsided by the bullshit?

Why did everything surprise her and shake her and devastate her?

Love rose to her feet. Three sets of concerned eyes fell on her. "Ladies' room," she explained, turning to make her way down the hall.

"Poor baby. When she gonna learn?" she heard June whisper.

"I hated to be the one to tell her . . . but I had to. Right?" Tashi asked, her voice not much lower.

"You had to, girl."

Love was glad to close the bathroom door behind her and lock it before she slumped down onto the closed lid of the commode. She dropped her head into her hands, and her entire body shook as the tears flowed from her like she was trying to fill a river overnight.

Rewind Three Weeks

"I really shouldn't be this happy about one of my brides damn near being left at the altar." Love sighed as she adjusted her aviator shades on her face before undoing her bikini top and laying back to let the Bahaman sun kiss her nipples.

"If her wedding happened yesterday, we wouldn't have been able to charter this yacht and spend the night making love in the middle of the ocean," Maleek reminded her, lifting up off his stomach to lean over and outline her deep brown aureole with his tongue.

Both of her nipples tightened into buds as goose bumps raced across her body. "Maybe one year we can sail the summer away, huh?" she asked as she brought her hands up to massage the back of his head as he replaced his tongue with his lips.

Maleek lifted his head to look at her. "Definitely," he agreed.

Love moved her hand to stroke his face. "Are we crazy to even talk about the future?" she asked.

"We would be crazy not to."

She caressed his strong face, looked into his dreamy eyes, and smiled with all the happiness she felt.

"You ready, brothah? Maleek. Maleek? You ready? You're on in five. Maleek?"

He finally focused his eyes on Brad's reflection in the mirror behind him. "I'm ready," he said, his voice cold.

Brad held up his hands. "Okay. A'ight man," he said.

Maleek didn't mean to be an ass, but the last thing he wanted was to be interviewed by Jimmy Kimmel. He didn't want to be doing a damn thing.

Especially thinking about Love.

Not anymore.

Damn, he thought. *We didn't even last the whole summer.*

"Now, he may ask you about your relationship with Nylah Lovely—"

Maleek shoved his hands into the pockets of his slacks, his hands clenching and unclenching with the same wrenching of his gut. "It's over. Love and I are over."

It hurt to say the words and feel the loss, but what ate at him the most was her thinking that he hadn't kept his promise. That he dropped the ball. That he let her down. That he didn't appreciate the risk she took for him.

That she didn't trust and believe in him.

* * *

Love licked her lips before she took another sip of her wine as she eyed the dozen different glossy magazines spread out over her bed. Either cover photos or features inside replaying her summer with Maleek. Out to dinner. Out shopping. At one of the outdoor festivals at Prospect Park. Even sunbathing on her rooftop.

The blog posts on YBF, Necole Bitchie, and Bossip were just as numerous. She didn't dare venture into the comment sections. Tashi had warned her against it because the blog commentators were . . . *outspoken* with their opinions.

One of the mags even questioned Byron about his opinion on her new relationship. Love could only sigh in relief when his publicist released a brief statement wishing her nothing but the best.

The entertainment shows had had a ball running through Maleek's long list of "reported" girlfriends. That had been . . . interesting—especially when Maleek had been honest about which of the reports were true.

Love used her foot to kick the magazines to the floor and slammed the laptop closed before she climbed out of bed. Her steps out of the room paused when she saw a pair of Maleek's size-fifteen sneakers by the closet door. She extended her leg and nudged one of the soles with her bare foot, hating the sadness that weighed her shoulders down. The shoes and God knows what else were in her house, just like his presence lingered in her life.

Love brought her hands up to wipe the weariness from her face. "All the signs say that, ever since the day that we laid eyes on each other, baby, you're the one for me," she sang in a whisper.

She looked up at her reflection in the mirror and laughed bitterly.

Rewind Two Weeks

"Maleek, if it's not true, then why are there pictures of you smiling like a fool with this woman damn near in your lap?"

"She was a fan who asked me to pose for a picture at the same party I asked you to attend . . . and you didn't."

"The same night you didn't come back to my house."

"Because I had a carload of groupies on my damn tail and my sister's house in the gated community is more secure than yours," Maleek explained . . . again. "That's why I rented this house for the summer. To protect you."

Love looked around at the living room. "Listen, you said you wouldn't ask too much of me," she reminded him, lowering her voice.

Maleek dropped his keys onto the table as he leveled his eyes on her. "Have I asked too much?"

Love took a deep steadying breath before she answered. "Yes," she said softly.

Maleek frowned deeply.

"I moved out of my house for the summer to spend time with you in peace," she began, ticking points off on each finger. "I have the press bombarding my phone lines with questions and interrupting my business. When we go out, I have groupies and shit stampeding me to get to you. And now on top of the garbage that press is lying about, I'm getting these random ass e-mails and phone calls from some *chick that knows a helluva lot about you and your every move. It's too much, Maleek. It's too damn much!"*

Maleek paced the length of the spacious living room almost as quickly as he ran the length of a basketball court. He shook his head in disbelief as he looked over at her standing in front of the fireplace. "Have I done one damn thing to make you not trust me?" he asked, coming to stand in front of her. His presence and his anger were overwhelming.

Love felt her happiness slipping through her fingers like sand. It scared the shit out of her.

"Have I?" he roared, his eyes blazing.

Love looked up at him and shook her head. She felt tired and drained from the arguing, from the press. From all the changes in her life.

Maleek threw his hands up in the air and stalked across the room, away from her.

She felt the distance as if it were a hundred miles. "How did she know that you went to the Vanity Fair *party and left early? Huh?"*

Maleek looked at her like he didn't know her.

"And the day you went to the graveyard with Ayannah, was the press there?"

Maleek bit his bottom lip. "No."

"I guess she spotted you there too, right?"

"So no matter what I say, you're gonna beat me in the head with this bullshit?" he asked, his voice actually tinged with pain and disappointment.

BZZZZZZ . . . BZZZZZZ . . . BZZZZZZ . . .

Love stiffened as her BlackBerry vibrated and lit up on the table. Her eyes shifted to the clock. It was close to midnight.

What the hell? *she thought.*

Bzzzzzz . . . Bzzzzzz . . . Bzzzzzz . . .

She snatched it up and opened her messages. She couldn't do anything but laugh. "Wow, guess who?" she snapped, holding up her BlackBerry. "Another update from maleeksprungonthis at yahoo dot com."

Maleek came across the room. "Don't open that bullshit, Love. Don't let whoever that is mess this up," he said, his tone serious.

Love wanted to fling the BlackBerry against the wall, but she fought hard to regain some of her composure. "You said you wouldn't ask me for too much," she repeated.

Maleek's eyes squinted as he looked at her. "And you said you would give me all that you could," he countered.

Love looked incredulous. "What more do you want from me?" she asked.

"Your trust. For you to believe in my actions and my words. To not fall for the bullshit. To have my back."

Love stepped close to him, her finger pointed at her chest. "I moved out of my home to stay here with you. I'm getting e-mails from your groupies whether they are lying or not. I am not the celebrity, big-time superstar loving the lights, camera, and action. All I wanted out of this was you . . . not the rest of this shit, and you knew that, Maleek!"

He patted his chest with both of his strong hands before he opened his arms wide. "And you have me. You have all of me," Maleek told her with conviction that was written all over his face.

Love wanted nothing more than to step forward and wrap her arms around him so tightly and close her eyes and pretend like everything would be fine. But she couldn't. "This isn't just about the groupie e-mails or whatever. It's everything. It's too much, Maleek. It's . . . the . . . life."

Maleek dropped his strong arms to his sides and stepped back from her until there was nearly two or three feet between them. "I won't beg you to be in my life anymore," he said, his face serious.

Love's heart broke in two as she stood there looking at this man who had so quickly captured her. As the silence between them continued, she grabbed her keys, pocketbook, and cell phone before walking to the door.

"Go ahead and run, Love. You weren't ever ready for this anyway," he said angrily.

Love opened the front door.

"But I'll tell you this, there was nothing no one could have said or done to make me walk away from what we have."

Love looked down at her cell phone and opened the e-mail.

Tell my man I'll see him in Hollywood tomorrow.

Maleek indeed was flying to the West Coast for some television interviews in the morning.

On that note, Love stepped out the door and closed it behind her.

"Are you sure you want me to go instead?"

Maleek nodded, not taking his eyes off the movie screen even though for the life of him he had no clue what film he was watching in their theater room.

"Even though I'm happy to see you so much, you can't sit in this house all day . . . every day," Ayannah said, coming deeper into the room to sit on the arm of the theater chair he reclined in.

"Thank God your camp at St. John's is coming up. And the party."

He missed the hell out of Love. He missed her and he felt hurt that she threw his affections back in his face. He just wanted to get through what turned out to be the worst summer of his life and get back to some normalcy on the basketball court. "I'm straight," he lied, ignoring the dull ache in his chest.

"Liar," she said affectionately and with a touch of sadness as she rubbed the back of his head before she rose to her feet and left the room to go handle the favor he requested of her.

Love arranged and rearranged the items on her desk a million times in the last twenty minutes. Her nerves were shot and she didn't know what to do with herself. She looked out the window at the soft drizzle of rain.

Bzzz . . .

"Ms. Lovely, your eleven o'clock appointment is here."

She rose from her seat and smoothed her pencil skirt over her hips before coming around the desk to open the door. Her heart pounded so loudly that she thought she might go deaf.

"Thank you, Faryn," she said into the intercom, her palms sweating with nerves.

Moments later there was a double knock on her door before it opened.

Love busied herself sliding on her glasses, looking up to find Ayannah standing before her. Love's eyes quickly shifted to the empty space behind her.

Ayannah gave her a sad smile. "Uhm, he's not here. He sent me instead."

Love tried her best to recover quickly. "Sure, that's understandable," she said, hating that she stammered.

Ayannah stepped forward.

Love rose to her feet long enough to wave at one of the empty club chairs before her desk.

"There's just some last-minute decisions with it being less than two weeks before the party," Ayannah said.

He doesn't want to see me. He didn't even want to lay eyes on me.

That stung and she blinked her eyes rapidly to keep a tear from even welling up in her eyes. It didn't work.

"Oh, Love." Ayannah sighed, standing up to come around the desk and wrap her arm around Love's shoulders. "Girl, we need to talk."

And the dam broke with Love burying her head against Ayannah's shoulder as her own shook with her sobs.

Chapter 11

"Happy Summertime"—R. Kelly

Two Weeks Later
The End of Summer

"Love, I *have* it."

She looked up from her clipboard as Faryn gently tugged it from her hands.

"I have it," she said again with a reassuring smile. "But are you sure you want to miss this?"

Love nodded as she looked out at her handiwork transforming the Fifth Avenue rooftop garden of a trendy nightclub into a summer oasis that was both elegant and entertaining. The event decor was in place. Flowers picked for their scent and color were in huge arranged formations throughout. The candles were lit. A slight bit of the summer breeze blew the bright red satinlike streamers against the New York skyline of bright lights. There was an area for dancing. An area for conversations via smaller ottomans grouped together. A huge ice sculpture in the shape of Maleek's MT logo. A fully stocked bar. A DJ. The works.

The only other thing needing supervision was making sure plenty of heavy appetizers and drinks were doled out by the uniformed staff—things she knew Faryn could handle. The red carpet was all set up downstairs. Plenty of press should be on the way. That was on Brad's end, and although Love had found the little man strange, she had heard great things about him.

Love knew that everything was set. She knew that Maleek would like it, but she would miss that moment that she enjoyed so much as a planner. The reveal of the room to her clients was important to her. The truth of their opinion was always in their eyes that instant after they first saw the event site.

She would miss that moment with Maleek.

At the thought of him, Love allowed herself a few precious seconds to reflect on the last couple of months they had shared. The summer they shared. He had taught her to take some time for herself. To not give her all to her business. To be happy. To be a little less serious.

Love smiled a bit softly at a memory of him doing the running man naked around her bedroom. She had laughed so hard until she thought she was going to have an asthma attack.

Maleek.

Forcing herself back to the present, Love grabbed

her Coach duffel bag. "Of course, if an emergency arises, do not hesitate to—"

"I know," Faryn said, squeezing her hand reassuringly. "But we both know nothing will go wrong."

"You know, Faryn, I learned that nothing in life is guaranteed," Love said, sliding her hands into the pockets of her fitted denims as she did a complete turn. "Whether by fate or the design of others, nothing ever goes smoothly. But if you're prepared and ready, you can at least recover from it. Right?" she asked, smiling at her young assistant.

With one last look over her shoulder, Love hurried from the rooftop and onto the elevator headed straight to the lower level. The elevator doors slid open. Love pushed off the wall. She just wanted to get the hell out of Dodge before she had any chance of running into anyone.

Maleek nodded his head in approval as he walked the entire length of the rooftop, his unlit cigar between his even white teeth. There was no denying that Love was a true professional. Everything was better than he imagined, and to know that it all was from Love's vision made it all the more impressive. He could see why celebrities called on her to make their events memorable.

Coming to a stop between two of the small canopies, Maleek slid his hands into the pockets of his tailored tuxedo pants, hitching his broad shoulders a bit as he looked out at the Manhattan skyline and took a deep breath of the smell of summer and flowers in the air.

"Is everything to your liking?"

Maleek tensed a bit as he turned to look down at Faryn through his dark aviator shades worn completely for style since the sun had said good-bye. He nodded, pulling one hand from his pocket to remove his cigar. "Yes, it's excellent. I might have to make this an annual affair," he said, his eyes squinting as he watched her.

Faryn nodded. "Of course, you know, I hope you go with Lovely Events again," she said with a smile. "Is there anything I can get for you before I check on some last-minute details?"

Maleek stuck his cigar back between his teeth and shook his head.

"Don't forget we need to go back down in a bit for your 'official' arrival," Faryn reminded him with a very polite but efficient clap that reminded him of Love.

As he shifted his eyes back to the view, he remembered a look on Love's face once as he made love to her. It had been like it was the first—or last—time he made love to a woman.

He smiled around his cigar. After Love he never wanted to make love to another woman again.

"Hey, Maleek, is Love here?"

He turned his head again. This time to find Tashi standing there. "No, her . . . uh . . . her assistant said she wasn't here," he said, reaching into the inner pocket for his monogrammed lighter. He lit his cigar, eyeing her over the rising smoke. "You're a little early, but I'm glad you could make it."

Tashi patted the back of her head, smoothing her updo. "Me too," she said with a polite smile.

"I'll have to save you a dance," he said with a smile.

"I was hoping for that," she said softly, giving him a coy look with a hint of a smile at her lips.

Maleek squinted as he eyed her. "Really?"

She took a step closer to him, wrapping her arms around his and pressing her breasts against him. "Yes, Love has been keeping you all to herself, but . . . I haven't forgotten you since we met at her house that day," she said, seductively biting her bottom lip as she reached up and gently pried the cigar from his mouth before sucking half the length of it into her own mouth.

Maleek's brows raised in surprise. "Wooow, you just gon' do it like that, huh?" he asked.

"Oh *that's* nothing," Tashi said.

"And what about Love?" he asked.

Tashi took a small puff from the cigar and released a smoke ring that she flickered with her tongue, dissolving it. "What about her?" she asked simply. "She won't be here tonight. I asked her. We could leave a little early and, uhm, get to know each other better."

Maleek reached in his pocket for his cigar holder, removing a new one to light. "I enjoyed your e-mails," he said, before tilting his head back to blow smoke rings upward.

"You . . . huh . . . what?" she said.

Maleek cut his eyes over at her before he smiled. "I liked how you went after what you wanted," he said, watching her closely.

Tashi's eyes squinted. "Listen, I'm not sure what e-mails you're talking about."

Maleek laughed. "I had the e-mail account investigated and it led straight back to you."

Tashi's body stiffened with alarm.

Maleek bit down on the cigar with his teeth as he shoved his hands back into the pockets of his pants and turned to face her. "It's cool. I've had plenty of women pull all kinds of stunts to get my attention. You wanted it. Now you have it. So what's up, Tashi?" he asked in suggestion.

She looked hesitant before she spoke. "What about you and Love?"

"What about her?" he asked, giving her back her own words.

"Yes, Tashi. What about me?"

Tashi froze and then turned to find Love and Ayannah stepping out of the nearby cabana. Tashi smiled nervously. "Love, you . . . you . . . you're . . . you . . . you are here."

Love nodded as she walked up to them looking beautiful and elegant and sexy in a fitted one-shoulder sheath in a vibrant red that enhanced the bronzed tone of her skin. "You know, when Ayannah suggested that someone close to me was sending the e-mails, we thought it out and thought it was Faryn. Wow. You know, I thought it was my little assistant having an *All About Eve* moment, you know?"

"Humph," Ayannah said, giving a frightened-looking Tashi a once-over like the woman had tried to step to her man.

"The more we went over all those e-mails and

compared some things I told you or Faryn, it all just started to make sense," Love said, coming to stand before Tashi.

"We knew if we gave one of you half the chance to get near Maleek that the guilty party would take the bait," Ayannah added.

Love's eyes saddened. "Or prove to me that I'm not such a bad judge of character," she added with a smile tinged with an odd mix of sadness and bitterness.

"I don't have to stand here and be accused like a child," Tashi said. "Or set up like a criminal."

Love's face stiffened. "You're lucky I have too much class, otherwise your ass would be laid out with a busted lip," she said in a hard little voice.

"In *what* life?" Tashi snapped.

Maleek stepped in between them. "Alright, baby, you got your proof—"

Tashi's eyes nearly popped out of her head. "Ba-*by*?" she snapped, her eyes shifting from Maleek to Love. "But you said y'all were through . . ."

Love reached up to stroke the side of Maleek's face with soft eyes. "I lied," she said. "Didn't I, baby?"

"Not to me," he added, reaching down to pull her body close to his.

"No, never to you."

Maleek never felt more alive in his life as he picked Love up against the length of his body and kissed her as she wrapped her arms around his neck. Just like their first moments together, it was hard to ignore or deny passion was there. And they were lost in it. Enjoying it. Realizing that they never wanted to lose it. Absence had made their hearts grow fonder.

"Close your mouth, dear," Ayannah said, gently guiding Tashi by the elbow as she signaled with her free hand for Yuri. "I'm sure you know by now your invite has been revoked. And if you are still as completely clueless as you look, Maleek and Love got back together last week. The disgusting things you did to destroy them eventually made them stronger."

Tashi looked back over her shoulder at Maleek and Love still embraced and kissing under the summer moonlight just before Yuri escorted her off the rooftop and out of their lives.

"I'm sorry, Maleek," Love whispered into the heated air between their parted lips as they lay naked in the middle of the bed. "I was so stupid not to trust you—"

"Ssssh." He dipped his head a dozen times to kiss every bit of her mouth.

Maleek used his hands to spread Love's legs wide as he used his hips to guide his thick dick in and out of her core. He bit his bottom lip as his eyes shifted from watching the sweet contortions of her face to dipping down to watch his slick and hard inches surrounded by her lips as he pumped away like a well-oiled piston.

"Wait, baby, wait. Too deep," she moaned, reaching out blindly to place a hand on his rigid stomach.

Maleek gave her a salacious grin that was almost wolfish as he panted deeply. "I can't get enough," he breathed heavily, bending down to suck her mouth into his.

"You love this pussy, don't you?" she breathed into his open mouth hotly before she sucked his mouth in return. She brought her legs down and pressed her feet into the bed to raise her hips and circle her wet and rigid core around his hardness.

"Oh shit," Maleek gasped, his face filling with surprise and pleasure as her walls massaged the length of him.

He loved how she was a mix of sophistication and sex. Innocence and boldness. Lady and freak.

Love closed her eyes as she purred like a kitten at the feel of his hardness, the heat, the steady and palpable pulsing of that thick vein that she loved to lick. "Maleek. Uhmmmmm. Maleek," she gasped.

His face became fierce as he watched the emotions flooding over her face and felt her core wet him more. "Don't stop, baby. Get that nut. Get it," he whispered against her face. "I'm gon' come with you."

She looked up at him, her face filled with rapture as she grasped his hard and sweaty buttocks tightly. "Here we go," she told him with a sassy smile.

Maleek licked her chin before he bit it lightly. "Here we go?" he asked.

Love nodded and gasped with a little cry as she continued to work her hips like she was hula-hooping. She was relentless. Spasms filled her core, and wave after wave of pleasure shimmied over her body from the feel of Maleek circling her body with his arms and holding her tightly as he buried his face in her neck, releasing a guttural cry against her flesh as his dick throbbed with his explosive release.

"I love you. I love you so much," he whispered against her throat, between feverish kisses.

She leaned back from him and caressed the side of his handsome mocha face. "And I love you," she countered huskily.

"We have to make this work," Maleek whispered down to her as he stroked her scalp.

Love nodded. "By any means necessary," she promised him.

Epilogue

One Year Later

Love smiled a little as she walked the entire length of the rooftop, her hand dragging along the edge as she looked out on Harlem. Her haven. Once upon a time. When she was wounded and thought only its embrace could heal her.

But then she found love. Real love.

"If my lover could be the summer sun, I would lay naked beneath him, exposed and waiting for him to reach out to kiss and caress my skin as his heat would fill my body and his light would elevate my moods." Love smiled lazily as a summer breeze caressed her upturned cheek. "If only my lover could be the summer sun, I would have no regrets and our love would last a lifetime. I would even share his brilliance with millions as long as he stayed available for me upon request."

She sighed just a little sadly because she would miss her brownstone and her life there in Harlem, but the sadness was replaced by a pure happiness.

She took a chance on love and it was working. They were working. And so she was taking another chance by moving to Denver with Maleek.

"Can you believe all the press downstairs?" Maleek asked, walking up beside her.

"They'll get bored and leave," she said, looking down the street at the church whose gospel choir's voices would fill the streets on Sundays.

"Who knew it would be you to advise me on the press?" Maleek joked, his voice seeming to rumble in his chest as he wrapped his arms around her and pressed her body back against his.

Love just smiled as she dropped her head to her chest. It was then that she saw the diamond ring he held in his hand. The summer sun glinted off it, and Love was blinded to the sight of it for a second. Her heart pounded wildly as she turned to face him. "Maleek . . ."

He smiled at her even though his eyes were filled with a serious intent that made her shiver as he spoke. "We spent a good majority of last summer in this brownstone. We fell in love in this brownstone . . . and I was trying to figure out the perfect place to ask you to spend the rest of your life with me."

Love forced herself to breathe slowly as emotions flooded her and she trembled like a leaf in the wind.

Maleek nodded as he bent his tall and muscular frame down on one knee and took her left hand in his. "Thank you for loving me. Thank you for supporting me. Thank you for understanding that when I lose a game I am grouchy as hell. Thank you for making me understand that life is about more than the game. Thank you for working hard with me to make all the miles between us feel like nothing. And then thank you for moving to Denver with me."

Love stroked the side of his clean-shaven face as she looked down into his slanted eyes.

"And I want to be able to thank you fifty years from now for making my life complete," Maleek said, almost looking nervous. "Say you'll marry me, Love. Tell me that you will be my wife."

Love nodded. "Yes, Maleek, I will marry you in a heartbeat," she whispered to him as he slid the heavy ring onto her finger and rose to pull her body against his.

Their kiss was all things. It was love and tenderness. Moments of passion and fire. It was filled with their joy and their expectations. It was made of their love and devotion. It was fueled by their desire and commitment.

"We're really doing this, huh?" Love asked him, leaning back in his embrace to smile up at him as she wiped her lip gloss from his mouth with her thumb.

Maleek nodded and rocked her side to side, her feet swaying in the wind. "I wonder who will plan it?"

"Lovely Events of Denver, of course," she said. "But we are getting married in New York, right?"

"Definitely," Maleek said, kissing her brow.

Love played with her ring, holding her hand out in front of her. She loved that it was a simple three-carat ring in an antique setting that was more about his show of love for her than the garish ten-carat ring her ex bought—a showpiece for him. Maleek understood what was important to her. He paid attention. He knew her. He loved her.

Maleek pulled her over to the edge of the rooftop. The lights of the press and paparazzi immediately began to flash.

"She said yes," he hollered down, holding her left hand high into the air.

Love just smiled down at them all and wiggled her fingers playfully.

Too Hot to Handle

Zuri Day

Chapter 1

Hot. Sticky. Both the muggy New York night and her dark caramel skin. Choice McKinley hurried up the subway station steps and navigated through the Times Square crowd on the way to her destination, the Empire State Building or, more specifically, its air-conditioned interior.

What? Choice's eyes widened as she saw the temperature scroll across a building in bright white neon. *Ninety-eight degrees? This time of night? No wonder I feel like I've wet my pants and my titties are raining.* Choice could feel steady streams of sweat trickling from the crevice of her weighty breasts, over her flat stomach, and into the band of her jeans. She hadn't watched the news before dressing for her best friend's Fourth of July party. Had she done so, she would have chosen different apparel, and learned that this was set to become the hottest day in Manhattan, ever.

But knowing her friend's year-round penchant for keeping her Brooklyn brownstone's thermostat at a cool seventy, and the New York subway system's tendency to be even colder, Choice had dressed in slim-legged black jeans, a yellow cap-sleeved tee, and a multicolored cotton jacket that could easily be stuffed into her oversized bag. As she walked the last block to her destination, she had a strong inclination to also stuff her jeans inside it and walk down the street bare-butt and fancy-free. Choice laughed at the visual her thoughts created, just as she reached for the building's glass door and entered the quiet, cool lobby.

Hum. Where's Dave? Choice scanned the lobby for the amicable, white-haired security guard who'd worked in the building for almost thirty years. He wasn't at his usual post; in fact, the building was eerily quiet, and only partially lit. Choice bit back a slight wave of fear at being almost totally alone in this huge city landmark. Thoughts of terrorists, rapists, muggers, and such scampered across her mind like skaters across the ice rink at Rockefeller Center. "Girl, you watch too much Lifetime," she mumbled, hurrying toward the bank of elevators and searching for the office key at the same time. She replaced the negative thoughts with a more positive one, the reason she was braving record-breaking heat and near-empty office buildings instead of partying the holiday night away with friends—her dad's surprise birthday party. Charles McKinley was turning the big six-o tomorrow, and his only daughter wanted everything about the rest of the week, from the office celebration to the evening with family and friends to her gift to him— a trip to Vegas in a chartered jet with three of his best friends—to be perfect.

The elevator doors opened and Choice stepped inside, smiling as she imagined her dad's reaction when she dropped him off at Kennedy Airport to board the private jet. Not that her father hadn't experienced such luxury before. To the contrary, for the founders and co-owners of McKinley Black Enterprises, Charles McKinley and Jeffrey Black, opulence was normal. But it was the presence of three friends Choice had worked hard to not only locate but secure their presence for the top-notch getaway, that had her showing all of her pearly whites.

Choice watched the shiny steel doors as they slowly closed—which is why she knew the exact moment a large hand reached between the sliding metal, stopping its motion. Choice's smile fled. Her mouth went dry and fear clutched her heart. This large, brawny hand with manicured nails did not belong to Dave, the trusty Irish security guard. This hand belonged to a stranger. And Choice was alone. The negative thoughts returned full force. Choice remembered the pepper spray in her purse, but at the moment was too terrified to move. The doors reopened, and the stranger stepped inside. Choice's heart rate increased as the doors closed.

And then the stranger smiled.

Choice's heart continued to pitter-patter at a mile a minute. But now the acceleration was hardly because of fear. It was six feet three inches and about one hundred and ninety pounds of butterscotch perfection that made her have to remember to breathe and caused moisture in places that had nothing to do with the scorching outdoor temperatures. No, there was another heat wave coming on.

Choice realized that she was staring, and that the succulent-looking lips that she stared at were moving.

"Uh, excuse me?" she asked, feeling like a fool. No one should have to repeat a one-word greeting.

The stranger pressed a number on the floor panel and blessed Choice with another smile. "I said hello."

"Oh. Hello." Choice looked down, chastising herself for behaving like an idiot. In her thirty-five years on the planet, she'd been around professional athletes, wealthy trust-fund men, and handsome celebrities. Yet she'd never had such an overwhelming physical reaction to another man, nor such instant desire. *Choice Alyssa McKinley! Get ahold of yourself!* "You scared me," she finished, hoping the man would believe it was shock and not awe that caused her erratic breathing.

The stranger appeared to not notice her angst. "Can you believe this weather? Still almost a hundred degrees, even after the sun's gone down!"

"No," Choice answered, having calmed herself enough to raise her eyes as she spoke. She forced herself not to react to his curly black hair and mesmerizing green eyes set below thick brows and long lashes. "I don't think I've ever been this hot." She immediately recognized the double entendre and quickly rephrased. "I mean, the weather . . . I don't think the weather has ever been so brutal."

"It hasn't," Mr. Wet-Your-Panties-with-a-Single-Glance responded, thankfully not reacting to Choice's verbal faux pas. "Today broke a record that has stood for sixty-nine years."

"Sixty-nine, huh?" Choice said. *Now there's a thought* . . .

She smiled, and the stranger took in a set of dimples amid what appeared to be buttery smooth skin. He scanned her body quickly, surreptitiously, and liked what he saw. Not that he was looking for a woman, or even a date for that matter. Trey Scott's focus was singular and absolute—to become a multimillionaire by his thirtieth birthday—just ten short months away. He'd just landed the job that could help make this happen, and he didn't intend to be distracted by anything . . . even when "anything" looked good enough to eat.

Choice adopted the standard elevator pose—body hugging the wall opposite the other lone occupant, eyes affixed to the escalating numbers over the elevator doors. Trey's phone beeped, and he became absorbed in the task of rapidly typing his response.

As they neared the floor Trey had pressed, Choice took one last look at the morsel of a man beside her. An unmerited yet unmistakable ache at the thought of not seeing him again rose within her. She immediately tamped down the feeling. *Don't even go there.* Choice's first boyfriend had taught her that behind every man who looked like this stranger was normally not just one good woman, but a gaggle of them. Her latest lover proved that sometimes another woman was the least of one's worries. She frowned, thinking of the man who taught her this lesson—Remington Black. Remington was her father's partner, Jeffrey Black's son, heir to the Black fortune, and if her parents had their way, their future son-in-law.

Trey noticed they had neared the floor he'd pressed, where a bank of high-end vending machines was housed, and stepped forward to exit. Without warning, the elevator made a jolting motion, and then suddenly stopped. Choice stumbled into Trey, knocking the phone from his hand. Seconds later, the lights went out. They were thrown into utter darkness.

A loud gasp permeated the air as panic swept through Choice, full and complete. She'd never been a fan of total darkness; had slept with either a nightlight or burning candle her entire adult life. Additionally, she tended to become claustrophobic in small, enclosed spaces. Engulfed in fear, she almost didn't notice the hardness of the arm on which she leaned, almost didn't smell the woodsy scent emanating from the body beside her. But Choice was frightened, not dead. As she forced herself away from Adonis, she deduced that even a corpse would rise if placed near a body that exuded such raw sexuality. She thought of the Michael Jackson *Thriller* video and imagined a motley crew of partially limbed zombies following this guy through Times Square. The thought brought levity, forced back reality, and temporarily staved off a panic attack.

"Are you okay?" Trey asked.

"Not really. I'm not a fan of the dark, at least . . . not like this."

Trey heard the tremor in Choice's voice. His voice dropped—becoming soft, comforting. He had the inexplicable urge to reach out and touch her, fold her into his arms, make her feel better. "It's probably just a temporary glitch. I'm sure we'll get going again soon."

Ten seconds ticked by. Thirty. More.

"There's an emergency phone," Choice began.

"I was just thinking the same thing." Trey moved stealthily in the darkness. "Ah, yes, here it is."

Choice held her breath as metal clinked against hard plastic. She hoped someone would answer quickly.

Trey rattled the phone hinge. "There's no dial tone."

"Would there be? I mean, it's an emergency phone connected directly to the front desk. I think it rings on their end without a tone."

Seconds seemed like hours. The silence was deafening.

"Still no one?" Choice felt as if she were drowning in the darkness. Her voice sounded tentative, distant to her own ears.

"Nothing." Trey sighed. "I'll find my phone and dial nine-one-one."

"Good idea. I have mine." Choice reached into her bag, glad to feel useful. She quickly punched in the number. **No signal available.** "I'm not getting a signal," she said, after trying twice more.

Meanwhile, Trey had been on the floor in his Sean John originals, searching for his satellite phone. "Just found mine," he said, dialing the emergency number, sure it would work. Unfortunately, his result was the same as Choice's—nada. "Okay, let's just . . . stay calm," he continued, trying to call out yet again. "All of these buildings have backup generators, emergency equipment . . . there's no way we'll be here for long."

"I feel like I'm suffocating," Choice responded. "I . . . I can't breathe."

Trey took two steps and bumped into her. Even in the seriousness of the situation, he took in the soft yet firm breasts that met his chest, begging for a rendezvous. He forced himself to simply take her hands, instead of wrapping his arms around her like he wanted to do, and he spoke in the low, calm, authoritative tone he used when under intense pressure, or about to make love.

"Take a deep breath, no, don't panic. Listen to me. What's your name?"

"Choice," she ground out through gritted teeth.

"Choice, that's an interesting name."

She took a deep breath. "I have interesting parents."

Trey laughed, a deep, rumbling sound that hit Choice's core and spread its warm tentacles throughout her body. She shivered, but nerves were only a part of it. Unfortunately, they were the most dominant part.

"I can't breathe!" she cried again, her voice reverberating against the thick steel walls.

"C'mon, now. Everything is going to be all right." Trey could no longer resist, and he pulled her curvaceous body into his arms, inhaling a combination of gardenia and something citrusy, feeling the heat that pulsed from inside her. "My name's Trey," he whispered against her ear.

His breath was hot, wet against her earlobe.

Choice found her arms wrapping around his waist of their own volition. Before she could acknowledge the yellow caution light flashing in her head, her hands had begun an exploration of his back, up his broad shoulders and back down to his narrow waist. Just before she lost her mind and cupped what she felt sure were hard, firm buttocks, she pulled away.

"I'm sorry. I'm okay." She backed into a corner, and instantly missed his touch.

"Yeah, right. Cool." Trey remained where he was, feeling bereft and alone without Choice in his arms. He blamed his somewhat discombobulated state on the alcohol he'd consumed at his parent's Long Island home. He'd tried to miss the event altogether, but he knew that not showing up for his mother's annual Fourth of July picnic would have caused an entirely different set of fireworks than those powered by TNT. He shook his head, ran a hand over his increasingly wet brow, and wished he had taken his mother up on her offer to "fix him a plate to eat while he worked." Trey had no idea how long whatever was happening would last, but the thought of a rib soaking up leftover traces of Hennessy sounded pretty good right about now. Instead he'd decided to grab a sandwich from a vending machine, and now even that was not an option.

"You okay?" Trey queried, after about ten minutes of silence that seemed an eternity.

No response.

"Choice, are you all right?"

"Not really." Choice felt more nauseated by the minute. "I'm burning up and about to be sick."

"You're probably dehydrated and overheating. Do you have any water?"

Trey heard rummaging around in a bag before Choice responded. "Yes."

"Good. Take sips and place some at your temples and the back of your neck. Then we'll have to take steps to get you as cool as possible."

Choice snorted sarcastically. "How do you propose we do that? By opening a window?"

"No," Trey answered. "By taking off those tight, hot jeans that are probably cutting off your circulation. Strip down to your underwear."

"Excuse me?" Choice said, incredulity lacing her voice. Very few people talked to Charles McKinley's daughter with anything less than the utmost respect, and this man's suggestion bordered on insulting.

"You heard me." Trey's voice was low, soft, authoritative, like the one he used when he was under intense pressure, or about to make love. "Take off your clothes."

Chapter 2

Silence followed Choice's emphatic one-word refusal to disrobe. The elevator became hotter by the minute, almost cloying. Choice swept her shoulder-length hair off her neck, fashioned it into a loose braid, and bundled it on top of her head. She wondered what Trey was doing, what he was thinking. The unmistakable sound of a belt being unbuckled was her first clue that he was taking his own advice.

"What are you doing?" Choice knew she was asking the obvious, but she had to say something to quell the surge of excitement that coursed through her at the thought of Trey in the nude.

"I don't know how long we're going to be in here," Trey calmly replied. He unzipped his cargo shorts and soon the swooshing sound of fabric hitting marble was heard. "You can be stubborn if you want to, but I've seen the effects of someone whose body has overheated. I'm going to do whatever it takes to keep my body right." The black T-shirt that

Trey wore soon joined the shorts on the floor. "Ah, that feels a little better."

Choice heard the sound of water being poured, and then a hand being patted over a taut, muscled frame. She closed her eyes and imagined the rivulets running down his skin. *Is he wearing shorts or briefs? What color are they? Wait . . . is he wearing anything at all?* A wave of heat burst from Choice's nana, shooting up to her neck and down to her toes. She reached for her bag, pulled out a flyer on the city's cultural arts programs she'd picked up in the subway, and began to fan herself. The air that brushed her face was hot and moist, but it provided a type of relief from her misery. With her other hand, she again dialed emergency. Still no signal, and on top of that, after being out all day, her battery was on one bar. It sounded like Trey had sat on the floor. But the elevator was pitch-black. She couldn't even see her hand in front of her.

Two minutes passed. Three. Five.

Choice's tee was wet with perspiration and she never thought she'd experience sweating feet. But her leather sandals had created their own type of furnace, causing her to feel like a hot, wet mess. She slid down to the floor, took off her sandals, and found temporary nirvana when her feet touched the somewhat still cool marble floor.

"Feels better, doesn't it?"

"Yes, it does." Choice had the urge to reach out and touch Trey. He sounded close but felt far away, even though he was only on the other side of the box. She pulled up her knees, wrapped her arms around them, and rested her chin. "I'm getting scared, Trey," she admitted, remembering a year ago and the terrorist who drove a truck of explosives into the heart of Times Square and almost succeeded in setting it off—mere blocks from where they now sat trapped. Choice had lunched in the area that day, and had been scared senseless. "What do you think is going on?"

"Obviously some kind of electrical malfunction."

"But like you said, they have backup generators for that. Why aren't the lights back on already, and why aren't we moving?"

"I don't know."

"Well, one thing's for sure. This can't go on forever. Tomorrow is Thursday, a work day, so at the very least we'll only be here for a few hours. That's not so bad, I guess." Choice had hoped to convince herself of this possibility while making the statement, but was only partially successful.

"Yeah," Trey agreed. He balled up his clothing, placed it under his head and stretched out as much as he could. "Might as well get comfortable, darling, since as you say, we're going to be here awhile."

Choice continued to sit on the floor, even though the flyer with which she'd fanned herself was becoming less and less effective. She raised her top enough to let air in, fanned the flyer back and forth, enjoying the air that felt cool across her sweaty skin. She raised up her top a little more. *Maybe taking my bra off will help.* She did, and her breasts seemed to applaud their freedom. They swayed perkily as she felt for her bag and placed the black lacy number inside it. Once again she raised her top, this time, over her breasts. The wind hit her wet orbs, bringing sudden yet temporary relief. The darkness was like crude oil, thick and solid. Still, Choice felt exposed and wanton. She was no prude by any stretch of the imagination, but neither was she given to striping naked in front of strangers and imagining the thrill of having a one-night stand. But in this moment, taking off her clothes and mounting Trey shamelessly—thus assuaging the nine months of celibacy she'd endured since ending her last relationship—took on an exciting, naughty appeal.

Throwing caution to the wind and engaging in the forbidden, exhilarating world of raw, spontaneous sex was something she'd never ever even think about in the light of day, much less do. After all, she was the daughter of Charles McKinley, heir to the McKinley fortune—and to whom much was given, much was required. She'd been groomed since childhood to know that what she did affected not only herself, but her family and their good name. Her parents had divorced when she was twelve years old, but one thing Charles and Arnetta had done right was continue to act civil for the sake of their child. When it came to how Choice was raised, the two adults were in total agreement. Arnetta McKinley-Baron was all about appearances and had done everything humanly feasible to make sure her daughter knew only the best life. Choice had been given etiquette classes as a child and teen, attended private school, came out as a debutante, graduated from an East Coast school, and then for her graduation present had spent one year abroad. There, in Milan, Spain, she not only became fluent in Spanish, but fell in love with fashion. That was also where the hitch in the giddyup occurred— when she decided to design clothes instead of buildings, much to her father's dismay. He'd dreamed of handing over the reins to his only child when the time was right, but Choice had the same determination to fulfill her dreams as her dad had had to fulfill his, and the same tenacity that had made McKinley Black one of the leading architectural firms in the nation. For the past ten years, Choice had anonymously built a stellar reputation and A-list following under the label Chai. This alter ego was never seen without sunglasses, long, flowing wigs, and her signature fashion statement: over-sized tops, skin-tight pants, and high heels. Only a handful of people knew that the mysterious Chai and Choice McKinley were one and the same. That's just the way she liked it.

"I can't believe this," Choice muttered.

Trey yawned as he answered. "Me either."

"Is the heat making you sleepy?"

"No, I'd have to blame that on the alcohol I consumed at my parents' party." Trey stretched out on the cool stone floor. "Trust me, I'm more comfortable than you are."

Choice took a few sips of her precious and dwindling water supply, then wiped her face with the hem of her shirt. She shifted positions, undid the button on her jeans, and unzipped them.

Time stopped on the other side of the elevator. Trey held his breath, waiting for the sound of denim sliding down skin. Given that he could have any female he wanted, Trey wasn't prone to fantasies.

But he'd been envisioning the cocoa cutie, sans clothes, since her soft, round body had fallen against his lean, hard one. For some inexplicable reason, it became very important to Trey that Choice be naked. He convinced himself that it was for her health.

Trey shifted to a cooler section of marble, one a little closer to Choice, and asked, "How's your water supply?"

"I'm trying to save it, but I feel like I'm in an oven."

"It's the clothes you're wearing, especially the jeans," Trey replied, trying to sound as a doctor might when telling his patient to disrobe and don a gown. "No telling how long we'll be in here. It may be morning before help arrives." His comments were met with silence. "Can you see me?"

Choice frowned at such a frivolous query. She'd never experienced such abject darkness in her entire life. "Don't you think the answer to that question is pretty obvious?"

"Doesn't look like it. Not from the way you're huddled up in the corner like a virginal school girl, willing to chance overheating and dehydration to getting out of those clothes and giving your body the air it needs."

Choice's curt comeback died on her lips. She wasn't so sure he couldn't see her. After all, she *was* huddled up in the corner, and braless state aside, *did* feel like a virginal school girl all aflutter after finding herself alone in the company of the top jock. His spot-on assessment embarrassed her. She was a grown woman who, as a designer, saw naked bodies all of the time. *So what's the problem?*

"Then again, I understand your hesitation," Trey drawled, his voice becoming lower, softer. "Brothah like me might have you thinking all kinds of thoughts once you get your clothes off . . . if you haven't thought them already."

"Are you always this arrogant?" Choice's embarrassment turned to anger. *The nerve of this guy!*

"Not arrogance, baby, insight. I read people pretty well. You're attracted to me, and it scares you."

"Don't flatter yourself."

Trey's chuckle was low, deep, knowing.

Choice pushed off the wall and stood. Before she could give herself time to think, she grabbed the waistband of her jeans and pulled the fabric over her thighs. Then she reached for the hem of each leg, pulling out of one and then the other. Through the heat of her chagrin came the warmth of reality—that she was nearly naked and within very close proximity to a gorgeous hunk of a man in a similar state of undress. *An arrogant, egotistical man,* she reminded herself to calm a growing horniness. *A man who is probably a very good lover,* she also acknowledged.

"Feel better?" Trey asked, after a pause.

"Actually, it does."

A few moments of silence passed before Trey continued. "So, what has you here on a holiday night?"

"Dropping off something for a friend," Choice quickly replied. Even though Trey had pushed the button to another floor, she knew that his knowing of her father was a distinct possibility. It was enough that he knew her name, a very unusual one that with just a few more bits of information would give Trey more facts than she wanted him to know. When people found out she was Charles Mc-Kinley's daughter, they treated her differently. "What about you?"

Trey shrugged in the darkness. "Wrapping up a few business matters, getting a jump on next week." He purposely avoided telling Choice where he was employed. Trey wasn't vain, per se, but he wasn't naïve either. His looks made women clamor after him, and if they succeeded in getting his attention, his economic status made them not want to leave. Trey loved all things female, but was discriminating in his choices of romantic partners. This year, while he made a name for himself at McKinley Black, he would stick to those women who he'd already schooled on how he handled his business—those who knew his good loving came with no meal tickets and no strings attached.

For a few hours, Trey and Choice conversed about casual matters: the Obama White House, why Choice loved Brooklyn and Trey adored Manhattan, and the crazy, unpredictable weather that both thought could be responsible for their present predicament. Choice learned that like her, Troy loved traveling internationally. They talked extensively about places they'd visited and places they'd like to see. At one point, Choice almost slipped and told Trey about Chai Fashion. Even in her near-naked state, she became comfortable with the easy-going man who seemed as intelligent as he was fine. She'd managed to tamp down the erotic images that kept presenting themselves in her mind, all of which included her being wrapped in Trey's arms.

Trey didn't try to rein in his imagination. The more he knew about this woman with the unusual name, the more he wanted to know. She talked openly enough, but Trey got the distinct impression that there was more to her than met the eye, and layers beneath those she chose to show him. And then there was his manhood, with a life of its own, twitching its agreement at Trey's copulative considerations, even as it momentarily hardened when Trey caught a whiff of Choice's flowery perfume.

I bet he tastes so good, Choice thought, after Trey's laughter brought to mind the smile that lit up the elevator when he'd stepped inside it. She moved a little closer to the sound that seemed to echo in the darkness.

If I roll over and stretch, I'll probably touch her. I'll just say it was an accident. Trey rolled over, making the appropriate stretching sounds as he stretched and searched.

In the next instant, neither needed excuses to make a closer connection. A large boom, followed by a rattling of the building akin to an earthquake, threw the almost-but-not-quite strangers into each other's arms.

Chapter 3

Choice screamed as her body collided with Trey, who'd sat up amid the brief shaking. She clung to him unashamedly. "What's happening?" she cried.

"I don't know," Trey whispered, every nerve in his body alert. His arms tightened around Choice, and he worked to still his breathing. "Shh," he said, when Choice came close to tears. "I think it's stopped."

The shaking had stopped, but the sirens had only begun. In their dark enclosure fifty-five floors above the ground, sounds were faint, yet unmistakable. Police horns wailed, followed by those of fire trucks. Soon, a helicopter was heard overhead.

Choice began shaking. "I'm starting to freak out," she said, shifting her body more closely into Trey's. "We've got to get out of here!"

Trey didn't want to voice his first thought after the blast—that another terrorist attack had struck their city. He chose to pin the events on nature, even though an earthquake could potentially be more destructive than a bomb. "It felt like an earthquake," he finally said.

"In New York?"

"It's happened before." Granted, the last major one occurred in the 1800s, but the possibility for another major shakeup existed. "I remember feeling a tremor five years ago. I was at a friend's house on Long Island. We were in the backyard, and I was lying in a hammock when I felt the strangest sensation and looked up to see the leaves shaking in a different way than when the wind blows. My friends thought I was tripping, but later the news reports confirmed my suspicion."

"I can't imagine being in an earthquake. It's one of the reasons I'd never consider moving to LA."

"I think us getting a major quake is highly unlikely. The 125th Street Fault here is nothing like the San Andreas fault in Southern California. Unlike the movie *The Day After Tomorrow*, I don't foresee the Statue of Liberty falling into the Atlantic."

"Oh my gosh," Choice moaned, snuggling even closer to Trey and burying her face in his neck. "Why did you have to go and mention that movie? I could barely sleep the night I watched it."

Trey couldn't answer. All of his senses were suddenly trained on the woman in his arms: the feel of her supple body curled against his, her scent wafting across his nose, the soft blasts of warm breath against his neck. His manhood hardened, and he shifted instinctively, settling Choice's lush gluteus maximus between his legs. He ground his hardness against her, used his finger to gently lift her lips to his, and pressed his lips to hers.

There was a blackout in the city, but inside this elevator, Trey's touch was electric. Choice's breath caught as his plush lips made contact with her equally full ones. The kiss was light, full of promise. He kissed one side of her mouth, and then the other; placed whispery kisses near the pulse point on her neck, and the tip of her nose. Choice closed her eyes, reveling in the moment. His actions, the way his mouth touched her body, made her feel cherished and special. After feathery kisses near her temples and still more along the side of her face, Trey brushed his lips over Choice's again. Choice's stomach clenched, her body fairly shook in anticipation of something wonderful happening, something more explosive than a cherry bomb, more mind-blowing than the fireworks finale she'd seen last year near the Statue of Liberty. She opened her mouth, wanting more, needing more, and ever so lightly swiped the tip of her tongue between his lips.

Trey groaned, opened his mouth, and met her tongue with his own. Their organs became dancing partners—swirling, twirling, circling—with the beauty of a well-choreographed ballet and the leisurely elegance of an old-school slow dance in a blue light–lit basement. Their noses touched, breath mingled, as the two deepened the kiss and their exploration of each other. Trey slid his strong hand down the length of Choice's arm before sweeping his fingernails back up to her shoulder and over to her weighty globes. He drew lazy circles around her areola, tweaked her nipple between his thumb and forefinger. Goose pimples instantly broke out on Choice's body, and she shivered in spite of the heat. She moaned into his mouth and shifted her body to give them both better access to each other. Trey took control, stretching his body out to its full length and effortlessly melding Choice against him. Choice wrapped one arm around his neck while the other delighted in the sculpted contours of a perfect frame that rippled with muscles. She ran her hand over his back and finally dared to caress the butt she'd admired. It was as she'd suspected—hard and round. Trey pulled her even closer to him, ground his massive hardness against her. The kiss continued. One minute. Two. Five. More. Their bodies communicated in a way that made words unnecessary. Which was good, considering that with what Trey's tongue was doing to her body, Choice couldn't formulate an intelligible sentence if she tried.

"Ah," she sighed, as Trey dipped his head and sucked a hardened nipple into his mouth. A flash of yellow, and through Choice's lust-induced haze came this thought: *Stop!* This, even as she skimmed her hands over the silky cotton of Trey's briefs and lightly cupped his substantial package.

"Umm," Trey breathed, removing her hand from his stick of dynamite and wrapping her arm around his waist. As much as he wanted to make love to the woman in his arms, he knew it wouldn't happen. At least not right now. He didn't have a condom, and even if he did have one, he didn't believe in anonymous sex. He knew nothing about the sistah who'd just thrown her leg over his thigh, cushioning his dick in the valley of her contentment. But one thing was for sure. He wanted to.

Trey shifted onto his back, bringing Choice with him. The kiss continued as he ran his hands along the graceful slope of Choice's back, finally cupping his destination—her firm, round, thong-exposed backside. He palmed it, squeezed it, imagined it bouncing above his hips. He knew he needed to end this dance of seduction before things got out of control. But for the life of him, Trey seemed unable to pull his tongue away from Choice's mouth or his hands from her body. And the way Choice's body was gently grinding against his, it seemed as if she was experiencing the same difficulty.

Oh, what the hell. Why fight fate? Throwing both caution and common sense to the wind, Trey parted his legs, allowing Choice's body to settle between them as if that was exactly where she belonged. His hardness teased her nether lips, causing Choice to become wet and full of wanting. She knew what was happening could not happen, but she seemed powerless to resist the magnetic pull that existed between her and this man she'd met just hours before. *What if this blackout is from some sort of attack? What if there's no way out, and I die tonight? Would I rather die with society's definition of dignity or with the memory of the best night of lovemaking I've ever known?* Because there was no doubt in Choice's mind that the sex would be as explosive as it was exquisite. Her other lovers had been adequate, but she'd never seen stars or had her world rocked. Until now. With Trey, Choice was having an out-of-body experience . . . and all he'd done was kiss her!

"I want to bury myself deep inside you," Trey softly admitted. He pressed the exclamation mark of his desire against Choice's heat. "I know it's crazy, but . . . do you want this?"

Yes! Every fiber of Choice's being screamed this affirmation. Choice wanted to do nothing more than give herself fully and completely to the man in whose arms she now rested, and against whose body she'd found peace. Stuck in an elevator, hundreds of feet above the earth, Choice felt safe and secure, protected and strangely . . . loved. "I want you so much," she whispered. "But I . . ."

The rest of her sentence was cut off by Trey's sword-like tongue plundering her mouth and scalding its insides with passion. He rolled them over, and Choice reveled in opposing sensations—the heat of flesh and the coolness of marble, the caution of logic and the spontaneity of desire, her body's yes and her mind's no. His kiss seemed to envelope her entire body and spread love's warmth through every muscle, fiber, and tissue. It was crazy, it was illogical, but Choice could taste the love this man had to give. She could taste the love and feel the promise. Her hands itched to slide inside his briefs, feel the flesh pulsating against her stomach, guide it to her opening, and let love rule. *Life is short, and no day is promised.* She pressed her hand to the band of his briefs, slowly pushed her hands under the cotton, and then something happened.

The lights came on.

Chapter 4

Trey's eyes flew open. In light of the, well, light, a wave of disappointment overtook him. He never thought he'd be sorry to have whatever malfunction had occurred come to an end, but he was. He and Choice had been wrapped in a cocoon that felt magical—where no holds were barred and everything was possible. But now the fluorescence of reality chased away that illusion, and Trey wondered if he could ever get it back.

Choice squeezed her eyes shut. As long as she didn't actually see him, she could imagine that this was a dream from which she'd awaken to find herself in her bed, clothed, and even more important, alone. Embarrassment replaced longing. The return of common sense brought with it the reality of consequence. She was Choice "Chai" McKinley: daughter of a nationally known architect father and a socialite mother, designer and owner of an up-and-coming clothing line, and an out-of-her-mind woman who'd come within seconds of giving up the nookie to a stranger in the elevator of one of the most famous buildings in the Big Apple. This thought, the now moving elevator, and Trey's quick actions jolted Choice out of her momentary immobility.

"Shit!" Trey muttered as he jumped to his feet. He jumped into his shorts and slipped his feet into his sandals while simultaneously reaching for his T-shirt and hurriedly pulling it over his head. *What in the hell was I thinking?* Trey rarely allowed himself to lose control and immediately became angry at his lack of discipline. This was where he worked, the place that would help him secure the future he desired and the life he fully intended to live. He couldn't deny Choice's beauty or his attraction to her. Nor could he dare think about what might have happened had they been in the very act of copulation when the lights came on, along with the cameras that Trey believed permeated the building. Fine female notwithstanding, Trey couldn't believe that he had almost let happen what almost happened! *On the floor? In public? Man, you're tripping for real.* An image quickly entered his mind—a glistening rump hovering over and between creamy spread legs. At his place of employment. With someone he'd met just hours before. It was not a pretty sight. He blinked his eyes to erase the image. Suddenly Trey wanted to be anywhere but here, with anyone but her. He looked at his watch: 6:07. He had just enough time to run home, shower, and change, get to work before eight, and try to forget the moment that he almost lost control.

Choice had managed to pull on her now wrinkled tee, but struggled with her snug, straight-legged jeans.

"Hurry up!" Trey hissed through gritted teeth, while reaching to pick up his phone.

"I'm trying," Choice panted.

Trey reached her in one long stride, yanked the denim up over her hips, and gathered her sandals from opposite sides of the metal square. "We've got to hurry. I, we, damn, I hope nobody's out there." Trey spoke quickly, watching the numbers as the elevator descended to the first floor.

"I'm not so thrilled to be seen with you either, my *brothah*," Choice fired back, immediately copping an attitude. She reached into her bag, quickly snatched out her jacket and scurried into it.

"No, I didn't mean it like that. I—"

"—know what you meant. I mean it too." The elevator's ding put a period to her sentence. The doors opened. "It's been . . . interesting," she said, tossing the words over her shoulder as she exited the elevator.

"Choice, wait!" Trey had spoken with urgency, but softly. He had no idea who was in the building. He waited one beat, two, and then eased out of the elevator. He peeked into the hallway and saw no sign of Choice or anyone else. *She ran out of here as if the devil himself were chasing her. Oh well. Probably best. It looks like the coast is clear.* Trey squared his shoulders and quickly moved toward the exit. *No one will ever know about the foolishness I almost got into. No one!* Trey reached the exit door and placed his hand on the bar. "I'm outta here."

He stepped into the humid, early-morning air. The street was quiet. There was no sign of Choice. He looked around for something, anything that could explain what had happened, why the elevator malfunctioned, the phones went blank, and sirens had blared through part of the night. Seeing nothing, Trey shrugged his shoulders. Whatever happened was obviously over. It was time for him to get back on track, refocus, *and try to forget about her.* Trey saw a taxi, motioned it over, and shifted his mind to the day's goals, now doubled, because what he'd planned to accomplish at the office last night hadn't happened. But what *did* happen . . . Trey settled back into the cab and allowed the thoughts to come. There was no use trying to dismiss images of the woman who'd made him feel things he'd never felt before. *Choice.* An uncommon name for an uncommon woman. One he wouldn't forget easily . . . if at all.

Chapter 5

"It's really a wonderful thing you've done for your father, dear. You are a kind, thoughtful young woman and I'm very proud of you." Arnetta McKinley-Baron sat in the tastefully decorated conference room of her ex-husband's firm, perfectly put together in an off-white designer suit, with matching shoes and bag that cost more than the average person made in six months. The bold, colorful scoop-necked shell she wore was a nod to her daughter and a show of support. Her silk Chai original made the entire ensemble come alive.

"I'm glad you could make it, Mom," Choice replied. "And really, the thanks should go to Denise. She did most of the work." Which was a good thing, Choice thought, since she'd been able to think of little other than hot, sticky elevators and deep, wet kisses all morning. She'd totally forgotten her mission, to place her father's surprise gift in his top desk drawer so that it would be the first thing he saw today. Now, she'd have to give it to him following the luncheon.

"With pleasure, I'm sure," Arnetta drawled, cutting a quick glance at the attractive, forty-something assistant who'd been with the firm for ten years as Charles McKinley's valued executive assistant. Or more, as both Arnetta and Choice had thought at one time or another. "Have you spoken to Remington?"

"No." Choice prayed that her one-word answer would be the end of this topic of conversation, but if that happened, she'd know that the world was getting ready to end. When it came to Remington Black, and his being the perfect choice as a son-in-law, both her parents were in agreement. He'd be *perfect*. Never mind that Choice had dated him last year, for three months, and decided that they simply were not compatible. Granted, Remington was successful, educated, and attractive. But he also would have fit better had he been born in the fifties. His ways were older than old school, more like *Leave It to Beaver* or *Father Knows Best*. In Remington's world, women were meant to be attractive arm ornaments, barefoot baby makers, and perfect hostesses and keepers of the home. Men, in turn, were to be the sole providers, rule makers, and absolute kings of the castle. He was only five years older than Choice, but treated her as if she were a child instead of an equal. After three months where she swore her tongue had shortened from biting it so much, she'd thrown in the towel. She hadn't dated anyone seriously since.

Arnetta looked thoughtfully at her daughter. "I saw him earlier and I swear that man gets better looking every time I see him. He reminds me a lot of Charles," she continued, her voice wistful as she remembered better days with her ex. "Hard-working, driven, a perfect gentleman. I don't know what happened between you two, honey, but Remington is still very attracted to you. Please keep an open mind. Sometimes we don't know what's good for us even when it's staring us in the face."

Choice was saved from having to respond when Denise walked over to where the two women sat. "Everyone will be arriving in about five minutes," she said, a bit breathlessly. "I told Charles that many of the staff had been called away for a mandatory meeting regarding emergency evacuation procedures. Yesterday's blackout made that ruse sound perfectly legit. He'll be coming here at twelve thirty for what he believes to be a conference with the building inspectors."

She'd barely finished the sentence when Remington Black walked through the door. Choice couldn't deny that her childhood friend was a handsome man. At six foot one, he was a portrait of mocha-hued masculinity, with a toned, solid build and perfectly shaped bald head. He wore a tidy goatee, laced with subtle hints of gray, and dressed impeccably. His eyes were dark chocolate orbs that bore into their target and twinkled when he laughed. At one time, Choice had been quite enamored of him. And then he'd opened his mouth.

"How are two of the loveliest ladies in all of America?" he asked as he sauntered over to the table. He first kissed Arnetta on the cheek, before sitting down next to Choice, taking her hands in his, and kissing each one. "You look ravishing," he said sincerely, and then leaned over to plant a kiss on her cheek. "This is a wonderful thing to do for your father. Your mother taught you well, prepared you to be a great wife and mother."

"Funny, Remington, but we were just discussing how—"

"Please excuse me for interrupting," Choice said, effectively cutting off her mother. "But the caterer is looking my way. I think he has a question." Before either Remington or Arnetta could respond, Choice rose from her chair and made a beeline for the lavish luncheon spread on the other side of the room.

Within minutes, the conference room filled up with twenty-five of the thirty-plus persons employed at McKinley Black. While it had not been requested, many brought gifts, which were recorded and then placed atop a table at the opposite end of the large, rectangular room. Some coworkers chatted amicably among themselves, mostly about the blackout, while others nibbled on hors d'oeuvres. At 12:27 PM, Denise motioned everyone to be quiet and at exactly 12:29 PM, the ever-punctual Charles McKinley stepped through the conference room doors.

"Surprise!"

Later, Choice would count the candid shot the hired photographer captured of her dad at this moment among her most treasured possessions. There were few things that surprised Charles McKinley, and nothing happened on the ninety-fifth floor that he didn't know about. Well, almost nothing. The genuinely shocked look that followed the chorused greeting was proof that Charles had been totally caught off guard.

He recovered quickly, narrowing his eyes as he

looked around the room for his assistant, Denise. *She's got to be the one who organized this,* he thought, with just a bit of chagrin, and something else he chose not to try to identify. Outside of Arnetta, no one knew him better than Denise, which meant that she knew that he did not like surprises or to be fussed over in any way. While lethal in the boardroom, Charles the man was reserved, almost shy—which is why there hadn't been a birthday party or any other party for him in the past fifteen years.

Within seconds, Charles spotted Denise and raised his brows in question. She shrugged and nodded toward the front of the room. Only then did Charles see Arnetta and Choice. He broke out in a broad smile as Choice stood and walked to his side of the room. "We know you'd rather we didn't, but this was a big one, Dad," she whispered, as she gave him a hug. "Happy birthday."

Chapter 6

While the festivities took place on one side of the building, hard work was happening on the other side. Trey knew his presence had been requested in the conference room, and he really wanted to make his boss's birthday party, but he was in the middle of snagging an appointment with the players in charge of real estate development at Ground Zero, New York City's most revered piece of real estate since 9/11. They were looking at architectural firms to design a prominent expanse of buildings that would surround the Twin Tower Memorial design. Trey knew if he could place McKinley Black in the mix of this site's rebirth, not only would his future be assured, but he'd reach his goal—millionaire status by the time he turned thirty.

That he was holding his own on this important telephone call was a feat in itself. From the time he'd stepped from the cool Empire State Building into the sultry morning air, he'd thought of little else but the tempting morsel he'd left behind. A passionate, provocative woman named Choice had pushed her way into his consciousness all morning long: as he hailed a taxi to take him the short, ten-minute ride to his apartment, while he stroked himself to release in the shower, while deciding what to wear (settling on the deep tan suit that reminded him of the color of her skin), and while trying to gather his thoughts for what could be the most important deal of his life. As he'd neared the Empire State Building's bank of elevators, Trey could have sworn he smelled her fragrance. And as he'd leaned against the cool, steel walls, he'd remembered his back pressed against them with her in his arms—writhing, moaning, feeling better than anything he'd ever held in his life. He'd told himself all morning that thinking about her was hopeless, that he'd never see her again. How could he? He didn't even know her last name. And while she'd said she was doing a favor for a friend, he didn't know where this friend worked. *No, best to forget about that little tryst and get on with what matters . . . taking care of business.*

Ten minutes later, a satisfied Trey Scott stepped into the lively conference room. He zeroed in on Charles immediately and crossed the room. "Sorry I'm late, sir," he said, extending a hand as he reached Charles' side. "Important business call; couldn't be helped. Happy birthday."

"You're on the right path, Trey," Charles responded. "Business always comes before pleasure." The two men continued to converse, with Trey relaying the good news of his upcoming meeting regarding office buildings around Ground Zero. "I don't have to tell you how much of a coupe that will be for us to secure such a contract," Charles finished. "Not even a month into the job, and you'd almost be able to write your own ticket in this firm."

Remington, who in a bid to rekindle their relationship had barely left Choice's side during the luncheon, noticed Charles and Trey talking intensely across the room. His eyes narrowed as he pondered what they were discussing. There were few men who intimidated Remington, and he'd never admit that Trey Scott was one of them. But something about the cocky, twenty-something Ivy-league whiz made Remington want to step up an already extraordinary game. On the surface, there appeared to be no reason for competition. Remington was one of the firm's top architects and a partner. Trey was merely the director of business development. Remington had been by his father's side since he began interning at McKinley Black during his junior year of college. His continued presence at the firm was guaranteed for as long as the company was in business, and he was being openly groomed to become CEO whenever his father chose to relinquish that position. Trey had an exceptional work record, especially for someone so young, but came to the firm with lots to prove amid a competitive, cutthroat field with hundreds of thousands of dollars in commission on the line. Still, there was something about Trey that unnerved Remington. Maybe it was how the women in the office looked at Trey the way they used to look at him. Maybe it was the young man's confident swagger, his self-assured demeanor, and the fact that he dressed as impeccably as Remington did, which was no small feat. Quite simply, the man seemed almost too good to be true, which is why Remington had decided that Trey Scott was an employee that bore close scrutiny . . . until he decided otherwise.

Choice turned to see who had caught Remington's eye. In the same moment, a pair of intense, deep green eyes looked over at her. Choice's mouth went dry. Her heart stopped. That she was surprised was a gross understatement. *What is Trey doing here, talking to my father?* A troublesome thought followed. *Did he know who I was in the elevator, and is that why he was so ready to get me out of my clothes?* More than once, an ambitious soul had mistaken Choice for a rung on the ladder to McKinley Black success, had assumed that, one, sleeping with the boss's daughter was an option and that, two, securing said option would ensure their success. They'd been wrong on both counts. Charles McKinley was a hard man to please when it came to suitors for Choice; and his apple/daughter hadn't fallen far from the tree.

It's her! As soon as he'd seen Choice, Trey's legs had moved of their own volition. He'd barely uttered an "excuse me" to Charles before moving slowly yet purposefully to where she stood. Now, he worked to connect his mouth to his brain, so that he could keep his cool under the watchful eye of Remington Black, a man who Trey knew had been watching him from day one.

"Choice, meet McKinley Black's newest director, Trey Scott," Remington said. "Trey, this is Choice McKinley."

"Choice," he said softly, taking her hand and

placing a gentle kiss atop her knuckles. "Interesting name."

Choice's stomach flip-flopped as his lips touched her skin, and she immediately felt heat spread through her core. It was crazy to get this turned on by a simple touch, in the middle of the day, in the middle of a crowded conference room, with her parents mere feet away. Especially with a man who could have an ulterior motive where charming her was concerned. She forced herself to smile and respond somewhat dryly, "I have interesting parents."

Their eyes caught and held, and for a moment they were the only two people in the room. The air fairly crackled between them, and seconds later, Choice realized that Trey was still holding her hand. Massaging it with his fingers the way he'd earlier massaged her mouth with his tongue.

She snatched her hand away. Remington noticed, frowned, and placed a protective arm around her shoulders. "Choice and I have known each other since we were children," he said, looking at her in a way that suggested admiration if not love.

"Yes, we have," Choice added. She wanted to be wrapped in Trey's arms instead of Remington's, wanted Remington to release the firm grip he had on her. "Our parents are close."

Remington chuckled, squeezed her tighter, and placed a kiss on her temple. "Our parents aren't the only ones."

As if on cue, Arnetta walked over to the trio. "Darling, thanks again for putting together such a wonderful surprise for your father." She turned to

Trey. "I don't believe we've met. I'm Arnetta McKinley-Baron."

"It's a pleasure, Mrs. McKinley-Baron," Trey said, shaking her hand.

"Choice, you will join us for dinner this evening, won't you? We're dining at your father's."

Choice nodded. "Sure, Mom."

Arnetta turned to Remington. "And we'll see you as well?"

Remington beamed. "Of course."

"And your mother is bringing her to-die-for carrot cake?" Arnetta queried.

Remington winked. "By special request."

With a nod to Trey and air kisses to Choice and Remington, Arnetta waltzed out of the room, leaving Choice to marvel at her mother's cunning ways. She'd invited Choice to dinner, knowing that she'd never turn down an invite to her father's private birthday dinner, and then, without Choice having known beforehand, had invited Remington as well. And for her to drop this little tidbit in Trey's presence? Mere coincidence or strategic planning? Choice's bet was on the latter.

Chapter 7

"Choice!"

Trey's voice pierced through the din that was midtown Manhattan, stopping Choice in her tracks. She spun around. "What?"

Trey was taken aback by her harsh response. "And you're angry with me because . . ."

"Because I don't appreciate being used to further a man's career."

Now it was Trey's turn to be angry. "And I don't appreciate being accused of something for which I'm not guilty."

"Are you saying you had no idea who I was when you entered the elevator last night?"

Trey took a step closer. "That's exactly what I'm saying." Fiery green eyes bore into sparkling brown ones. Trey noticed how Choice's nostrils flared slightly when she was angry, and how her rapidly rising and falling breasts strained against the soft-looking material that covered them the way his hands longed to. "How could I have known who you were last night?"

"My father has a picture of me in his office."

"An office I've only stepped into once, and that was during my initial interview with Charles." Trey placed a hand on Choice's shoulder and guided them toward the outer wall of a business and away from the middle of the busy sidewalk.

"And you don't remember seeing my picture?"

"That morning I had one thing on my mind, and one thing only: becoming the next director of business development at McKinley Black. Baby, *you* could have been in the room that day . . . and I wouldn't have remembered. Let alone your picture." His gaze was unwavering, his eyes shone with sincerity. "Now, are you ready to apologize?"

A hint of a smile crossed Choice's lips. She liked this guy. Where Remington's confidence seemed somehow contrived, Trey wore swagger as his due. "I'll think about it."

Trey smiled, and for the first time, Choice noticed a hint of a dimple in his right cheek. "You'll do more than that. You'll give me your phone number, and then you'll have a drink with me. Tonight. Ten o'clock. Don't give me that look, and don't even think about turning me down. I'm not taking no for an answer."

"You heard my mother earlier. I'm dining with my parents tonight."

"And that fool, Remington. Yes, I heard. Which is why I said ten, instead of nine. You can have dinner with them. But dessert is with me."

"How do you know that he and I aren't dating? Or that there isn't someone else? Aren't you afraid of treading on another man's territory?"

Trey reached for her left hand, looked pointedly at the bare third finger. "The territory I'm interested in, that I tasted last night and this morning, belongs to nobody but you." His voice was firm and laced with meaning. "So if Remington has plans to claim you, or some other brothah has plans to keep you, then they'd better bring their A game."

At 10:27 PM, Choice entered the swanky confines of Flute Midtown. The bar Trey had chosen was one of her favorite spots, causing her to once again wonder just how much he knew about her. She looked around the room, not wanting to appear anxious and not wanting to show how excited she was to see Trey again. It had taken her forever to get away from her father's home, and even longer to get away from Remington, who judiciously promised Charles and Arnetta to "see their daughter home safely." She stepped farther into the crowded space and looked around. Trey was nowhere in sight. Her heart dropped. She thought to call him, then decided against it. *He's probably mad and thinks I stood him up. I'll just get voice mail.* She turned and walked back toward the door.

A hand on her arm stopped her. "Where are you going?"

"Trey!"

"Surprised, huh. You know I should have left."

"I couldn't get away."

"And you couldn't call and say you'd be late?" He slid his hand down to her elbow and guided them to a booth. "Don't even bother to answer, woman.

Just keep racking up the infractions," Trey drawled, his eyes twinkling with merriment as he sat across from her. "Because I'm going to enjoy delivering your punishment."

"Infractions, huh," Choice murmured, enjoying this salacious banter. "Punishment. You sound like a dangerous man. I don't do pain."

"You'll like my kind."

And just like that, the atmosphere changed. The electricity of their magnetism could have lit up the room, could have fixed the power outage that spawned their alliance. Choice was thankful when the waiter chose that moment to stop by their table.

During the time it took to place their orders, Choice found her calm. "So, Trey Scott . . . who exactly are you?"

Trey leaned back in the booth. "That answer could take a while."

"I've got time."

"Okay. My name is Trey Scott, but you know that already. I was born and raised in Omaha—"

"Nebraska?"

"Yes, and . . . ?"

Choice shrugged. "And nothing. I just would never have guessed that you grew up in the Midwest. I thought you were East Coast, born and bred."

"Ha! I feel like I should have been, but I didn't come here until my sixteenth birthday. After my parents divorced, my mom stayed in Omaha while my dad moved here. I'd gotten to be quite a handful by the time I was fifteen, and when I was sixteen, my mother followed through on an oft-uttered threat and sent me to live with my father. It was one of the best things she could have done."

"That you were a problem child doesn't surprise me."

"It wouldn't surprise me to find out you were one either."

"I've never caused my parents a moment's worry."

Trey looked thoughtfully at Choice. "That could be the problem."

Choice was immediately defensive. "What problem?"

"I'm just messing with you, girl. But yeah, I did act out when my pops left. Like many children, I went through the phase of thinking it was my fault, then the other of blaming my mom for Dad leaving. Sports were my saving grace, kept me out of bigger problems like drugs and crime . . . but I just grew too big for Virginia Scott to handle. Especially after she remarried. I'd been the man of the house for six years. I guess you could say that our home wasn't big enough for two bosses."

For a moment, Choice saw past the gorgeous, chiseled hunk of a man and peeped at the frightened, vulnerable yet defiant child that Trey must have been during this time. She imagined that it was here that he honed his confident façade, the ability to never let anyone see him sweat. *Except, perhaps, in tight, suspended elevators amid all kinds of heat . . .*

After the waiter had delivered their drinks, a Remy neat for him, a chocolate martini for her, Choice learned more about Trey. That a tennis scholarship had landed him in the hallowed halls of Harvard University, and his 4.0 GPA had kept him there, where he earned a business degree in three short years. That, as the oldest of three children, he felt obligated to be a major success, and that his natural sales ability, along with a chance conversation with a college friend's father, had set him on his current path. He gave a brief rundown of the three jobs he'd held in ten years, and how he'd been recruited by McKinley Black.

"So that's the short version," Trey concluded. "Basically, what you see is what you get."

"Not so fast," Choice retorted, feeling more and more relaxed with each martini sip. "You've told me about your career. What about your personal life?" Again, his intense green eyes bore into hers with such voracity that Choice wanted to squirm. But she forced herself to remain still and meet his gaze.

"What do you want to know?"

"Are there any currents, exes, baby mamas, kids?"

"No, yes, no, and no."

After waiting a beat, Choice pressed further. "That's all you're going to say?"

"Isn't that all you need to hear?" Trey swirled the drink he'd barely touched. "What about you, Ms. Choice *McKinley*. Why didn't you tell me who you were last night?"

"And when do you propose I was supposed to do that?"

"When I asked what brought you out on a holiday. You said you were doing a favor for a friend, when what you could have said is that your father was co-owner of the largest, most successful African-American architectural firm ever, and that you were there to visit his office."

"And if I had, do you think that what happened would have happened?"

Trey hesitated for just a moment. "Honestly, I don't know. But I think we both have to admit that the attraction between us would be rather hard to ignore, whenever and however we would have met."

There it was, out in the open. The first acknowledgment that he was indeed attracted, and that what happened in the elevator hadn't been a random act of horniness.

"All my life I've had to work to establish my identity," Choice continued after a pause. "To be someone other than the daughter of Charles and Arnetta McKinley, or the heir to the MB fortune, or the debutante or honor student or any of those other titles that described but didn't define." Choice shrugged. "I guess truth be told, I'm still working on it."

"Is your not working at your father's firm part of this desire for individualism?"

"Partly. But more than that, it's because of my passion. My dad loves to design buildings while I love to design clothes."

"Cool! So you're a fashion designer? Do you work for one of the major houses or one of the high-end chains? I can take one look at you and tell that your stuff is high-end."

"Please," Choice chided, though she warmed at the compliment. "Some of my looks are high fashion, but I also design for the working woman, the eclectic artist, and the sistah who is everyday. I try to cover the gambit. And no, I don't work for someone else's house. I work for my own."

"What does that mean? You sell your stuff online, or through eBay, or what?"

Choice took a long look at Trey and yet again did something that was totally unlike her. *What is it with this man? He forces me totally outside of my comfort zone and makes me glad to be there.* "I'm the visionary and designer behind Chai Fashion."

"You're Chai? The weave-wearing sistah with the loud clothes and big shades?"

"Ha! That is not the description I'd offer as PR, and those are wigs, not weaves."

"My bad, I meant no disrespect. It's just that . . . my sister loves your stuff. So does my mom. I saw you as a guest judge on *Project Runway*."

Choice was amazed. "You watch that show?"

"Only because my mom forced me into it!" When Choice cracked up laughing, Trey came clean. "Okay, maybe I like it a little bit on my own."

They spent the next two hours talking, laughing, and getting to know each other. At the end of the night two things were clear. One, the sizzle between them was no passing fancy, and two, both wanted to replace the fireworks they'd missed last night . . . with their own.

Chapter 8

Remington tapped the computer keys, scrolling through a document he still couldn't believe he was reading. But here it was, in black and white. *How could human resources have missed this?* Remington knew for a fact that all potential employees were scrupulously screened, background checks and credit checks were conducted, and extensive reference checks were made. At least that is what was normally done. Somehow, he deduced, this suave-talking Trey Scott had slipped through the cracks. His model good looks and Harvard degree had somehow overshadowed and/or hidden a more telling if not impressive title—felon.

Turning toward the window, Remington looked out on the deceptively gorgeous day; the bright blue sky and silky clouds masking the brutal heat waves that pulsated from the roads and sidewalks of the city's concrete jungle. Inside his large corner office, Remington's outer calm also masked the unease boiling inside him—an unease he'd felt since meeting Trey, and which had escalated when he saw the way he and Choice looked at each other.

A knock on his office door cut through Remington's meandering thoughts. "Yes?"

Trey opened Remington's door. "You wanted to meet with me?"

"Yes, come on in." Remington quickly closed the window he was viewing.

It was seven o'clock in the evening, but neither man was surprised that the other was still on their grind. Working long hours was expected at McKinley Black, sixty-hour weeks were the average, and even eighty hours not outside the norm. Trey reached Remington's desk and sat down in one of the dark brown leather chairs facing it. He placed his right ankle over his left knee, sat back, and waited. *You called me,* his body language conveyed. But when Remington remained silent, Trey looked at his watch and finally asked, "What's on your mind?"

Remington noted the small victory. He wanted this young player to know that he was dealing with a master of corporate politics and a force to be reckoned with at McKinley Black. Trey might be a director, but Remington was a VP. *This newbie had better recognize!* Especially since Remington was fully aware that if Trey pulled off getting the account at Ground Zero, his star would not only be on the rise, it would be a meteor zooming straight to the top.

"I talked with Charles. He told me about the potential project at Ground Zero. He's excited about the possibility, yet is understandably reserved as to the likelihood of our securing such a large contract given the list of players already vying for the limited jobs around that site. Still, we haven't talked in depth since you were hired. I thought now would be a good time for me to get in this loop, make sure that MB is positioned correctly, and get a timeline for this project's advancement." Actually, Remington wanted to find out as much about the players in said project as possible and position himself to meet all of them so that when they fired Trey for lying on his application, Remington could ride in on his white horse and save the day.

Trey nodded but remained silent.

"So . . . how did you get a meeting with the big boys? I've talked to several of my contacts who'd believed all of the contracts regarding that location had been sewn up years ago."

Trey shrugged. "A bit of networking here, researching there. A good friend of mine is on the city council, another works in Bloomberg's office. I'm young, only ten years into my professional career. But I've used the time wisely, made friends and contacts strategically. Those contacts will pay huge dividends in the next few months."

Remington leaned back, acting nonchalant. "Exactly who do you know on the council? I know a couple guys myself."

Trey leaned back as well, his body an equal mask of relaxation. "I know several of them actually, along with some heavy hitters in city construction. And I appreciate your interest. But I'm a bit superstitious when it comes to getting ahead of myself and revealing information prematurely. In a few months, everything will be laid out on the table, after Charles and Jeffrey have joined me to seal the deal."

Remington stroked his goatee, admitting a very slight and begrudging respect for the man sitting in front of him. Remington thought Trey an old soul . . . older than his years. He decided to change tactics. Trey wasn't going to be intimidated or fooled. So Remington turned the corner and tried the camaraderie route. After speaking briefly about a few more potential clients, he changed the subject. "Nice party for the chief yesterday."

"Yes, it was. Are there many social functions at the firm?"

"Not really. The holiday bash around Christmastime is the biggest event, one where we invite our clients, families . . . and speaking of family, I'm sure you were impressed with Charles's daughter, Choice."

Oh, so now we're getting to the real reason for the visit. "I didn't talk with her much."

"Brothah don't need to talk much around a woman like her."

"She is quite attractive."

"She's also quite off-limits."

Trey's brow rose. "Oh?"

Remington sat forward. "Look, what I'm about to say is off the record, man to man. But the reason there was an opening for a business development director is because the last one made a move on Charles's daughter."

Trey's piercing eyes gazed at Remington. "Is Charles protecting her? Or are you?"

Remington smiled, reared back in his chair, and clasped his hands behind his head. "There's an interesting history where Choice and I are concerned. As you heard from Arnetta, we grew up together and our families are very close. Charles has been after me for years to marry his daughter; forge a dynasty of sorts."

"And you've resisted because . . . ?"

Remington laughed. "Who says I'm resisting? Choice and I will be together, of that I have no doubt. I'm just giving her a chance to spread her wings a little bit before she settles down and starts having my babies."

"Well, I wish you the best, man," Trey said, rising. "It's been a long day, so if that's it, I'll be on my way."

Remington rose as well. "Keep me posted on the Ground Zero accounts. When we get the job, I'll be working closely with Charles and my dad, so I want to be prepared."

Trey said good-bye and headed out the door. There was somewhere he needed to be. Because while Choice may be having Remington's babies in the future, she was having dinner with him tonight.

Chapter 9

After she'd unlocked the metal door to let him in, Trey placed a kiss on Choice's temple. "I'm glad to see you."

"Me too," she answered, walking down a short hall to a flight of steps and beginning to climb them. Trey followed. "Although I can't believe I'm doing this."

"What?"

"Letting you come into my hallowed space, especially now, at such a critical juncture."

"Critical?"

"Yes. We're preparing for the biggest show of the year, Fashion Week at Bryant Park."

They reached the third floor and walked to the double doors at the end of the hall. Choice opened the door to the brightly lit room, and Trey thought he'd stepped into another world. Colors burst forth from everywhere: the walls, ceilings, floors, and from the rows and rows of fabrics in every texture imaginable. Mannequins around the room were in various stages of dress, tables held partially cut pieces, and a corner desk was laden with books and magazines. The room's far wall resembled a craft store, with buttons, ribbons, thread, zippers, and various other knickknacks and accessories carefully organized in see-through bins. A sultry neo-soul tune played lightly in the background.

"Wow," Trey finally said, after a moment of taking it all in. "You've really got it going on here."

"This is where the magic happens," Choice said, her eyes shining as she looked around the room. Sometimes she still found it hard to believe that her dream of being a fashion designer had come true.

Choice led them down a hallway, where Trey noted a storage room on one side and a bathroom on the other. The back room had been made into a break room of sorts, with a mini-fridge, microwave, and bar table for two. He set down the sack of Thai food he carried and began lifting out containers. "I hope you're hungry."

Choice eyed Trey from behind, taking in his broad, strong back and tight, round butt. "Starved."

Trey stopped and turned around to catch Choice's eye. She quickly averted them to the containers of food, but Trey had gotten the message anyway. He placed the large drinks of Thai tea on the table and enveloped Choice in his arms. "I'm hungry too," he said, before crushing his lips against Choice's in a ravenous kiss. She gasped, and Trey immediately took advantage of the opening. He swept his tongue into her mouth, swirling it around seductively until he had found her tongue. The dance began again, even more fervent than when it had started just a little over forty-eight hours ago, fifty-five floors above ground. Choice felt like she couldn't think or breathe. She was drowning in passion, almost choking on a desire so strong it scared her. She'd just met this man, barely knew him, but had an aching desire to become totally his in every way. Warning bells went off in her head, but she ignored them. All she wanted was Trey, all of him. Here. Now. Forever.

Trey pressed his hardened shaft against Choice's stomach. His hands slid from her waist and cupped her luscious booty. He wanted to be inside her, pounding away, claiming her territory as his own. He felt that once he started making love to her, it would go on forever. But when it happened, his logical mind reasoned, it wouldn't be in her studio on the break room floor. She deserved better than that. She deserved everything that he could give her. As much as he wanted to do otherwise, Trey abruptly broke off the kiss and stepped back. "I'm sorry," he said, breathing heavily. "I almost got carried away."

Choice fought to catch her breath as well. "I almost wanted you to."

Trey looked deeply into Choice's eyes. "Baby, there's nothing I want to do more than to make love to you, nice and slow, and for a long, long time. But . . . I don't know. You're different than the other women I've been with. It feels more special with you. So when we take this to the next level, I want to do it right."

Choice, having regained her breath and her composure, stepped to the table and began opening the containers. "What exactly is *this*," she asked, "and what next level are you talking about?"

Trey pulled two paper plates from a separate sack, along with forks and napkins. "I guess that's what we need to talk about. "So," he began, after taking a hearty bite of his Pad Thai chicken, "what's up with you and Remington?"

Choice knew that the question was coming. Trey had hinted about her and Remington's possible connection the night before. *Might as well get it out of the way.* "We used to date," she answered simply.

Trey took a moment to let this news digest. The noodles had gone down easier. "For how long, and how long ago?"

"For about three months, nine months ago." Choice took a bite of her Kung Ping shrimp, savored the taste of the chili lime garlic sauce. "It was inevitable, really. I've known Rem my whole life, though he's been married throughout much of my adulthood."

"Remington is married?"

"Past tense, he divorced about five years ago. He was married ten years and has an eight-year-old daughter."

"Why didn't you two hook up after his divorce?"

"He wanted to, but I was in a relationship. When that ended, I took a break from dating, needed to get *me* back, you know? Remington and I talked a lot during this time, as friends. Then finally, I agreed to give him and me a try. He's a good man, and we'll always love each other, but romantically, he's not the man for me."

"Does he know that?"

"He's having a hard time believing anyone can say no to the great Remington Black."

"What about your father?"

Choice's face was a puzzle. "What about him?"

"How does he feel about the fact that you and Remington aren't together?"

Choice sighed. "Sometimes it takes a while for parents to understand that their children have minds of their own and lives to live based on their own decisions. I'm constantly reminding them that I'm my own person."

"Like your being here instead of at McKinley Black."

"While defiance may have played a role initially, I'd like to believe that my love of clothes is the biggest reason I'm here. But maybe, somewhere deep inside, I just didn't want the pressure of my father's legacy on my shoulders. Thankfully, Remington's are big enough to carry the mantle for both of our fathers."

Trey didn't like Choice commenting on Remington's broad shoulders and tried switching the subject. But Choice wasn't about to let him off so easy. "Before we talk about the ongoing heat wave, there's something I'd like to know."

"What's that?"

"Why isn't there a special lady in your life?"

"I have other priorities right now."

"Has there ever been anyone special?"

Trey's countenance grew serious. "Everyone has a past, Choice. I don't like to talk about mine."

Whoa, what's with the attitude? Choice knew she'd

hit a sensitive spot but couldn't back off. Not just yet. They were both way past grown, had both had relationships. *So what's up with the secrecy?* "Why? I've told you about Remington and that there was someone before him. Have you ever been married or in a serious relationship?"

"Yes, I have. But the present is all you need to worry about, and like I said, there's no one special in my life right now." This time when Trey switched subjects, Choice went along. They finished their dinner, and then Choice stood and began placing their empty containers in the trash. "Thanks for dinner, Trey, but I've got to get back to work."

"Work? It's eight thirty. I was hoping we could go out and catch a jam session, maybe go to Harlem."

"That sounds great, really, but I've got too much to do. I'm launching a men's line this year and . . . hey!" Choice stood back, looked at Trey with a critical eye. "Turn around," she commanded, suddenly the designer checking out a potential model for her clothes. She ran her hands across shoulders that were even broader than Remington's, ran her hands down his back and clenched his waist. "How tall are you?" she asked, turning Trey back around to face her and holding his arms out from his sides.

"Six-three, why?"

"Because I think you'd make a terrific Chai Guy and would make my clothes look good on the runway."

"You want me to model?"

Choice nodded.

"No, baby girl, that's not my thing."

"I know. But it's my thing. It's super easy and

you'd be great. Would you think about doing it for me?" Choice fixed her face with a pseudo-pout and batted her eyes.

"What do I get out of it?" Trey's eyes darkened as they roamed Choice's body.

"A suit?" Choice eked out.

Trey shook his head. "Uh-uh, I have enough clothes."

"Umm, a day at the spa?"

Trey took two steps and was face-to-face with Choice. "No, that incentive doesn't excite me."

"Well, what would excite you?" Choice asked, her nana tingling in anticipation of his answer.

Trey tweaked her nipple through the soft cotton fabric of her tee, even as he placed his mouth close to her ear. "A night with you."

Choice swallowed hard and resisted the urge to tear off her top and bury Trey's head between her breasts. "I'll think about it," she whispered, relishing Trey's tongue as it traced her earlobe before he placed nibbling kisses down the side of her face to her neck.

"You do that," Trey replied, and then once again buried his tongue in Choice's wet mouth while dreaming about burying it elsewhere.

Chapter 10

There was pep in Trey's steps as he walked down the halls of McKinley Black on the way to his office. The weekend had brought with it blessedly cooler temperatures, and not only that, his former college buddy and current tennis partner, Josh Meyers, had given him excellent news when they'd met on the court. His dad's firm had checked out MB and was going to be calling this week to set up a meeting. Solomon Meyers was a fifth-generation Jew whose grandparents had fled their beloved Poland during the Hitler era and arrived on Ellis Island in 1944. He'd landed in the banking business before expanding to real estate, while his brother had taken a more nefarious route, making millions in Vegas and Atlantic City before venturing into politics. Now a family to be reckoned with, their children wanted for nothing. Josh was privileged, but he wasn't spoiled. He and Trey had met during their freshman year and hit it off right away. It was a connection that would continue to pay off for the rest of Trey's life.

And not only that, but Trey was in love. He wasn't ready to voice these words aloud, could barely believe it himself. Before meeting Choice McKinley, he would have said he didn't believe in love at first sight. But ever since meeting her, he'd thought of no one else. He'd only been in love one other time, and after that heartbreak, which had tragically ended when his fiancée drowned, Trey swore he'd never fall again. But fall he had, and he was in deep. The funny thing was that Trey had no desire to get out. Choice had come in and rocked Trey's world and now he couldn't see it spinning without her in it.

"You're here early." Remington stood in Trey's open doorway. Trey had been so deep into working that he'd not heard Remington walk up.

"I like to get a jump on the day."

"Any progress on the Ground Zero project?"

"I've got some irons in the fire this week. When anything breaks, Charles will be the first to know and then it will be his call to disseminate the information to appropriate personnel."

Aside from a slight narrowing of the eyes, Remington held his cool. *You sanctimonious asshole. You'd better hope you close this deal so that you can live off the commissions while you're unemployed!* Remington didn't know how it would happen, but he was sure that Trey's stay at MB would be short lived. He would see to it. The guy was a liar and too suave for his own good. *Get the Ground Zero project, get rid of*

Trey. In that order, and hopefully with one event quickly following the other. "Do I recall from your resume your having worked for a financial institution?"

"No," Trey answered without looking up.

"Hum, so you've never been involved in banking or credit unions or anything like that."

Aw, hell, not this again. Trey had dealt with an on-going problem for five years and was hoping the worst of it was behind him. Obviously not. "My work history is detailed on my resume. Would you like another copy?"

"I'm standing right here. Why don't you just tell me?"

"Because I have a meeting with Charles in one hour and I'd like to be prepared. So if you'll excuse me, Rem, I'd really like to get back to work."

Rem? Remington kept his face neutral while his mind whirled. Everybody in the office called him Remington; only Choice called him Rem. Which meant that Trey had seen her, and they'd discussed him. Remington gave a curt nod and left. He headed to his office to make some calls and come up with a game plan. If Trey thought he was going to waltz in off the street and take a Black property, he'd better think again. It had taken Remington years to realize that Choice was the woman for him, and now that he'd made that decision, he fully intended to make her his wife. He'd just have to work faster than he planned, and slow another brothah's roll.

At exactly nine am, Trey walked into Charles McKinley's massive corner office. The near floor-to-ceiling glass offered stunning views of the George

Washington Bridge and the midcity skyline, and the waters of the Atlantic Ocean sparkled in the distance. Charles's décor reflected the man: strong, solid, and simple yet refined. Charles stood from behind his desk and motioned Trey to join him in a sitting area at the other end of the room.

After trading a bit of small talk about the lingering effects of the blackout, the cooler temps, and the upcoming U.S. Open, Trey got right down to business. "I have good news, sir."

"Oh, yes?"

"Yes. I got a call from Solomon Meyers and we've scheduled a meeting for this Thursday. He expressed a desire for you to also attend that meeting. I told him I'd have to check your schedule, but—"

"I'm already there," Charles interrupted, excitement dancing in his eyes. "I've got to tell you, Trey, this is some kind of business you might bring to the firm, less than two weeks after being hired."

"It's why I got the job," Trey replied matter-of-factly. "You wouldn't have hired me if you didn't think I could deliver."

"You've got to have inside connections. My network in this city runs pretty deep, and I've only been able to ripple the waters around this site."

Trey told Charles about Josh Meyers and their ongoing friendship. He also mentioned his contacts at the city council, and his personal relationship with Mayor Bloomberg, who was also a tennis fan. "There's a rumor that they want to finalize this portion of the deal before the year is out," Trey finished. "Which is why we're moving so quickly. Plus, I'd already done my homework, had been scoping out this property and possible contracts months before being hired here. I actually started baiting this particular hook a year ago and told Josh that when I got hired here, I was coming after a chunk of that construction deal."

Charles reared back in his chair, respect for this young man growing with every conversation. "You were pretty sure of yourself then."

"I was hopeful," Trey replied. "I knew that I was qualified for the job, and that if given the chance, I'd do everything in my power to convince you of this fact. Plus, my mom is big on that whole positive thinking, visualization stuff. Drummed it into me from the time I was a child. A little of that rubbed off on me. I've seen myself working here for a long time."

Charles's phone rang. He reached for the extension on the table next to where he sat on the love seat. "Yes, Remington." He paused, looked at his watch. "Why don't we make it twelve thirty and meet for lunch." Another pause. "Fine, I'll see you then."

As Trey walked back to his office, his cell phone beeped. He smiled when he saw that it was a text from Choice.

Can you meet me at the warehouse around 6:30? For a fitting?

Trey reached his desk and typed in his reply.

Sure, I can't wait to have your hands all over me. But make it 7.

He clicked on his laptop to check e-mails while he awaited her answer. It came within seconds. 7 is cool. Come prepared to take your clothes off.

Trey laughed and typed. You too?

Almost a minute went by, and then came the response. We'll see.

Chapter 11

Charles was silent, intently studying the single sheet of paper Remington had placed before him. After another moment, he took off his wire-rimmed glasses and rubbed his eyes. "I can't believe this," he said softly. But it was there in black and white: Trey Scott, guilty: embezzlement, coercion, fraud.

"I'm not one hundred percent certain," Remington admitted. "I plan to have what I've learned investigated, but I wanted to bring it to your attention right away. I also plan to tell Dad as soon as he returns from vacation."

Charles nodded. The waiter brought his perfectly cooked filet mignon, but he had no appetite.

Not so with Remington. He dug into his lobster salad with relish. "What do you think is the best way to proceed?"

"Carefully, to say the least," Charles said, after a sip of tea. "I'd hate for us to get the Ground Zero job, be front and center in the spotlight, and then have it leaked that a convicted felon is on our team."

"Exactly. Which is why I've been thinking of how we can pull off the deal without him."

Charles looked at Remington a long moment. "I don't know about that, Remington. He's best friends with one of the major player's sons. That's how we got in so deeply, so quickly. We have to make sure we have all the facts, and then, if it comes to it, take care of this matter with a deft hand."

"In light of what I've uncovered on Trey, I think there is something else you should know." Charles looked at Remington quizzically and finally picked up his knife and fork to begin eating. "He's been seeing Choice."

Charles paused for a moment. "How do you know that?" He cut off a slice of steak and put the tender morsel into his mouth.

"I have my ways," Remington said, with a smile. "I care deeply about Choice and am more than a little protective when I see someone poised to potentially take advantage of her."

"So you think that rather than having a genuine interest in her, he's just trying to maneuver himself into the family." Charles had always thought Remington a perfect choice for his daughter, but the thought of Trey being possibility had crossed his mind. Of course, that was before receiving the news that his new star employee might be an ex-con.

"I think it's more than coincidence that the two have gotten so close so quickly. He's been at the job what, two weeks, and has already had a date with your daughter? I know you don't play that, Charles, and I'm sure as hell not going to stand back and watch some player make a move on my girl."

"So you and Choice are seeing each other again?"

"She is still showing that independent streak of hers and seems bound and determined to keep this little clothes hobby that she's cultivated. But, yes, we're getting back together."

Charles nodded in satisfaction. "She can be stubborn when she sets her mind to something, but you're a pretty determined young man yourself. I'd say you'd do well to handle your business. Because unless and until you uncover news to the contrary? I don't want Trey anywhere near my daughter." Charles fixed Remington with a knowing look. "And I mean that."

"Hey, baby."

"Hey."

Trey stepped inside Choice's shop and tried to give her a hug. But instead of melting into him as she normally did, she turned away and headed toward the stairs. "What's wrong?"

"We have to talk," she said over her shoulder, and then remained silent until they were in her work space and she'd closed the door. She walked over to a long work table piled high with silks, cottons, and jersey knits, turned around, leaned against it, and crossed her arms. "Are you a felon?" Since receiving her father's phone call hours earlier, and then searching his name online, she'd gone over various ways in her mind to approach this subject and had decided to do it straight out.

Trey took a step toward Choice, but stopped when she tensed up. "Where'd you hear that?"

"Never mind where I heard it. Is it true?"

Trey sighed. "No, Choice, it isn't true. I am not a felon. The only entanglements I've had with the law are a few speeding tickets and a few cases of being stopped for driving while black."

"Then how do you explain the articles about a man named Trey Scott, who sounds a lot like you, having been arrested for embezzling from his company and doing time in prison as a result?"

This time, Trey didn't stop when he walked toward Choice. "Can we sit down?" he asked, reaching for her hand. She nodded and walked with him to the break room. They sat opposite each other, Choice as still as a statue. Trey looked at her, saw the confusion in her eyes, and wanted to erase it.

"About seven years ago, a man named Trey E. Scott embezzled several hundred thousand dollars from a bank. He is African-American, about my age and complexion, and worse still, lived for a time in Nebraska. Just my luck, right?" When Trey's attempt to lighten the moment was met with Choice's silent stare, he continued. "A year or so later, when I got stopped for speeding, they ran my name and got his information. The dude was already in jail, but the traffic officers didn't know that. It obviously didn't come back on whatever information they received when they put me into the computer. So I was hauled off to jail and stayed there almost forty-eight hours before my attorney was able to straighten out this case of mistaken identity. His name is Tre' Eugene Scott. My name is Trey, with a Y. And my middle name is Edmond. I might be guilty of a few things, Choice, but committing a crime—white collar or otherwise—isn't one of them. I've never done drugs, never cheated on a woman, and never took anything that I did not buy. I've worked hard to be one of the few, good men, Choice. And that's why I'm looking for a real good woman to be by my side."

Choice put her chin in her hand as she gazed at Trey. He did seem like a good man. She believed it in her gut. But fortunately or unfortunately, she was Charles McKinley and Arnetta McKinley-Baron's daughter. So she couldn't risk any type of scandal sullying their good name. And no matter what she felt, her father and the Internet could be right. There was still the very real possibility that Trey was lying and was a felon after all. "I'm afraid you'll have to convince my father of that," she said softly, and proceeded to tell him about their conversation. "He doesn't want me to see you, Trey."

"Baby, I'm a grown-ass man, and you're a grown-ass woman. Nobody can tell us who to be with."

Choice's eyes filled unexpectedly with tears. "It'll mean your job, Trey. You just got hired and I know you've got big plans. We barely know each other, and while I admit that I'm as attracted to you as I think you are to me, that may be all this is—a physical attraction. It isn't easy getting into my dad's firm, and his reach is high and long for anybody who crosses him. Calling my dad overprotective is an understatement. Underneath that cool, calm façade is a pit bull. Go against what he feels best, and he could make both our lives a living hell."

Trey left Choice's workroom shortly after. Just to cool off, he walked several blocks before hailing a taxi, and when he got home, he was still pissed. He knew beyond a shadow of a doubt that Remington Black was somehow in the middle of this madness. And he knew something else: that he didn't want to have to decide between keeping his lucrative job and the woman of his dreams. *You were looking for a job when you got this one,* he thought sarcastically. But he'd beat out hundreds of applicants for his cushy spot as director of business development. And Choice? Women like her didn't come along every day. So Trey decided to toss his hat into the ring and play the game Remington had started. Not one for losing, Trey would be playing for keeps—winner take all.

Chapter 12

The week flew by, and Trey and Charles's meeting with Solomon Meyers & Company, one of the primary hiring firms for the Ground Zero building projects, was a huge success. Another meeting was being scheduled for the following week, with a request for initial floor plans to follow one month later. Charles's calm reserve was a perfect complement to Solomon's more boisterous personality, and Jeffrey Black's suave presence balanced the two. Trey's presentation had been flawless. He'd done his homework, and the players at Solomon Meyers were noticeably impressed.

Trey hung out with the boys on Friday night, played tennis with Josh on Saturday, and spent much of Sunday in the gym. Since their meeting, he'd called Choice a few times. The first time she'd answered, but they spoke only briefly. The next two times had gone to voice mail. Trey was angry and frustrated. If she was feeling him the way he was feeling her, why give up so easily? Why walk away from something that felt amazing? By the time

Monday rolled around, Trey had had enough of the standoff. One way or the other, he was going to see Choice.

In a totally uncharacteristic move, Trey began clearing his desk just after five PM. He figured Choice was working and hoped to catch her before she left. He'd just switched his phone to night service when Remington walked into his office.

"Leaving so soon?"

"Yep, have an appointment."

"Something to do with Ground Zero?"

None of your damn business, is what Trey thought. "No, something else," is what he said.

"Well, I hear congratulations are in order. Dad says that getting the contract for the Phase II set of buildings is all but in the bag."

"I don't like to count my chickens before they're hatched, but we all feel pretty good."

"What you're poised to achieve so soon into this job is nothing short of a miracle. Back in the day, a deal could only move that fast if a bunch of hands were greased." Remington chuckled to soften his implication that bribes had occurred.

"Good thing we're not still back in the day," Trey calmly replied, snapping shut his laptop bag and reaching for his briefcase. "In today's climate, it's not who you pay, but who you know." Secretly, Trey also knew it was still sometimes who you paid, but thanks to his friendship with Josh and his deep political connections, he hadn't had to go that route. "All right, Rem, don't work too hard. I'm out of here." He waited until Remington had followed him out of the office and then locked his door.

"Oh, and Trey," Remington said when they reached the end of the hall and he prepared to go in the opposite direction, "my name is Remington, and that is what I am called here at the office. Only one person calls me Rem, and she does it in the bedroom."

Trey's hand clenched around the briefcase handle, but his face showed a smile. "No worries, Mr. Black. Remington it is." With that, he turned and headed across the lobby.

Remington stroked his goatee as he watched Trey walk to the elevator. *What has Mr. Scott leaving the office so early?* Remington worked until seven or eight most evenings, and he couldn't remember leaving after Trey since the new guy had started working there. Suddenly, Remington had a thought. He walked purposely to his office and closed the door. Hitting the speed dial on his cell phone, he walked to the window and took in the famous New York skyline while awaiting an answer.

"Hello?"

"Ms. McKinley."

Choice smiled. "Mr. Black."

"Have dinner with me tonight."

"Remington . . ."

"I know. You don't think you're ready to try us again. But how will you know that I've changed unless we get together? I understand that you have to have your own thing, which is why I'll allow you to keep your clothing company, as long as it doesn't interfere with your social obligations as my wife."

"You'll *allow*?"

"Honey, let's not get caught up in semantics.

Meet me at the Top of the Tower, six o'clock. Wear something sexy."

"Remington, this has been a busy day and I still have a lot of work to do."

"Even a busy working woman needs to eat, right?"

Choice was hungry. She'd had a single helping of strawberry yogurt for breakfast and had barely stopped to chow down a salad for lunch. She looked at her watch. 5:15. Choice figured she could change into one of her samples, put on some makeup, and make it to midtown in an hour. She'd missed Trey immensely, and while she doubted the Remington lion could change his mane, he could feed her, at least, and take her mind off Trey for a little while. *It's for the best,* she reminded herself for the umpteenth time. "Okay, I'll see you in an hour."

Thirty minutes later, Choice stepped out of her building and almost ran into Trey. "Trey! What are you doing here?"

Trey's eyes feasted on Choice, looking simply sexy in a little black dress with strategic glimpses of skin through cuts in the dress's midsection. Her legs were bare and she wore jeweled, flat sandals. He wanted to ravish her on the spot. "I was coming for my fitting, but it looks like I'll be joining you for dinner instead."

"Fitting?"

"Yes. I'm your male model, remember? Just because you've decided to put the skids on our relationship doesn't mean we can't still be friends." When Choice didn't respond, Trey continued. "Does it?"

"No, I guess not."

"Well then, do you still want me to model or what?"

"Trey, I don't know if this is a good idea. We both know we're playing with fire."

"Yeah, baby, and I'm ready to get burned." Trey couldn't take it anymore. He reached out for Choice and crushed her in his arms. Her hands went around his waist of their own volition and their mouths met and opened, and tongues began swirling of their own accord.

What is it with this guy? Choice thought, as she flitted her tongue inside Trey's mouth like an addict looking for crack. That was it. Trey was like a drug and she was a user. She knew she wouldn't be satisfied until she'd had him. All of him. Completely. It was the only thing that explained why she was allowing a man to put his tongue down her throat in broad open daylight.

Damn, baby, you feel so good. Trey's hands roamed Choice's body, sliding over the soft, silky material, longing to feel her naked flesh. She moaned, squirmed, and he imagined the wetness at the apex of her thighs. Hardening instantly, he broke the kiss. It was either that or snatch Choice's keys, carry her to her work space, and make love amid yards of muslin, satin, and baldachin.

Choice knew exactly why Trey had broken off the kiss. And as much as she agreed that it was the right thing to do, her body screamed with unreleased passion. "You should have called," she blurted, forcing her mind to think and her legs to move. "I've, uh, I've got an appointment and I'm going to be late."

"Let's meet afterward. Have a drink with me. I miss you, Choice."

"I'll call you later," she replied, walking away as she did so. But as she reached the curb and hailed a taxi, Choice knew she'd left part of her heart on Trey's delectable lips.

Chapter 13

"You look lovely." Remington stood as Choice neared the table and leaned over to give her a kiss on the cheek before pulling out her chair.

"Thank you." Choice knew that Remington expected a return compliment and as always, he did look good. But try as she might to forget him, her heart was filled with Trey. She didn't want to offer Remington any false promises but hoped that they could remain friends. "Have you ordered?" she asked.

"I chose the wines, but decided to wait until you arrived to order the appetizers."

"Wines, plural? Remington, I told you. I'm *working*. I have an hour for dinner and then, really, I have to get back to the shop."

Remington reached over and grasped Choice's hand. "Okay," he said, kissing it softly. "But only if you'll agree to a more well-rounded date with me this Friday night."

Instead of answering, Choice watched as the sommelier walked over with Remington's wine choice. He poured the fruity sauvignon blanc into both their glasses, and then placed the wine into a silver ice bucket. "To friendship," she said, hoisting her glass before her.

"To love," Remington replied. They clinked glasses. "So, my darling, what has you working your fingers to the bone at this time of night?"

"Fashion Week," Choice replied. "It's the biggest time of year for designers, and this year, I get to do another full showing at Bryant Park."

"That reminds me. I'd like you to come over this weekend and have a look around the apartment. I'm thinking of totally redesigning the living and dining spaces and would like your input."

And just like that, what was important to Choice was forgotten, and Remington was off to the races with what mattered in his life. Choice learned about his latest golfing adventures, his latest architectural designs, becoming president of his fraternity, and his plans for them to spend Christmas in Hawaii. There was just a slight problem with this last idea; actually, two. One, he hadn't asked Choice, and two, someone named Trey was standing in the way of her saying yes. Choice pretended to listen intently, but inside she was imagining this as her life for the next forty years. Then she imagined herself sitting at their dining room table, a skeleton, and Remington so busy talking about himself that he wouldn't even notice. Choice began laughing, softly at first and then in full-out guffaws.

"Choice," Remington hissed. "People are watching."

Remington's aghast expression sent Choice into another peal of laughter. She took a drink of water to try to calm herself, caught a visual of Remington talking to a skeleton, oblivious to the fact that she'd died, and starting laughing again. So hard that she did the unthinkable—she snorted. Which, of course, sent her laughing again.

"Choice, *stop* that! What has gotten into you?"

"I'm so sorry, Rem," Choice said, wiping her eyes with the soft linen napkin. "Whew! I just thought of something funny and . . . I guess I'm a little sleep-deprived. I had a hard time controlling myself for a minute."

"I'll say."

You would. Remington reminded Choice of her mother. Arnetta would have been equally mortified to have Choice dare laugh out loud, in public, and would have possibly fainted at the snort. *Too bad you're not into older women and she's already remarried. Because you and my mother would be perfect together.*

Shortly after the laughing incident, the waiter arrived with their orders. After eating an absolutely succulent dinner and having two more glasses of wine and a fairly pleasant conversation, Choice thanked Remington for the dinner and insisted that she leave, alone, and take a cab back to her workplace. She was only partially surprised when the cab pulled up and she found Trey there . . . waiting for her.

Chapter 14

"Have you been waiting for me this whole time?" Choice asked as Trey paid the cab driver, as he'd insisted. They walked up to the main office door, and Choice unlocked it.

"No. I took care of some business in the area, and then decided to stop by here and see if you were back. Looks like my timing was perfect."

"Hum, I don't know. You're feeling kinda like a stalker right about now."

"Would that be so bad?" Trey was directly behind Choice as they mounted the stairs, his hot breath wet on her neck.

And right then, right at that moment, Choice knew how the night was going to end.

"I normally like to have my assistant here when I'm doing fittings," she said, taking long strides to increase the space between her and Trey. "But I guess I could make an exception."

"It's cool. I can come back tomorrow if you want me to." His lips said this, but his eyes told her that he wasn't planning on going anywhere.

Choice's breath quickened, her stomach tightened, her nana tingled. "That's okay," she said, her calm voice belying her roiling emotions within. "I guess I can handle this one by myself."

She walked across the room for her tape measure. Trey began undressing. "You do want me to take my clothes off, don't you?"

"Not everything," she answered, somewhat breathlessly. "Just your shirt and your, um, pants."

And it began. Trey's eyes never left Choice's as he unbuttoned the first button, and then the next . . . and the next. His countenance was serious, purposeful. Choice knew that this time there was no stopping, and no turning back. Not that she wanted to; not that she could if she tried. His neck and arm muscles rippled as he pulled off his shirt. His chest bulged inside the stark white sleeveless undershirt that covered it.

Choice didn't move and barely breathed.

Still watching her, Trey reached for his belt buckle and slowly undid it. Choice licked her lips, subtly, but Trey saw it anyway. The barest hint of a smile appeared before he unbuttoned the lone fastener at the top of his slacks, unzipped the zipper, and let the pants slide to the floor. Choice took one look at his massive package and almost slid to the floor herself. *Day-um!* Her feet seemed glued to the spot while her eyes remained fixed on Trey's manhood. Her mouth watered and her lips became dry. *He's just a man,* Choice told herself, willing herself to act professionally and to treat Trey as she would any other male model. *But this isn't just any male model. This is the man you want to screw you senseless!*

Choice broke her gaze and turned abruptly. "Let me get, um, I need to get something out of the back." And then she fairly ran out of the room, down the hall, and into the break room, where she opened the mini-fridge and proceeded to stick her head inside it. Her entire body was on fire; it was as if Choice was having an out-of-body experience. *It's got to be the wine,* she reasoned. *Yes, that's it. Trey isn't turning my world on its axis. No, never that. I'm just tipsy.* While continuing to convince herself of this, Choice reached inside the fridge and pulled out a bottle of tea.

"Do you want some tea?" she yelled out.

"No," Trey whispered from directly behind her. "All I want is you."

With that, Trey backed Choice against the wall and kissed her. But this time it was different. Instead of the ravenous, scorching kisses she'd come to expect from him, he decided to do a Roberta Flack and kill her softly. His body was pressed fully against her, but his lips grazed hers ever so lightly, once and then again. Like a serpent (or the python she felt between her legs), Trey flicked his tongue in and out, tiny licks, over her arms and neck, followed by soft kisses in the same areas. He ground himself into her as he did this, brushing his sculpted chest across her hard, sensitive nipples. The silky fabric between them acted as an accessory to his foreplay, feeling soft and cool against her body, masking the heat emanating from his.

And then, like a serpent, he struck—silent and deadly. His soft, feathery kiss became hard and demanding, his tongue a probing sword against her mouth's soft flesh. He lifted Choice against the wall and ran his hands underneath her dress. His touch was scalding hot against her tender thighs. Her legs opened without any directive from her, and the next thing she knew, they were wrapped around his waist.

"Uh-huh," he moaned into her mouth, taking a finger and swiping it down the center of her thong, before flicking her nub with his thumb. He ran his finger over the satiny fabric of her underwear. Choice became wetter and wetter with each brush. Trey placed a finger inside her heat and Choice gasped out loud. He placed a second one inside her, began stretching her softly, preparing her for the painful pleasure to come. Choice couldn't get enough of him, couldn't kiss him hard or deep enough, couldn't feel enough of his back, shoulders, and soft curly black hair. She began grinding against his stomach, wanting to feel him on her, in her, everywhere. She became wild with desire, reaching for the hem of her dress, working to pull it over her head. She was past the point of no return and she didn't care. *Maybe if we make love I can get him out of my system.* Choice knew that in trying not to be with him, she was losing her mind.

Trey eased her down gently, until her feet touched the floor. Then he turned her around, unzipped the dress, and helped her out of it. He placed his wet mouth on her lacy black bra, sucked her nipples through the sheer fabric, nipped one and then the other with his teeth, while his fingers once again found her paradise and began a journey of exploration. His mouth left her breasts and began its own journey, over her shoulders, down her arms, around to her stomach and farther down.

Oh, God, Choice thought. *Oh, no. I mean . . . yes.*

He teased the band of her thong with his teeth, while his finger made love to her. Suddenly, he reached for the thong, quickly pulled it down, and buried his head in her fur. Choice's legs buckled. "Wait," she whispered. "Let's go to . . . I have a . . . there's a couch, up front."

Trey lifted her off the floor and, like a warrior going to battle, marched them to the front of the workspace. With one motion, he swiped fabric and pattern pieces onto the floor and lay down on the sofa. "Sit on my face," he commanded.

Choice complied, and immediately knew what heaven was like.

"Oh my goodness, Trey, wait," Choice panted. It was too much. Could one die from pleasure? Choice attempted to lift herself from him, but Trey wasn't having it. He locked his arms around her legs and thrust his tongue inside her. Lapping, nipping, tonguing, oh my! Choice screamed as an orgasm more intense than she could have imagined erupted from deep within her. Her entire body pulsated with the intensity of her release, and tears sprang to her eyes. She'd never been loved so thoroughly, so completely. But Trey was just getting started.

He rolled them over, walked over to his pants, and pulled out a condom. "Put it on me," he growled. His eyes were forest green, almost black with longing. He stood like a king in his castle, legs spread, hands on hips, sword hard and poised for battle. Choice's hands shook as she unrolled the gargantuan prophylactic onto Trey's gloriously perfect dick. But not before she'd tasted him, placed the mushroom-shaped head into her mouth, and suckled gently. A long hiss escaped from Trey's mouth as he threw back his head and enjoyed her ministrations. As soon as she'd completed her task, he flipped her over onto her knees, then entered her slowly, gently, giving her body time to adjust to his size. Midway in, he pulled out to the tip and eased back in, over and again, until she was totally ready for him. And then he pushed in to the hilt, a long "ahhhhhh" accompanying the move.

"This is what I want," he whispered softly. "This is what I've wanted from the moment we met. What about you, baby?"

"Umm" was all Choice could say in reply. Did people actually talk in paradise?

It could have been moments, but it felt as if Trey made love to her for hours. Choice experienced so many orgasms that she lost count. And when Trey finally found his release (after asking her if she was satisfied and if it was all right for him to do so), he stayed inside her until his shaft quit pulsating, until he'd spilled every drop. And then he cuddled Choice into his arms, and they slept.

Chapter 15

The next morning, Trey entered the McKinley Black offices and headed straight for the coffeepot in the break room. He was not normally a java man, but then again, this hadn't been a normal twenty-four hours. He'd barely allowed Choice a chance to sleep, having awakened her once in the middle of the night to make love, and then again as the early-morning sun's rays painted the dawn. He couldn't get enough of her; even now she filled his thoughts. She was everything he thought she'd be and more: passionate, uninhibited, insatiable. Just like him. They were a perfect match.

He turned the corner into the break room and saw the last person with whom he wanted to start his day. But he was here now, so he sucked it up and proceeded to the coffee machine. "Good morning, Remington."

"'Morning, Trey."

"How are you doing?" Trey didn't really want to know but felt it was an obligatory question.

"Couldn't be better. Had dinner with my lovely

lady last night; going to take her on a mini-cruise this weekend."

"Sounds good."

"Yes, Choice really digs the water. I'm thinking about buying a yacht after we get married."

Marriage? Choice? That's where she was coming from last night, having dinner with Remington? Trey's flash of temper was immediately cooled by images of Choice writhing beneath him, out of her mind with pleasure. He smiled at the memory. *She may have had dinner with you, man. But I was her dessert.* Trey wanted so badly to voice this out loud, but unlike Remington, he didn't feel the need to put his business in the streets. Besides, Choice now said, more like screamed, *his* name in the bedroom. "Well, all right then, man. See you at the meeting later this morning."

"All right," Remington replied, stirring creamer into his coffee and pondering the satisfied look on Trey's face. "See you then."

Trey arrived at his office and turned on his laptop. Among the slew of office e-mails was one from McKinley's assistant, Denise. Thinking that it was concerning the meeting scheduled for later, Trey opened it up right away.

Trey, I'd like to stop by your office this morning, if you have time. I'll only need 5–10 minutes. Please e-mail back and let me know. D.

Trey paused, his hands hovering over the laptop keyboard. *What could Denise want to talk with me about?* Any time the subject had to do with a meeting or specific project, that fact was mentioned in the subject line. But this e-mail sounded different. It sounded personal. Shrugging his shoulders, Trey responded to the e-mail by telling her to drop by anytime after the meeting. Moments later, he was knee-deep in plans for his second meeting with Solomon Meyers & Company and two other smaller projects that had just come to his attention.

Denise took minutes for the meeting, and shortly after it was over, she knocked on Trey's door. "Hello, Trey."

Trey looked up from the report he was reading. "Hey, Denise. Come on in."

She did and closed the door.

Trey immediately became suspicious and hoped that he wasn't about to experience a come-on from his boss's secretary. He felt that Denise was smart and quite attractive. But she wasn't his type. Nobody was, except Choice. "Have a seat, Denise," he said, pointing to the chair in front of him. "And tell me what's on your mind."

Denise sat and nervously twirled a pen in her hand. She took a deep breath and began. "I'm taking a bit of a risk in coming here and sharing what I'm about to say. But I think you're an excellent employee, Trey, and I like you. That's why I feel it in your best interest to know what's going on."

This cryptic intro immediately got Trey's attention. He leaned forward and rested his chin on steepled hands. "Okay. Talk to me."

"Well, there's some information going around about you. Not widely," Denise hurriedly added. "Just among the partners."

"What type of information, Denise?"

"Your criminal background," she said.

"Oh. That."

"Yes, Trey. That is a very big deal in a company that prides itself on a stellar reputation and above-board players on our team. Charles has planned a meeting with the human resources manager tomorrow to chew her out for missing this major detail about you in the screening process. It just might get her terminated. Things could get ugly . . ."

"Denise, I can explain." Trey's voice was low and calm as he leaned back in his seat. He believed he had a very good idea of how this information had come to Charles' attention, and why so much was being made of it. *You've never been involved in banking or credit unions or anything like that?* Remington's probing questions came back to Trey with clarity. But one question remained. Did Remington simply want him out of Choice's life or out of the company?

"The report that is being circulated, presumably on me, is a case of mistaken identity. But I'm glad you let me know what's happening so that I can clear things up."

"Charles can't know that I told you this. He wanted to . . . get his ducks in a row before he talked to you." There was someone else Denise didn't want to know about her conversation with Trey—Remington. While many speculated on whether or not she was sleeping with her boss, Charles, Denise had actually carried a torch for Remington Black since first meeting him ten years ago, shortly after she was hired at the firm. He was married at the time, so her interactions with him were strictly professional, and basically remained so until this day. Except for last year, at the Christmas party, when they'd slow danced to a golden oldie and shared a good-night kiss. She knew he fancied Choice McKinley, but Choice had confided her feelings to Denise shortly before breaking things off with him. She had felt stifled beneath Remington's domineering personality, while Denise would like nothing more than to quit work and embrace full-time the role of being Mrs. Remington Black.

"Don't worry," Trey said, after a pause. "I'll make sure that this seems all my idea, something I want to clear up just in case Charles hears rumors—the industry being cliquish and all. I'm not planning on going anywhere any time soon, Denise, or on getting people fired. I appreciate your giving me the heads-up though. I owe you one."

Keep Choice away from Remington and you won't owe me anything, is what Denise thought. "Thank you," is what she said.

Denise left Trey's office and headed straight for Remington's well-appointed domain. She was confident in her appearance: her ultra-short haircut was stylishly chic, as were the tan-colored suit with a skirt stopping two inches above the knee and her three-inch pumps. Denise was the mother of a teenaged son, but she still felt that she had something she was working with. She added just a touch of sway into her walk as she reached Remington's office and, after a light tap on his outer door, stepped inside. "Hey, you."

Remington smiled as he looked up. "Denise, what can I do for you?"

"You can save me from going solo tonight and attend a gala at the Met. It's a private showing," she went on, knowing how much Remington appreciated fine art. "The tickets include a sit-down dinner with the artist."

"That sounds nice," Remington said, stroking his goatee as he clicked open his electronic calendar. "Let me see what I've got planned." He knew what wouldn't be happening tonight—seeing Choice. He'd called her twice and gotten voice mail each time. During the meeting, she'd finally returned his call, saying that she was swamped and wouldn't be able to join him for dinner. She'd said how busy she was, some kind of fashion show, if he remembered correctly. But was sewing the something that was taking up all her time? Or was it someone? No matter, Remington decided. Sooner or later, Choice would be his. It wouldn't hurt to enjoy some harmless flirtation with Denise in the meantime. "Looks like I'm free," he told her.

"Great," Denise replied, veiling her enthusiasm. "I'll meet you there at seven."

While Denise was making plans with Remington on one end of the building, Trey was walking toward Charles McKinley's office at the other end. Seeing Denise's chair empty but Charles' door open, he tapped on the door. "Charles, do you have a minute?"

"Sure, Trey. Come on in."

Trey sat in a chair facing Charles' desk. "I wanted to make you aware of something that I thought had been handled a few years ago. But recently, a colleague of mine informed me that there might be some loose ends I still need to tie up." Charles remained silent, and in that moment, Trey realized that Choice had her father's eyes. "It's regarding my name, and the fact that someone else, with the same name, committed a felony some years ago. Now, like I said, this matter was supposedly cleared up through my attorney's office, with photos, and the addition of my full middle name to online accounts." Trey stopped, handed Charles a folder, and continued. "As ironic as it seems, both this guy and I have the same initials—T. E. S. But his middle name is Eugene. Mine is Edmond." Trey became silent then, giving Charles time to scan the documents corroborating the story he'd just told.

"Why didn't you reveal this at the time you were hired?"

"I didn't think it necessary, sir. I thought the matter was behind me and that there would be no future mix-ups. I know how this firm prides itself on being above reproach and would never want to do anything to tarnish its name. That's why before coming here, I again contacted my attorney to make sure this matter had been handled. But with the Internet, it's a continuous job to make sure that pages containing unauthorized information don't get put back up. There's no way to control it, really. So I've taken matters into my own hands and brought the proof directly to you, to ensure that everybody understands that I am exactly who my resume says I am."

Charles looked at the folder's contents another moment before closing it and placing it on the desk. "You say a colleague brought this to your attention?"

"Yes," Trey said, figuring the universe would forgive him for this white lie. "He knows about my upcoming projects and asked if I was aware that some search engines still linked my face, my image, to that crime. I've now hired a Web expert to try to sort this mess out. I only hope he can succeed where my attorney did not."

"I appreciate your coming to me with this information," Charles said, shuffling papers on his desk as a sign that the impromptu meeting was over. "Good luck on getting everything straightened out."

"Thank you, sir."

Trey exited Charles's office and found Denise sitting at her desk. He spoke to her and gave her a subtle thumbs-up. Now, he was headed to his desk to make sure Choice had plans for the weekend, ones that did not include Remington Black. Trey smiled as he thought of how they might pass the time. *Winner takes all.*

Chapter 16

Choice breathed audibly as her phone rang again. "Remington, I am not going with you!" she muttered before mashing the talk button without checking the ID. He'd called every day since Tuesday and twice on Friday, trying to convince her to join him for a weekend cruise to Martha's Vineyard. On this rainy Saturday morning, Choice was in no mood for coercion. One of her assistants had quit, run off to Italy with a lover she'd just met, and another had called in sick. On top of that, two of the vital fabrics needed for her men's line had not arrived, and the jewelry designer had raised his prices. If one more bad thing happened, she'd lose it for real. She snatched up the phone. "I said no, okay? Now please stop calling. I've got to work!"

"Work is why I'm calling, baby girl," a low, sultry voice responded. "I'm sorry for being so busy the rest of the week. But I'm ready to come down for the fitting that was so wonderfully interrupted earlier."

The moment she heard Trey's voice, Choice's mood instantly changed. Only now did she realize that of all the situations that had put her in a bad mood, not seeing Trey since their hot encounter on Monday night, the one that had flowed seamlessly into Tuesday morning, was probably the truest reason for her funk. "Any other time, I'd fire a model for being a no-show," she said, a smile evident in her voice. "But I guess I could make an exception."

"Have you eaten breakfast?"

"No, but don't even ask me to leave the shop, and don't expect to dally when you come down. There's enough work for three people on these tables and I'm the only one here. So this visit is strictly business, okay?"

"Sure, baby. Strictly business."

"I mean it, Trey. If you can't abide by my wishes . . . then don't come down."

Trey hung up without answering.

Choice looked at the phone before she tossed it aside and continued laying out the pattern of the one-shoulder, form-fitting evening gown that she knew would see a red carpet within the next year. *It's better that he doesn't come down here,* she thought, trying to appease the empty feeling in the pit of her stomach at the thought of not seeing Trey. *I need to stay focused.*

Forty-five minutes later, the downstairs doorbell sounded. "It's about time," Choice muttered, as she stomped down the hall to let in the assistant complaining of food poisoning. *But why didn't he use his key?* Choice looked through the peephole. Her heartbeat raced as she beheld the vision of beauty on the other side. She opened the door. "You came?"

"Sure I did," Trey said casually, brushing past

Choice and taking the steps two at a time. "You think you can scare me with that funky attitude?"

"No, you didn't," Choice indignantly responded.

"Yes, I did. A fluffy cheese omelet and your choice of bagel: cinnamon raisin or blueberry." He smiled as he faced her, having purposely misunderstood her previous statement. "You can thank me with a kiss." He closed his eyes and pursed his lips. Choice thought he looked perfectly devilish and delectable, all at once.

She walked over and kissed him on the cheek. "Thanks. I'm starved."

She unpacked the sack that also contained a bowl of fruit salad and two containers of orange juice. After washing her hands, she joined Trey at the break room table. "You know you're not supposed to be here. It's not cool to jeopardize your six-figure job for a modeling gig that at best will get you a free pair of pants."

"Oh, I squashed all that. Everything's cool. You can marry me now."

Choice's eyes widened. "Marry you?"

"Dang, girl, don't look so scared. I'm just teasing. But I did handle that rumor and the mistaken-identity situation. You know that information I e-mailed over to you, proving I'm Trey Edmond and not Tre' Eugene? I gave a printed version to your dad as proof against what Remington had told him about me."

"How do you know Remington had anything to do with it?"

"Please. Who else could it have been?" Trey took a bite of his food. "It doesn't matter. In fact, I'm glad it happened. Otherwise I wouldn't have been aware that the problem still existed. Now everybody knows what's going on, and there will be no surprises at a crucial moment to potentially screw up a deal.

"But enough about me and McKinley Black. I've been dealing with that all week. What's going on in the world of fashion?"

Choice was silently amazed. Trey and Remington couldn't be more different. Where she couldn't remember the last time Remington initiated a conversation about her work, if ever, Trey seemed genuinely interested in her world. Her heart swelled with love for him, and her kitty meowed with wanting.

"It's crazy," she began, and spent the next fifteen minutes giving him the brief version of what had happened the past week. "So I'm actually glad you called," she finished, gathering up their empty wrappers and placing them in the trash. "I can fit you, and then at least get started on the toile for the first suit."

"What's a toile?"

"It's like a dummy design, so I can test out the pattern before cutting the more expensive cloth."

"Oh."

They walked back to the main area of the shop, where Choice instructed Trey to strip down to his undies. This time she practiced restraint, resisted the urge to sculpt him with her hands, and quickly took his measurements. "Okay, we're all done."

"Cool." Trey dressed and leaned against the cutting table. "What can I do now?"

"What do you mean, what can you do?"

"I've got a few hours before my match with Josh. You said you're running behind. How can I help?"

"Trey, that's so sweet. No one I've ever da . . . I mean, you're the first person to ask me that."

"You can say it, baby. We're dating."

"I don't know, Trey. Granted, I am very attracted to you. It's almost scary. But we're both at crucial times in our careers. Do you really think we have the time to commit to a relationship?"

"We'll take the time."

Choice turned back to the table and began cutting around the pattern placed there. "It sounds easy. But relationships have a way of turning complicated."

"That's because you were dating the wrong dude!"

"Ha! Oh, that's it."

"Umm, it sure is." Trey slid behind Choice, ground himself into her butt, and nibbled her ear.

"Trey. Don't. Start."

"Just one kiss, baby."

"No! I mean it. I'm going to count to three, and if you haven't stopped, I'm going to have to ask you to leave!"

Trey squeezed her butt cheek. "Can you put about a minute between the one and the two?"

"Trey!"

"All right," Trey said, laughing. He stepped away from Choice's plump onion, even though he wanted nothing more than to take a bite. "If you're not going to give me any loving, then put me to work."

He had no background in design, but Trey did manage to trace the outlines of four paperboard patterns onto muslin, and using a chart that Choice had designed, matched various accessories—buttons, piping, lace, etc.—with the corresponding fabric swatches for that garment. During this time, Trey and Choice chatted like old friends who'd known each other for years, and Choice shared more about her fashion goals than she'd ever shared with anyone else. Remington called again. She let it go to voice mail. In spending time with Trey, Choice discovered that while she appreciated hearing about and supporting others' dreams, she also relished talking about her own with someone who seemed genuinely interested. For the past ten years, her dream had been to be a force to be reckoned with in the world of fashion. Now she had another dream . . . to spend the rest of her life with the man who'd simply asked, "How can I help?"

Chapter 17

Choice hummed a nonsensical tune as she browsed the aisle of her local market. She didn't cook much, but Trey's suggestion for them to spend a cozy night indoors on this rainy day had brought out the domestic side of her. So here she stood, in the produce aisle, getting fixings for a salad to go with the meatball sandwiches and chips that would round out their meal.

Once home Choice was reminded why she loved her brownstone in the Prospect Heights section of Brooklyn. Lots of windows allowed in plenty of sunlight, which bounced off her polished oak floors and the walls, which were painted a soft minty green. Live plants abounded in the combined living and dining room area, and colorful artwork and framed fabric swatches graced the walls. A mannequin in the corner gave further nod to her profession, while an ottoman was home to dozens of fashion magazines. Anyone walking into her place immediately felt right at home.

After a quick shower, Choice walked into the kitchen, and within minutes, the smell of sautéing onions danced deliciously with the sounds of Vivian Green. Choice prepared the meatballs, placed them in a tangy sauce, and then turned the burner to simmer so that they could cook low and slow. She put together the salad, poured the dressing from its store-bought container into a server, and then buttered the kaiser rolls that would be toasted later. Satisfied that all was ready, she poured herself a glass of wine, walked to her couch, and planned to relax.

The ringing doorbell awakened her. Startled, Choice looked at her watch and realized she'd been asleep for only ten minutes. *He's right on time*, she thought, dancing to the doorway. She placed her hand on the knob, peered through her peephole . . . and froze. *Remington? No!*

Choice leaned against the door, pondering what to do. She thought about not answering the door, but knew that with the sound of music clearly audible, a determined Remington would not leave until he'd seen her. Praying that Trey was running late, she took a deep breath and opened the door . . . barely.

"Remington," she said through the tiny crack. "What are you doing here?"

"Coming to see you," he said, holding out a bottle of wine. "I figured that with your crazy schedule you could use a little R & R. I'm glad to have found you at home." Choice remained silent. She knew that her lips should be moving, but honestly, she couldn't think of what to say. "Well . . . aren't you going to invite me in?"

"I wish you'd called, Rem. I'm expecting company."

Remington squared his shoulders. "Oh, really?"

"Look, don't give me that patronizing tone. You are not my father. You are a man who I used to date and I don't owe you an explanation."

"Wow," Remington mused, as if to himself. "She's reduced thirty years' worth of friendship to 'a man she used to date.'"

Choice opened the door wider. "I'm sorry, Remington. You know I didn't mean that how it sounded. I will always love you, but it's just not going to work for us. I'm . . ." *Sorry* died on her lips as Trey came into view, looking up at the numbers as he walked. He didn't have to find Choice's address. Seeing Remington standing there told him that he was in the right place.

Trey walked up the stairs as if he lived there, a bouquet of exotic flowers in one hand, a bag of goodies in the other. "Hey, man," he said to Remington, as if he were greeting a delivery guy. Remington turned but did not move away from the door.

Trey stood toe-to-toe with Remington. "Excuse me."

"I thought I told you that Choice was off-limits."

"Yeah, well, I figured that decision was left up to Choice."

Remington turned to Choice. "Has he told you

everything you need to know? Like the fact that he's a criminal who's done time in the pen?"

"Yes, Remington, he's told me everything. Trey, come on in."

"Oh, I'm standing on the sidewalk like a stranger, but he gets to come on in?"

Trey walked around Remington and adopted a protective stance, placing Choice slightly behind him. "That's what happens when you're invited to someone's home as opposed to just showing up."

"Man, you'd better watch your mouth. I'm just about two seconds from jacking you up!"

"Dog, you don't scare me."

Choice forced herself between them. "Guys, please! I deal with enough drama at my work. I don't need it showing up at my front door." She took a deep breath. "Remington, I appreciate your thinking about me, but I invited Trey over. Could you please leave? Peacefully?"

If looks were fire, both Choice and Trey would have been burned to a crisp.

"I hope you've got a good nest egg in your savings account," Remington said through clenched teeth. "Because your days are numbered at McKinley Black."

Trey watched Remington get into his car before closing the door. "I'm sorry that happened, baby," he said, pulling a rattled Choice into his arms. "Let's put it out of our minds, okay?"

"How can I, Trey? Remington doesn't issue veiled

threats, and he's the son of the company's co-owner. You're going to get fired, and it's all my fault."

"Shh. You let me worry about that, huh? Right now I'm smelling some good home cooking, I've got my girl in my arms and some movie classics in the bag. The worst of the evening just happened, love. The rest of the night belongs to us, and it's going to be magic."

Chapter 18

"Dad, I'm telling you. It's either him or me."
Two days had passed, but a still livid Remington
paced the office where Jeffrey Black and Charles
McKinley sat.

"Remington, this isn't like you." Jeffrey eyed his
son as he continued to wear holes in the carpet.
"You need to calm down."

"Charles, I told you what he was doing. Told you
he was making a play for Choice. You think he loves
her after knowing her for just three weeks? And
already coming over to the house with wine and
flowers? He was setting the stage for seduction,
pure and simple. With someone using your daughter like that, I'm surprised that you're so calm."

"And I'm surprised that you're letting a personal
beef impact a professional decision. This isn't about
Trey's work as business development director. It
isn't about his education, experience, or skills. This
is about you being angry because Choice chose to
go out with him instead of you. I'm her father, and

even I say that who Choice goes out with is her own business."

"Oh, really? You weren't saying that last week when you thought he was a felon."

Charles fixed Remington with a look, his voice controlled. "I'm saying it now."

Jeffrey tried to be the voice of reason. "This is crazy, son. It's not how we do business. If Trey messes up, gets out of line in any way regarding MB, then he's gone. But to just up and fire him . . ."

"Then put together a severance package. I'll contribute to paying him off myself. I mean it when I tell you that I don't want him around here." It wasn't often that the confident, debonair Remington Black acted like a spoiled, pampered, petulant child. But now was one of those times.

"Let me and Charles talk it over," Jeffrey finally said. "We'll come up with something by the end of the week."

The days flew, and by Friday, Charles and Jeffrey had made the difficult decision to release Trey. Remington had convinced them that he could snag the Ground Zero project without him, that he'd work around the clock to ensure that McKinley Black got the bid. No one was happy with the position that Remington had put them in, even Remington. Because deep down he knew that even with Trey gone, Trey would still have Choice.

While the partners had been busy preparing Trey's departure, Trey had been equally busy ensuring that he'd stay around. He'd worked his network, met with Solomon Meyers & Company, and now had a proposal that McKinley Black would be crazy to refuse. But if they did, he would go to a firm that would appreciate his hard work.

Just as Trey was organizing the last of his papers in a folder, his phone rang. "Hey, Denise."

"Hi, Trey. Charles would like to see you . . . now."

"Cool, because I was just getting ready to call and request a quick meeting. I'm on my way."

Trey walked into Charles's office looking like a million bucks. He'd purposely dressed to impress in a tailored black suit, stark white shirt, and designer tie. His hair was freshly cut and his skin carried the glow of someone who'd recently visited an esthetician. Anyone looking at him would understand why Choice wanted him walking the runway in her clothes.

He entered Charles' office and was only mildly surprised to see that Jeffrey was there as well. "Denise said you wanted to see me?"

Charles nodded, his face grim. "Have a seat." Once Trey joined them in the sitting area, Charles got right down to business. "There's no easy way for me to say this, Trey. Your work here has been very good, and personally, I've enjoyed having you on our team. But one of the major players—"

"Remington," Trey interjected.

"Yes, Remington, doesn't feel that you're working out. As Jeffrey's son and a junior partner in this firm, his word carries weight. We've prepared a generous severance package and will write glowing recommendations for your future job search, but . . . we're going to have to let you go." Charles reached for a folder lying on the table and handed it to Trey.

"That's too bad," Trey replied calmly, putting down the folder that Charles had just handed him and opening his own. "Because I came to deliver some very good news." He handed a single sheet of paper to Charles and one to Jeffrey, and then he sat back while they read.

It was so quiet in the ensuing moments that one could hear a mosquito flap its wings. Trey was the epitome of calm. He was in a win-win situation. If McKinley Black was stupid enough to can him today, Friday, he'd have another job by Monday afternoon. He looked out of the window, beheld the beautiful blue sky and a plane in the distance flying toward JFK Airport, and thought about how his corner office would have a similar view.

"What is this?" Charles asked, even as he read the obvious for the third time.

"Just what it says," Trey replied. "This project moves forward only with me as project manager, either with McKinley Black . . . or another firm."

"This is illegal," Jeffrey snapped. "The bid has to go to a firm, a corporation, not a person."

"Correct, but there can be stipulations placed on said bid, and that's what this letter outlines. That whichever firm gets this particular project must have me heading it up." Trey leaned forward slightly. "Gentlemen, this victory didn't happen overnight. I cultivated these contacts for years, some since college. I've done my homework. This document is airtight. And since I have no desire to stay where I'm not wanted, I'll accept your severance package. Please consider this my two-week notice, unless you'd like for me to clean out my desk right now." Trey reached for the folder Charles had initially offered him and stood to leave.

"Now, wait," Jeffrey sputtered. "Let's not be too hasty."

"Obviously this development . . . sheds new light on our decision," Charles added.

"I'm not sure it changes mine," Trey said. "Because while I'm shedding light, Mr. McKinley, there's something else you should know. I'm in love with your daughter and have no plans to stop seeing her. I understand that there's a rule that men who work here can't date her—that is, except for Remington. So while you gentlemen discuss your opinion on my fate, know this. That when it comes to deciding between this job and the woman I love . . . that's an easy . . . *choice*." Trey looked at Jeffrey, and then at Charles, nodded curtly, and left the room.

Chapter 19

"Baby, put on something sexy and meet me in Midtown."

"Trey, wait!"

"Don't argue with me, woman! We're going out to celebrate!"

Choice giggled. Trey was obviously excited and his joy was infectious. "What are we celebrating?"

"My continuing to work at McKinley Black . . . and us."

"Huh?"

"I'll explain everything when I see you. I'll meet you in an hour."

"Make it two; I just got home."

"I can't wait that long. An hour and a half." Trey gave her the address. "Take a taxi."

An hour and fifteen minutes later, Choice arrived at a hotel near Times Square. Trey met her in the lobby and enveloped her in his signature tight embrace before planting a quick kiss on her mouth.

"Trey, what in the world is going on?"

"You'll see. Wait here." Trey walked to the concierge and then came back for Choice. "Let's have a drink."

They stepped into the cozy bar and found a booth. Trey moved to let Choice slide in first, and then slid so close next to her that there wasn't even room for air between them.

"You're crazy," Choice said, unable to wipe the smile off her face. "What are you up to?"

"Girl, let me taste those juicy lips. You know what I need as soon as I see you."

Choice complied, and after a long, wet lip-lock, Trey nestled Choice into his arms and told her about his summary dismissal the week before.

"I knew it," Choice exclaimed. "I knew that Remington would have you fired. Trey, I'm so sorry."

"No worries, baby girl. I had an ace up my sleeve." Trey then told Choice about the proposal and the partners' about-face when they realized what the firm stood to lose. He figured he could tell her later about what Denise had confided in him . . . that Remington had asked her to join him in Hawaii for the holidays, and that she'd agreed.

She squealed. "Oh. My. Goodness. I would love to have seen the look on my father's and Jeffrey's faces when you told them that. What did they do?"

"Started stumbling over their words like a baby learning to crawl. I could tell your dad didn't really want to let me go," Trey continued. He glanced at Choice. "I'm surprised Charles didn't have more backbone and stand up for what he thought was right."

Choice turned and looked at Trey. "He didn't have a choice." She then told Trey about her father's humble beginnings and how instrumental Jeffrey Black's family had been in helping him become a success, how Jeffrey's father became the one Charles never had, mentoring and sponsoring him throughout his high school and college years. About how when it came to the business, Jeffrey and Charles would always have each other's back; that it was McKinley and Black against the world. Their word was gospel and anyone with those last names had the power to make their word law. "My dad is loyal to a fault," Choice finished. "But he means well."

"No worries. It's all good." Trey looked at his watch. "Okay, come on. Let's go."

"Where are we going?"

Trey turned mischievous eyes in her direction. "That's for me to know and you to find out."

They walked to the bank of elevators. Trey punched the number for the top floor. The doors closed and Trey's hands were immediately all over Choice. "Baby, we never did get to finish what we started in that elevator." He tried to put his hands under her dress.

"Trey, stop!" Choice hissed. "I don't want somebody seeing me with my dress hiked all up around my waist."

The elevator bell dinged and Trey stepped away from her. "I'ma let you off the hook . . . for now."

They stepped through the doors and were immediately assailed by the wind created from a helicopter's swirling wings and the drone of its engine.

"Is this for us?" Choice squealed. "I always wanted to take a helicopter ride!"

Five minutes later, Trey and Choice were enjoying

amazingly scenic views of some of New York's most iconic landmarks: the three famous bridges, the United Nations and Chrysler buildings, Yankee Stadium, Times Square, Central Park, and of course, a close-up of the Statute of Liberty. The private ride lasted for twenty-five minutes and was one of the most amazing things Choice had ever done in her life.

"That was wonderful," she said once the helicopter had landed and she and Trey had stepped out. She threw her arms around his neck. "Thank you."

Trey placed a soft kiss on her lips. "You're welcome."

They walked to the bank of elevators. One immediately opened up, but when Choice turned to step into it, Trey stopped her. "Wait a minute. Let's take another one."

"Why? There was no one in that one. Trey . . ."

"Look, just chill, okay? I didn't feel good about that elevator."

Choice looked at him questioningly but said nothing further. Soon, another elevator door opened and a hotel employee stepped out. Trey greeted the gentleman, shook his hand, and then motioned for Choice to get inside. The elevator had just begun its descent when it stopped suddenly.

Choice's eyes widened. "Oh no. What happened?"

Trey looked at the row of numbers. They were stuck on the thirty-ninth floor. "I don't know. We're not moving."

"Obviously . . . but why?" Choice fought the urge to panic and reached for the phone.

"Uh, hold up, baby. Let me call the front desk

from my cell phone." Trey punched in a set of
numbers, told the person who answered that they
were stuck in the elevator. "They said not to worry,"
he told Choice once he'd hung up, taking off his
jacket as he stepped toward her.

"What are you doing?" Choice asked, stepping
back until she hit the elevator wall.

"I'm . . . feeling rather hot," Trey said. He let his
jacket hit the floor and began unbuttoning his shirt.

"Trey, it's not that hot in here. How long did they
say it would be before help arrived?"

Trey shrugged. "A half hour, hour . . . they didn't
know." He reached for his belt buckle. Seconds
later, his pants hit the floor. "Aren't you hot, baby?"
Trey placed his hands on either side of Choice's
head, his body pinning hers to the wall. "Umm, you
feel hot," he whispered, as he began a slow grind
against her midsection.

"Trey," Choice said, swallowing hard. "I . . . don't
know if . . . this is such a good idea." Even so, her
legs spread at Trey's urging, and soon his fingers
had found her paradise.

Trey stopped and abruptly pulled Choice's dress
over her head. He unclasped her bra and ripped
off her thong. His movements were methodical,
decisive, like a man on a mission. The blatant show
of alpha maleness turned Choice on. She dropped
to her knees and licked his already rigid weapon
into further hardness. Trey entangled his fingers
in her hair, reveling in her actions. But not for
long. He wanted to be inside her, had dreamed of
this moment since the Fourth of July. He stepped
away from her, whipped out a condom, and then in

one fluid motion, he lifted Choice and pinned her against the wall.

"Later, we'll do it nice and easy," he whispered. "But right now, I want it hard and rough."

Choice nodded her agreement. Trey poised his weapon at her point of entry and then eased her down onto nine inches of pure ecstasy. They settled into a frantic rhythm, with Choice's whimpers and Trey's grunts piercing the silence. Choice grabbed the bar behind her, allowing Trey to grab her hips and take control of the ride. His thrusts were strong and unrelenting, branding her from front to back and side to side. All Trey could think of was how perfectly she sheathed his sword, and he wanted to "fence" forever.

But Choice's trembling legs told him it was not to be, at least not right now. She wrapped her arms tightly around his shoulders and buried her head in his neck to keep from crying out. Her body bucked with the intensity of the orgasm, and soon Trey grimaced with his own noteworthy release. They slid to the cool floor, totally spent.

"Hey, haven't we been here before?" Trey asked.

"We've been close," Choice said. "But nothing has ever felt like this."

Once they'd regained their breathing, they quickly dressed. Trey used the key that the employee he'd bribed had given him, and Choice frantically searched her purse for some perfume. By the time the elevator dinged on the first floor, they stepped out looking like a normal, respectable couple. Hand in hand they left the hotel, got into a cab, and then burst out laughing.

"You're dangerous," Choice said, pointing an accusing finger at Trey. "I can't believe I just did that with you."

"Hmph, you're the one who's dangerous . . . got a brothah trippin'." Trey gave Choice a sideways look, his pole twitching from the pleasure it had just experienced. "I think you might be just a little too hot to handle."

"Well, you know what they say," Choice innocently countered. "If you can't stand the heat, get out of the kitchen."

Trey scooted over and pulled Choice into his arms. "Naw, I like playing with fire," he whispered, rolling his tongue around Choice's earlobe and getting her excited all over again. "If a flame is the analogy for this love we're feeling? Then, baby, I say let it burn."

More of the Hottest
African-American Fiction from
Dafina Books

Look For These Other
Dafina Novels

If I Could
0-7582-0131-1

by Donna Hill
$6.99US/**$9.99**CAN

Thunderland
0-7582-0247-4

by Brandon Massey
$6.99US/**$9.99**CAN

June In Winter
0-7582-0375-6

by Pat Phillips
$6.99US/**$9.99**CAN

Yo Yo Love
0-7582-0239-3

by Daaimah S. Poole
$6.99US/**$9.99**CAN

When Twilight Comes
0-7582-0033-1

by Gwynne Forster
$6.99US/**$9.99**CAN

It's A Thin Line
0-7582-0354-3

by Kimberla Lawson Roby
$6.99US/**$9.99**CAN

Perfect Timing
0-7582-0029-3

by Brenda Jackson
$6.99US/**$9.99**CAN

Never Again Once More
0-7582-0021-8

by Mary B. Morrison
$6.99US/**$8.99**CAN

Available Wherever Books Are Sold!

Check out our website at www.kensingtonbooks.com.